A KILLER CONVERSATION

DI Ravenscroft & Professor Laing
Book 1

ANGELA C NURSE

Cover design by GetCovers

First e-book edition January 2025
First paperback edition January 2025

ISBN 978-1-914597-15-2 (paperback)
ISBN 978-1-914597-16-9 (ebook)

www.angelacnurse.com

A Note from the Author

This book is written by a British author and is set in
Scotland. All spellings are the British version

Chapter 1

Somewhere a phone rang, startling Sylvia, she flicked her head up, eyes darting around the carpark confirming that she was alone. The ringing had stopped, she shook her head, laughing at herself for being so jumpy. She threw her bag onto the passenger seat and was about to get in the car when the sound came again.

An unfamiliar ringtone, she paused holding on to the open driver's door in her right hand trying to get a fix on where the sound was coming from. She should leave, this wasn't her problem and she had somewhere to be. But, she thought, if she'd dropped her phone and someone had the opportunity to pick it up and help, she would really appreciate it.

The ring came again, she closed the car door and walked towards the sound, it was clearly coming from inside the large green clothes donation bin.

There was a telephone number on the front of the bin, calling it now would only result in her talking to an answering machine. The ringing had stopped and started four times now, someone was desperately trying to get in touch with the owner of this phone.

Sylvia climbed on an upturned bread crate, perhaps with a little extra height she'd be able to see inside. From her elevated position, pulling down the access hatch and peering inside was easy. Letting go of the handle, it clanged shut, echoing into the night, Sylvia turned away, retching, and then gulping in fresh air. Pull yourself together woman, she told herself.

Reopening the hatch and using her mobile phone as a torch illuminated the drop shelf inside, dark brown lines streaked the green metal - blood. After three summers working in her uncle's butchers the smell of meat on the turn was seared into her nostrils.

Sylvia's hands trembled dialling 999 into her phone.

'Police please, I think I've found a body.'

Chapter 2

DAY ONE, MONDAY

Nancy looked at her reflection in the mirror of the toilet block wall. The night was dark and still, she'd made an effort to not crunch through the campsite gravel close to any of the holiday makers. She'd thought about not bothering, but she wasn't about to turn up on her first day back without at least brushing her teeth. Perhaps cutting her long dark hair off had been a mistake, the hairdresser she'd gone to in order to get it cut into some sort of style had clearly thought she'd lost it, though she did a very good job with the cut, now a neat bob sitting just below her chin.

She pulled on the door handle of her campervan to satisfy herself that her home was properly locked before getting into her car and driving slowly out of the site.

There were only a couple of other cars on the coastal roads she took to get her back into Dunfermline, she drove quicker than normal trying to get to the crime scene whilst it was still fresh. She'd dropped her driver's side window down a crack, air conditioning was all well and good but there was nothing like the cold costal breeze blasting against your cheeks to wake you up.

Forty-five minutes later Nancy pulled into the car park, showing her badge to the uniformed officer standing guard at the entrance. The crime scene was a hive of activity. The door of the donations bin had been prised open and the forensic team clad in white suits were carefully emptying the contents. Nancy stood back and observed for a moment.

'What are we looking at?' she said to the group in front of her.

The taller of the two men jumped slightly and turned to face her, 'sorry miss this is a crime scene, I'm going to have to ask you to leave,' he took her gently by the elbow as if to encourage her away.

Nancy resisted, 'please don't do that,' she shook herself free of his grip and took pity on the confused face above her. 'We haven't been introduced. DI Nancy Ravenscroft, nice to meet you.'

His cheeks flushed scarlet, 'Oh shit, sorry…I mean…we didn't…' his shoulders slumped, 'Sorry boss, I'm DS Callum Tung, my friends call me Cal.'

'Ten out of ten for vigilance, zero out of ten for putting your hands on a woman you just met, but at least you're paying attention.' Nancy had a vague memory of an email about getting a new DS, the details were a little fussy though. Cal was younger than expected, when did they start giving out DS roles to teenagers. Oh God! I sound like bloody Cooper, Nancy thought. He was tall, but beanpole thin making Rob look positively enormous next to him. 'Would anyone like to get me up to speed?'

'Morning boss,' DS Rob MacDonald said, 'uniform responded to a call just after 2am, someone phoned it in saying they found a body. The belief was it was a hoax, but when they arrived there was a smell…' Rob realised there was little need to explain that further as the odour had already started to permeate the air around them.

'And what do we know about our victim?'

'Dr Clarke's here and we're waiting on an update.'

'Ooh she'll not be happy at this hour of the day,' Nancy smiled.

'There were definitely some expletives,' Rob smiled. Winding up Dr Lucy Clarke, pathologist, and old friend of his boss, was a personal pleasure.

'And the body was inside the donation bin?' Nancy asked.

Rob nodded.

'Do we know how it got in there?' Nancy spoke as she walked towards the forensic team.

Lucy didn't look up, 'In pieces, hence all the blood.' Dr Clarke stopped and glanced up. 'Nancy? I didn't realise it was you, no one said you were coming back today?'

'I took a week off, not a year long sabbatical,'

Dr Lucy Clarke looked like she'd walked straight off the pages of a magazine, her make-up a smoky eye with eyeliner flicked up at the edges, her signature red lipstick fully intact.

'We've got a body of a young man, hard to confirm age at this point.' Lucy said.

'Were you out on a date when this call came in?' Nancy asked.

'I have a life outside the job Nancy, you should try it.'

Nancy's face showed that her friend's words stung.

'Sorry,' Lucy said, realising a moment too late that her words hit too close to the bone. 'Sorry, you know I didn't mean…'

'Cause of death?' Nancy cut her off.

'Hard to say at the moment – I want to make sure we have the complete remains first.'

'When will the PM be done?'

'Tomorrow, 2pm, but I'm in court in the morning so it could be later, I could get Peter to do it, I know how you love working with him.' Lucy said, sarcasm in every word.

'I'll wait for you,' Nancy scowled. 'Can I get a quick look now?'

Lucy pulled back the plastic sheeting exposing the young man's face, blonde hair badly matted with dried blood. 'naked?' Nancy asked.

'Wrapped in a towel from the looks of it.'

'How long do you think he's been in there?'

'Hard to say, even at this time of year the heat in the bin would have been higher than the external temperature, and it's been unseasonably warm for March as it is. I'll know more when we've done the exam.' Lucy turned away indicating that even for an old friend the conversation was now over.

'What happened to the person who called 999?' Nancy asked Rob as they walked away from the scene.

'She had to go…'

Nancy opened her mouth to speak, but Rob continued talking.

'She was only in the carpark because she'd received a call from her father's nursing home, he'd taken a fall. She was heading to her car when she heard the phone ringing. Waiting for us to arrive had already significantly delayed her and she was desperate to go and check on her dad. Under the circumstances I made the decision to let her get on her way, we took all her details and arranged for her to come into the station later this morning.' Rob finished.

'Let's make sure we speak to her as soon as possible, we

don't know at this stage that she wasn't involved. Can you tell the team to get back to the station and we'll have a briefing and sort out a plan of action.'

'Sure,'

Nancy smiled, 'don't worry I'll be right behind you, need to make one stop on the way though.'

Chapter 3

Nancy made her way to her team, their room was a depressing shade of grey/green. Having given up asking DCI Ross Cooper to decorate it, maybe one day she'd go to B&Q, buy the paint and do it herself.

'I went past Stephens the Bakers, I've got pies, steak bridies, sausage rolls & pastries, help yourself.' The open box let the warm bakery smell waft through the air releasing one of those scents that most couldn't resist.

'Ya beauty,' Rob said taking a pie and a fudge doughnut. Back at his desk he cracked open the ring pull of a pound shop energy drink and took a large swig.

Nancy took a sausage roll, her hand hovering over the box trying to decide whether to lift a Yum Yum now or hope there was still one left later. One glance at the team made her decision, wrapping it in a paper napkin, it would make a good mid-morning snack.

'You know that stuff will rot your insides,' Nancy said to Rob.

'It's good to know you care boss,' Rob smiled. 'I'll have you know my body is a temple.'

She shook her head half laughing taking a bite out of the sausage roll, it was hotter than anticipated, forcing her to open her mouth and let the steam out, holding the mouthful on her curled tongue in the hopes it couldn't be seen by the rest of the room. That was the benefit of catching the bakery as it just opened, and its wares were fresh out of the ovens, the downside was risking incinerating the roof of your mouth. Nancy wiped her fingers of grease and stood to speak.

Back when Nancy had become a detective there would have been an actual board standing in the room displaying the photo of the victim, and as the case progressed the various leads that the team had chased. It was all digital now though and the only thing to share was the picture of the dead body taken on her phone at the crime scene. It looked bleak taking up the whole of the large screen on the wall.

'Anyone got any thoughts?'

'Murder,' DC Isla Shepherd said from the back of the room.

'Ya think?' Rob teased. 'I thought he might've chopped himself up and then jumped in that recycling bin.'

Isla stuck out her tongue.

Nancy ignored the exchange, it was this kind of light-hearted banter that helped them deal with the horrific things they saw. There was a line, of course, and as long as they never crossed it, they were free to wind each other up.

'We recovered a lot of clothes from the donations bin, might be an idea to see if any of them are his size, I know we believe the body was wrapped in a towel but that doesn't mean that his clothes weren't discarded as well.' Isla continued.

'Thanks Isla, can I leave you to liaise with forensics on that, and if they find anything then we could do some additional DNA swabs. Our victim's blood will have got onto most of the items but if we found sweat or skin cells on collars or cuffs that might give us something a bit more to go on.'

'I want to be able to put a name to this face by the end of the day if at all possible.'

They nodded.

'Now what about this phone, the one that our 999 caller heard, do we have anything back on that yet?' Nancy asked.

'It's with forensics for fingerprinting etc.'

'Can we at least get the details from it so we can start seeing what connection it has to our victim and why someone was calling him insistently at 2am.'

'I'll get on it,' Rob replied.

'Thank you. Cal can you start going through CCTV, there's several businesses in that section with cameras, and can we get uniformed officers to do a sweep of the houses on either side of the road, some might have CCTV or those camera doorbells. Anything that might have seen something.'

'How far do you want me to go back?'

'Let's start with the last twenty-four hours, until Dr Clarke tells us otherwise, we'll work on the assumption that he's not been there longer than that.'

Nancy considered for a moment suggesting to her new DS that he looked like a high school student in black trousers, white shirt, and tie and perhaps he should consider a more casual look, but decided against it. 'How long have you been a DS for?'

'This is my first time in role since getting the promotion,' he smiled.

'Who was your last boss?'

'DI Matthew Biden in Glasgow.'

Nancy didn't recognise the name. 'How old are you, if you don't mind me asking?'

'Twenty-six, I was on the grad scheme.'

Nancy smiled, 'Right, what was your degree in?'

'Criminology, my father wanted me to be a lawyer, but I always fancied the police.'

Rob caught her eye, neither of them had got degrees, they'd worked the beat and come up the ranks together, even been partners for a short while when they were both in uniform. Their careers had mirrored each other's so closely that she'd worried that when she got DI and Rob didn't it would affect their friendship and doubly so when he got moved to her team. But he was good natured and according to him there was too much paperwork and not enough door kicking in being a DI.

'Good for you,' was about all Nancy could muster as a response. 'Rob, can you go to missing persons and see if they recognise this man and if not start going through the data base.'

She sat back down at her desk and finished eating the sausage roll, staring at her computer screen. She closed the link between the PC and the large glass screen on the office wall. Cutting up a human body would take strength and time and make a whole load of mess. The question really was, why do it at all, if you weren't going to spread out the body parts then it wasn't a counter forensics measures.

Chapter 4

DCI Ross Cooper appeared at her office door, for a large man he was unusually stealthy, not that he was fat, he wasn't, but he was 6' 7" tall and built like a rugby player, when she'd first met him Nancy had been struck by how much more like a thug than a detective he looked.

'You keep going to Stephens the Bakers and your whole team will be knocked out by a coronary,' he said standing in the doorway making it feel dark and dingy inside.

'4am call out though, I think they needed it.'

'And you're alright being back?'

'From a week's holiday, of course.'

DCI Cooper took a step further into the office closing the door behind him, ensuring that their conversation couldn't be overheard. 'Nancy don't, not with me, you can do the brave face thing with the team if you want, but be real with me, at least.'

'Chris is having a baby with another woman, I moved out, what more do you want?'

'Have you got somewhere to stay?'

'Yes, I'm good.' She thought about the campervan she had parked in Cellardyke campsite sure that her DCI wouldn't agree that it was a long-term solution, but she was happy, and she'd think about something more permanent after this case was over.

'Have you spoken to your sister?'

'To say what? When I said you could stay with us for a little while I didn't realise I needed to actually tell you not to fuck my partner?'

'You can't avoid her forever though.'

'Watch me.' There was nothing anyone could say that could change her mind, they were both dead to her. The only time she'd waivered was when her 16-year-old step son, Dylan, had asked her not to go, it had broken her heart to leave him behind, she knew that deep down he understood, but still…

'Do you need any help getting your stuff?'

Nancy wasn't really one for stuff and she'd managed to pack most of her belongings into the holdall and backpack she'd taken with her. 'I'll let you know.'

'Alright then, where are we with this case?'

'We've started on CCTV and Missing Persons files, Rob and I will be attending the PM at 2, and we should know more about time and cause of death by then.'

'Fair enough, you'll let me know the outcome?'

'Will do.'

DCI Cooper opened the door and strode across the room almost colliding with Isla as she entered the pods, 'didn't see you there, DC Shepherd.' he said turning sideways to let her past him.

Nancy took a large swig of tea, then grimaced, it was cold, and she wasn't entirely sure it was hers. Tempted to spit the mouthful into the bin, she swallowed then hurriedly took a bite of the Yum Yum. 'Did you know these were Scottish? I read that on a cooking blog.' Nancy said as her DC entered her office.

Isla said nothing in reply.

'What's up?'

'I've just had a call from the lab, there's a few items of clothing they think fit the criteria I gave them, do you want me to go and check them out before we order any additional tests?'

Nancy chewed slowly thinking. Forensic tests are expensive, and she wasn't even sure what the budget was for this case, she should've asked Cooper when he was here, but better to ask for forgiveness than permission.

'Yes please, if you think there's an item, or items that warrant further testing then go ahead and arrange it.'

'Do you want to know the costings first?'

'No, just don't go crazy – stick to any items you think have the biggest likelihood of being our victim's clothes and I'll sign off the paperwork when you get back.'

Isla nodded and left.

Nancy took the half full mug of cold tea and walked across to the sink pouring the contents away. 'How are you getting on?' she asked Cal.

'I've got the CCTV for the grocery store and from the ATM, they have the best view of the entrance to the car park. I've been working my way backwards through it, but nothing suspicious so far. There is a significant blind spot near the recycling bins, which is a challenge as well as three other ways they can be approached. You can come down the side of the pub, down some stairs next to the shops, from the far side of the shops, but you'd need to walk in front of all the shops, plus that path is elevated and easily seen from both the road and the houses on the other side of the road, or you can cut through from the housing estate behind. If I was guessing I'd say that would be the best option, I think you could park in the estate, carry the body down the embankment and to the bins without being picked up on any CCTV.'

'Wouldn't that be risky though, given the body was in parts. Unless there were two people it might mean making a second trip from their car to the recycling bins, doubling the risk of being seen.'

'I don't see any other viable alternatives at the moment, but I've got a couple of uniforms doing a bit of door to door along the street where he, or should I say they, are most likely to have parked, looking for domestic CCTV and asking if anyone saw anything suspicious, but it's mid-day on a Monday so a lot of people are out.'

'Okay, I still think it's worth going through all the CCTV, you never know it might catch something. What about Missing Persons?'

'I've gone back three months so far, and I've a couple of candidates that I thought we could look at after the PM. And Dr Clarke rang, she said she's been delayed in court so PM is now 2.30.' Rob said.

There was a knock at the door and a young female detective poked her head around. 'I'm looking for DI Ravenscroft,' she said.

'Guilty as charged, and you are?'

'Sorry, DC Abbotts, I've recently joined DI Penman's team, but before that I was seconded to an international crime liaison team.' She said, her body still in the corridor.

'Do you want to come in and let me know why you're here?'

The whole team had stopped, distracted by the newcomer, all that was except for Rob, he'd looked up as

Grace came into the room and then looked away, his line of sight trained intently on the computer screen in front of him.

Grace flushed a bright pink 'My DI mentioned your homicide,' she rushed the words out before taking a breath and continuing. 'It made me think of a case I worked before, girl was Australian, Maria Fisher, throat slit, found naked and wrapped in a towel in a commercial bin behind one of those "massage parlours" in Edinburgh and I thought you might be interested.'

'What made you think of bringing this to me?'

'It was the victim being wrapped in a towel and put in a bin, I know totally different MO, but how many murderers wrap the naked body of their victims in a towel before they put them in the bin?

'Interesting, do you have a first name, DC Abbotts?'

'Grace.'

'What was the outcome of that case?'

'It's gone cold, consensus of opinion was that she was a sex worker who upset the wrong person?'

'What did you think?'

'I was just on the periphery, not sure my opinion counted for much.'

'Well, it does now.' Nancy said.

'I thought that the only evidence that she was a sex worker was highly circumstantial and if her body had been found anywhere else that angle wouldn't have been fixated on.'

'Thank you, Maria was Australian you said?'

'Yeah, she'd come over to Scotland to do some travelling, go to the festival, she was working in a club, but the day she went missing she'd gone to interview to be a nanny. When her mother hadn't heard from her in a week she began to panic, normally she text every day. She even came across herself to look for her, that was just before her body was found.'

'Was there any evidence that the nanny job actually existed?'

'Maria had forwarded a copy of the advertisement to her mum, but it was a dead end, phone number was a burner, and the email address didn't get us anywhere either.'

'Interesting, can you email me across the full file?'

Grace gave a short nod, 'will do ma'am,' and then sensing it was time left without saying anything further.

Nancy glanced at her watch, 12.45, enough time to read over the file on Maria Fisher before going to the lab for the PM. She was grateful for having had a big breakfast, she made it a point not to eat directly before. She looked into the office to see Rob heading to the microwave with what looked like left-over takeaway curry. She shook her head and laughed, the man had a Teflon coated stomach, she was sure of it.

On her computer screen she displayed the photo of Maria Fisher's dead body and the one her mother had provided when she made the missing person's report. She'd been a happy looking young woman when she'd left Australia, nine months later she was dead and disposed of in some back alley.

Mrs Fisher had phoned the police every day since she reported her daughter missing, and then until she was finally told there were no more leads in the murder case. Nancy opened Facebook and searched for Maria Fisher and her mother, it didn't take long to find the page 'Justice for Maria' that Mrs Fisher had made in the days after the case was shelved here in Scotland.

In the months following the discovery of her daughter's

body she had continued to campaign for new information, insisting that someone must have seen her daughter's murderer. And in the beginning, she'd received messages from other people from around the world who'd shared hostel dormitories with Maria, handed out leaflets for the Fringe Festival together, and had worked with her in the club, but no one that had seen her after the day of her interview.'

Chapter 5

The drive to the post-mortem took twenty minutes up the A92, Rob had seemed a little distracted and Nancy suspected it had something to do with DC Grace Abbotts, she didn't ask, figuring that some things were better left unknown.

Now sitting on the other side of the glass screen Nancy felt like she was watching a macabre production as Dr Lucy Clarke began the methodical process of the post mortem. Nancy fixed in on the details as Lucy spoke.

'I'll have a full tox screen done on the blood, liver and kidneys, there's no sign of injected drugs and his lungs are clean and tar free, he wasn't a smoker.'

Nancy glanced at Rob who was diligently taking notes, they'd get the full report first thing tomorrow, but he knew her well enough to know she'd want to talk it through with him and then the team later.

'Now this is interesting, this mark on the inside left wrist, not sure what this shape would be called, looks to me like one of those Jesus fishes but with a tail on each side. It looks like it's been burnt into the skin.' Lucy looked up, 'I think his killer branded him.'

'Sorry, *what?*' Nancy said leaning forward and speaking into the intercom system.

'I was saying the killer must've branded him, it's like an outline of a two tailed fish.'

'Can you show me in more detail?'

Lucy took the microscope over the area, displaying the markings in 50x magnification and waited.

'I've seen that exact mark before,' Nancy said.

'Where?' asked Rob.

'On the left shoulder of the dead body of Maria Fisher, who was found, throat slit, naked, wrapped in a towel in the bin in a back alley in Edinburgh a year ago and that can't be a coincidence. They were marked by the same person.' Nancy said.

Chapter 6

'The body was dismembered post mortem, I suppose we should be thankful for small mercies.' Lucy said. 'Cause of death was a single stab wound into the heart, blade was long, narrow and cylindrical.'

'Any idea what it might be?' Nancy asked.

'Your department, not mine, but if you get me some candidates I can do some tests to see if it's a match. Body was sawn in half by a bone saw, like this one.' She held up the one from the tray behind her.

'Someone with access to medical equipment then,' Rob said.

'And if you have access to medical equipment, maybe you have access to a lab like this one,' Nancy added.

'I hate to disappoint you both, but I have a cast iron alibi for the time in question, which was approximately 48 hours ago.'

'Killed elsewhere and then disposed of in the recycling bin.' Nancy stated. 'Any idea how long he'd been in there?'

'Given the temperature inside the bin I'd say he'd been

in there less that 12 hours, much longer and I suspect it would have been the smell rather than the telephone that would've been drawing attention.' Lucy replied.

'Thanks, let me know when the tox screens are back.'

'You hungry?' Rob asked as they walked back up the stairs into the main body of the hospital.

'I can't believe you can think about food after watching that.'

He shrugged, 'it's not like we were just at an abattoir and besides I'm a growing lad, you just ask my mum,' he smiled.

'How's your mum doing?' Nancy asked.

'You know how it is, she'd rather be fussing over everyone else and she doesn't like to talk about the illness. I think she's driving my dad round the bend,' Rob smiled, then changed the subject. 'Branding is a bit freaky don't you think, I mean I've heard of human traffickers doing it to mark a person as belonging to gangs or pimps in the US, but not something I've come across here. Has to be a link between our victim and the Australian girl though doesn't it.' Rob said.

'People don't get symbols burnt onto their skin by choice, the question is why is he marking them and why if he considered them his property did he kill them, and what's with the towels?' Nancy said.

'Do you think there will be more victims?' Rob asked.

'I hope not, but I don't want to rule it out yet.'

The cold March wind battered into them as they opened the doors out to the carpark.

'When we get back to the station, I want to look through any murders in the last year where the victim has been left naked or wrapped in a towel in any kind of bin.' Nancy said as she waited for Rob to press the button to unlock the doors.

'You're thinking this might be a serial killer?'

'Not necessarily, it's just a thread that needs tugged on a little bit harder to see if it unravels anything useful, and I'm going to ask to have Grace Abbotts assigned to our team for the duration of the case,' Nancy glanced across at Rob as he started the engine. 'That's not going to be a problem for you, is it?' she'd noticed the way Rob and Grace had deliberately avoided eye contact with each other this morning.

'Not for me.' He replied without looking at his boss.

'Do I need or want to know what happened?'

'I liked her, I thought she liked me, we hooked up a couple of times and then out of nowhere she just stopped replying to my texts.'

'So not awkward at all then,' Nancy said sarcastically.

'You know me boss, I'm a consummate professional.' He gave a half smile. He'd been hurt by Grace's actions, more than he'd cared to admit. It hadn't been merely his ego that had taken a bruising, he'd really liked her, and he'd thought it was mutual.

'Good, because we need all the help we can get.'

Chapter 7

Nancy knocked on DCI Cooper's office door before opening it without waiting to be invited in. Cooper said nothing, he looked at her, his eyes narrowing. 'Social visit or case update?' he asked.

'A favour.'

'What?' he asked.

'DC Grace Abbotts, I know she's not long joined DI Penman's team, but I'd like to borrow her for this case, she has prior investigative knowledge of an interconnected case, having her will save us a whole lot of work and an extra pair of hands wouldn't go amiss.'

'I think I might have remembered another dismembered body locally.'

'It's not exactly the same, but there are enough similarities that I think we'd be daft not to think the two are connected and if there's two then maybe there's more.' Nancy paused, scanning her boss' face trying to decide if her argument was winning him over. 'And if it's a serial killer then we don't want to waste any more time.'

'You can have her for one week starting tomorrow morning and if you haven't been able to prove you're looking at a serial killer, she goes back to Mhairi,' DCI Cooper said leaning back in his chair, arms crossed.

'And if I have proved it?' She was pushing her luck, but now was the time, she knew he was still feeling sorry for her, and Nancy was prepared to use that to her best advantage.

'Then you have her for the rest of your case, but she's Mhairi's resource, don't forget she may need one of your team in the future and I'll expect you to be equally accommodating.'

Nancy nodded, they both knew that she'd never give up one of her guys without a fight though. Now all she had to do was avoid Mhairi Penman for at least one week.

Isla was waiting for her when she re-joined the team, 'Sylvia Young is here,' she said.

Nancy looked at her confused.

'The woman who called in the dead body in the car park,' Isla replied. 'I've got her sitting in one of the interview rooms, do you want to speak to her or do you want me to do it.' Isla asked.

Nancy looked at her watch, 'Let's do it together.'

The two women entered the room and introduced themselves to Sylvia.

'Thanks for coming in, how's your dad doing?' Nancy asked remembering that Rob had let her go so she could get to him. The woman looked pale, dark circles making her eyes sink into her face.

'He's in hospital, they're not sure he'll wake up,' Sylvia said quietly.

'I'm so sorry to hear that. We'll try to be quick with this so you can get back to him.' Nancy said, the thought that helping them with their enquiries would be stealing precious moments from her witness.

'Thank you, I'm not sure that I can be of much help though.'

'Do you always park your car in that car park?' Nancy asked.

'I try not to, I live over the road and sometimes when I get home my neighbour has people round and I can't get parked anywhere near the house. It's a bloody nightmare, I've called the council so many times, but they just keep telling me there's nothing they can do.' Sylvia looked at Nancy. 'They've been awful since they moved in, parties, noise till all hours. My neighbour on the other side went round to complain and they threatened to smash his windows. Sorry I know you're not interested in that, but that's why I sometimes use that car park, I can't risk being blocked in if dad needs me.'

'And that night you didn't see anything out of the ordinary either when you parked up the first time or when you were walking across to your car?'

'No, but to be honest I'm not sure I would've noticed anything.' Sylvia said.

'You were in a rush, I understand,' Nancy said. 'Why did you bother looking for the phone then?'

'I don't know, I wasn't going to. I was so close to getting in my car and driving off except I had this nagging feeling, what if the owner of that phone was like me and someone they loved needed them and they couldn't get hold of them because they'd accidentally dropped their phone in that bin thing.'

'What did you do?'

'I thought I'll have a look, maybe it would be easy to

reach, I guess I wasn't really thinking about it beyond that.' Sylvia said.

'What made you think that there was a dead body in there?' Nancy asked.

'The smell, I worked in a butchers shop once and there's a smell when meat is going bad, I recognised it.' Sylvia said.

'Could've been a pack of mince though, why dead body?' Nancy pressed.

'It was a lot of blood, it would be hard to get that much blood from something that had been properly butchered. I suppose it might've been any kind of animal, there was just something that made me feel like it needed reporting and that's what I did.'

Nancy thanked Sylvia for coming in, there wasn't much to be gained from the woman's account of the evening and there was nothing in what she'd told them that had aroused Nancy's suspicions that she was anything other than what she presented as; a conscientious member of the public.

Keen to find out what her team had been doing in her absence she made her way across to Cal. 'How are you getting on with the neighbourhood door cams?'

'Still nothing new, I've asked uniform to go out again this evening to all the houses with camera doorbells that weren't home this morning.'

'Okay thanks, Isla any update on the clothes in the donation bin?'

'Nothing of any use, most of the donations are women and children's clothing, and none of the men's clothing looks like they would fit our victim.'

'Brilliant so we're no further forward than we were this morning?'

Cal raised his hand.

'You're not at school Cal, just speak if you have something to say,' Nancy managed without rolling her eyes.

'I know some of the guys in cyber forensics and I got them to give me a printout of the calls made and received, I've been having a look at the numbers. The one that he was receiving a call from on the night the body was found called our victim nine times, I'm trying to find out who the number belongs to, but you know what mobile companies can be like. There's only a couple of months' worth of calls on the phone, so looks like it was new to him, and it's a burner so no contract information.'

'Good work Cal, keep pushing on those numbers, we need to know who was so desperate to get in touch with him.'

Cal nodded, his black hair flopping about making him look even more like an enthusiastic schoolboy.

'I've had an email through from missing persons, they think they might have a match for our victim.' Rob said still staring at his mobile phone screen.

'Finally.' Nancy stood up, 'come on then,' she indicated to him, 'let's go.'

Contrary to what you often see on the television, the Missing Persons department was not located in the basement and watched over by a crumbling DI on the verge of retirement. Instead, it occupied a corner of a large open plan floor that looked like it had been given a budget for upgrading the décor.

'DI Ravenscroft,' Nancy announced herself as she approached the young woman sitting at the closest desk. 'We got a ping saying you might have information on our victim?'

'The binman?'

Nancy winced, she'd never been a fan of anything that

dehumanised a victim and reducing him to where his body was dumped felt wrong on every level.

'Your email said you had a possible match.' Rob stepped into the conversation.

'Yeah, hold on a second, and I'll bring him up.' A few keystrokes later and a face filled her computer screen. The man in the picture bore an uncanny resemblance to the victim, it would be hard to believe they weren't one and the same.

'When was he reported missing?' Nancy asked.

'Hmm, just over a week ago, went for a date and never came back. The sister was insistent that something must've happened to him, she was a bit of a pain in the arse if I'm being honest.' The officer looked up at them. 'I'll email across the whole file. Can you let us know if it turns out to be the binman, we'll update our records.'

'Thanks,' Rob said gently taking hold of his boss' arm and leading her away.

Nancy scowled at him.

'Look Nance, I'm saying this as your friend, are you sure you're in the right head space for being back at work, break-ups are shitty and what's happened to you, I can't imagine…' he trailed off.

'Not you as well, I've already had Cooper doing his softly, softly routine on me today.'

'I know you don't want to hear this, but you seem a little off today and what happened to your iron in your move, because that shirt definitely hasn't seen one.'

Nancy looked down at what she had to admit was a very crumpled shirt, sure that when she'd dressed this morning it hadn't looked that bad. 'I used my iron to clock the last DS that questioned my capability,' Nancy smiled. 'Thank you for caring, but I'm good and I'm more than able to do my job.'

'I wasn't questioning your investigative abilities, it was your interpersonal ones I had concerns about.'

'Fair point,' she knew that she'd been more irritable today, and being woken up in the middle of the night to look at a dead body in a car park wasn't enough of an excuse in her line of work. 'I'll do my best to be nicer to everyone.' Nancy forced a smile.

'Just don't bite anyone's head off, how about we aim for something achievable.'

Back in her office she opened the file from Missing Persons and looked at the face of Owen Fairmile, 32, missing for three weeks, reported by his sister Diane after she hadn't been able to contact him for over twenty four hours.

Owen had done twelve years in the Navy after leaving school at 16, in the following two years he'd had a string of jobs, none of which seemed to stick until he started working for a local estate agent. He'd been in between houses and had been crashing with his sister for the last couple of weeks which is why she'd become so worried when she hadn't been able to get in contact with him.

Nancy emailed the file on to Dr Clarke, if it was Owen then it would be easy enough to confirm

Chapter 8

Cal knocked on the open door, 'that number boss, the one that tried calling our victim so many times, it belongs to a Rachel Howgate.'

'That was quick, how did you get the mobile phone companies to release the information?'

'Oh, I didn't – I'm still waiting on them getting back to me.'

'So how do you know who called?'

'I thought I would type it into Google in case something came up, and it got a hit on Rachel Howgate.'

'And who is she?'

'I was wondering if she might be his partner, I found her because she's got her number attached to some of her social media, it's surprising how much you can find about someone if you just look.'

'Should I be worried or impressed?'

Cal smiled, 'I was hoping for impressed. I'd thought about going into cyber security before I joined the Police.'

Nancy nodded, 'good work.' She noticed his cheeks

flush peachy pink. 'What were you able to find out about her?'

'Not much, she posts a lot of pictures of eating out at restaurants, and she has a few gym pictures but nothing that really tells us very much. Her profiles says she works in finance but nothing specific and she checks-in at places within a fifty mile radius of Dunfermline, but I'd need to get some help to properly look into her.'

'Any photos of her with our victim?'

Cal shook his head, 'no photos of her with anyone.'

'Did you do one of those reverse image searches?'

'No not yet, what are you thinking?'

Nancy shrugged, 'I'm thinking that if our victim was her boyfriend there should be pictures of them together.'

'Could be they were just seeing each other.'

'What does that even mean,' Nancy realised her tone had been angrier than she intended. 'I just mean dating seems to be so much more complicated than it used to be.'

'Oft, showing you're age a bit there, boss,' Rob chuckled from her office doorway.

If she'd not had Cal stood in front of her, she would have stuck her middle finger up at Rob, she settled for a scowl.

'Do you have anything to add to this conversation or were you just lurking in the hopes of offending me?'

'That was an added bonus, Dr Clarke just phoned, she can confirm Owen Fairmile is our victim, he'd had dental x-rays done a month ago.'

'Alright then. We'd better go and inform the sister, Diane, wasn't it?'

Rob glanced down at the paperwork in his hand, 'that's right, Diane Bridlington, 36, divorced, 2 children, 10 and 16, works as a doctor's receptionist. It was in the mis-per file,' Rob added when he noticed his boss looking at him curiously.

'I take it we have an address?'

'Yeah, it's in The Heathery.'

The houses in The Heathery had been considered exclusive when they'd been built, the man that did the voice over for the 1980s tv programme Gladiators had even lived in one. Now though, whilst still very nice, they weren't quite as exclusive with the growth of houses in the Dunfermline area, and the fascination of the new build, meant they weren't as desirable as they'd once been.

As they pulled into the street Nancy thought about what attracted people to houses like these, they were nice, and big, but each one looked much like its neighbour, everyone playing keeping up with the Jones' when it came to new cars and soffit board lighting. She'd clocked at least seven Tesla Model 3s as they'd made their way to Diane Bridlington's house.

Nancy glanced down at her creased shirt, would she have paid more attention to it if she'd known she'd have been giving someone the worst news later that day? The truth was probably not, Diane wasn't going to remember what she looked like, she was only going to remember the feeling of devastation.

The door was answered by a teenage boy.

'Is your mum in?' Nancy asked.

He frowned, 'who are you?'

She took her warrant card from her pocket, 'I'm DI Nancy Ravenscroft and this is my colleague DS Rob MacDonald. Is your mum in?'

He nodded, 'have you come about Uncle Owen?'

'I think it's best we talk to your mum indoors, pal, if that's okay.' Rob said.

He disappeared from the open front door, in the background they heard him tell his mother that the police were at the door. A few moments later a woman appeared, she was tall and athletic looking, an image enhanced by her wearing a tracksuit.

They reintroduced themselves and Diane ushered them into the house and through to the living room. Nancy had expected pale wood floors and cream leather and was surprised to see a plush blue carpet and well used brown leather sofas. Nancy and Rob sat awkwardly on the two seater sofa together.

'Michael take your brother upstairs and look after him,' Diane said to the older boy. He hesitated, clearly torn between following his mother's directions and wanting to be there for her. 'I'll be fine, go on. Noah, go with your brother, if you're lucky he'll give you a shot on his Playstation.'

'Really?' the younger boy said clearly not understanding the gravity of the situation.

'Yeah, come on.' Michael said, putting up no protest against a directive that would ordinarily have caused an all-out teenage tantrum..

'Thank you,' Diane looked at her oldest son smiling weakly.

How frequently did she lean on her son, Nancy wondered, that there wasn't the slightest hint of defiance.

The adults waited until after the living room door was closed and they were satisfied that the boys were out of earshot.

'You'll have come about Owen.' The words were matter of fact but the scratch in Diane's voice gave away her emotion.

'I'm sorry Mrs Bridlington, we have found Owen's body...'

Diane gasped and clutched her chest, opening her mouth to take in air without success. They sat in silence giving Diane the chance to regain her composure. 'Are you sure it's him?'

'We've had a positive dental match and with your permission we'll do a DNA match to be certain.'

'How…how did he die?'

Rob shot a glance at Nancy hoping that she was going to be the one to answer this question.

'We're treating Owen's death as suspicious,' Nancy said, it was better than saying murdered, not as harsh and for now she'd like to spare the woman some pain. 'Do you know if he had any enemies, had he had any fallings out with any of his mates?' Nancy asked.

'No, he had a tight knit group of mates, known most of them from school or the Navy.'

'What about his work?'

Nancy noticed a slight grimace on Diane's face.

'What is it?' she asked.

'Probably not important, Owen liked his job, he enjoyed meeting with people and helping them sell their houses.'

'But?'

'But a couple of months ago the company brought in a new guy, Owen said there was something off about him, he couldn't quite put his finger on it, he said he gave him an uneasy feeling.'

'Did he tell you this man's name?'

'Jake, but he never mentioned his last name, I'm sorry.'

'Don't be, you're doing great. You said in the missing person's report that Owen had been living with you, how did that come about.'

'His landlord gave him notice, he was selling the flat, gave Owen first refusal.'

'Owen wasn't interested?'

Diane lifted her shoulders in a half shrug, 'I think he thought buying a flat meant that he was tied down, settled. He still spoke about going traveling, him and Michael were meant to be taking a trip this summer to Australia, New Zealand and Thailand. Michael is going to be devastated, he idolised his uncle, they were so close.'

'Like a surrogate father?' Rob asked.

'No, it wasn't that kind of relationship they were just super close.'

'You didn't mind Owen coming to live with you?'

'He was easy to get along with, helped out with the boys, he'd do the ironing, better than me to be honest and it's not like I don't have the room. I was actually quite enjoying having another adult around.' She took a sharp inhalation of breath before tears streamed down her cheeks, the banks of her emotion had broken now.

'My sergeant will get you a cup of tea.' Nancy said.

'No, it's okay,' Diane dried her eyes on a paper handkerchief then blew her nose, 'I want to get through this, I want to help you find out who did this to my brother.'

'If you're sure?'

She nodded.

'Did Owen have a mobile phone?'

'Yes, an iPhone – I'm not sure which variety, I just know it was the latest one, he always kept up with technology, the only blessing was that he gave his hand me downs to the boys, with the upkeep of this place, my wages are spread pretty thin.'

'Do you know if he had it when he went out the last time you saw him.'

'Yes, he text me to say he was at the restaurant, joked

that his date was running late and that he might've been stood up.'

'Was that the first time he would've met this woman in person.'

'Yeah, they'd been messaging before for a while, he'd spoken to her on the phone. I think he liked her. When he didn't come home that night I assumed,' she blushed, 'you know that he'd got lucky, but I thought he'd be back the next day, when I hadn't heard from him by lunch time, I knew something was wrong. I tried calling his phone and it went straight to voicemail. I left a message telling him I was worried and not to be a dick and just let me know he was okay. I kept calling but nothing – Michael has Owen's last phone and they're still under the same Apple account, so he tried the find my phone thing, but it was like the phone was turned off and that's when I properly started to worry. I phoned round his friends and they hadn't heard from him then I tried the hospitals and nothing so I called the police and they said to come in and make a report.'

'Can we see Owen's bedroom?' Nancy asked.

'Of course, I'll take you up.'

The staircase twisted round a wide landing in the middle at the top of the stairs. Owen's bedroom was a decent size, with an ensuite, compared to Nancy's current living conditions this space was practically palatial.

Diane stood in the doorway looking as though crossing the threshold was some kind of betrayal.

'We'll be okay if you want to go and check on your boys,' Nancy said.

Diane said nothing before turning and heading towards a closed bedroom door.

'It doesn't even look like anyone was living in here, it's so neat and tidy.' Rob pulled open a drawer and looked at the row of neatly folded t-shirts, raising his eyebrows at the sight.

'He was in the Navy, they learn to iron and fold, I'm not sure this is as outrageous as you're implying.'

Rob pushed the drawer closed and continued looking.

Nancy sat at the pine desk and opened the MacBook, it was unsurprisingly password protected. 'We should bag this and see if the tech people can get access.'

The sound of crying could be heard now from the boy's bedroom then a door bashed against a wall and Michael appeared in the hallway. He shot an angry look in our direction before stomping down the stairs.

'What's that about do you think?' Nancy said to Rob.

'His favourite uncle is dead, he's a teenage boy, I think his reaction is fairly standard.'

Nancy sucked her tongue against her teeth, making a wet clicking sound, Rob curled his top lip in disgust. The look was enough to make his boss stop.

'I'm not sure we're going to find any answers in here,' Rob declared.

Nancy walked along the worn blue carpet towards the other bedroom, knocking gently on the open door. Noah was lying on the bed in the foetal position, the tip of his thumb secured in his mouth. Diane looked frozen, arms wrapped around her own body. Nancy gently touched her arm and the women jumped.

'Sorry,' Nancy said. 'We're going to leave you in peace just now. We've taken Owen's laptop and I'll have one of our family liaison officers out with you within the hour. If you think of anything else then please just call,' Nancy held out her business card waiting for Diane's glacial response to take it.

'I'm sorry about Michael,' she said as she took hold of the card. 'He's not normally like that.'

'It's been a horrible shock for him, he'll come round.'

'Do you have children?'

'Yes,' Nancy replied out of habit, but the word caught in her throat, was that even true anymore, was Dylan still her son? 'About the same age, hormones and emotions are a lot, he'll be okay, he's a good kid.' Diane smiled, but Nancy wasn't even sure she was still talking about Michael.

'You okay Nance,' Rob whispered as they descended the stairs. She nodded slowly, even though the thought of Dylan no longer being in her life had caused a gut wrenching sensation.

Outside Michael was sat on the pavement, legs crossed, the heels of his hands embedded in his eye sockets trying to contain his tears. Rob lowered himself to the ground, 'How are you doing?'

'Can I see him?'

'We can arrange that if you'd like to.' Rob knew that Nancy would have liked to kick him for agreeing to that.

'You and Owen were close.'

Michael wiped his face on the sleeve of his sweatshirt. 'He was the best, mum's fine, she tries, but she still thinks I'm a little kid, I think she forgets that I'm six years older than Noah, I'm practically an adult.'

'Owen treated you like an equal?' Rob suggested.

'We were going to go travelling this summer, mum said no in the beginning, but he persuaded her.' His head dropped and the crying began again. 'And now I'm going to be stuck here forever because she'll be afraid to let me out her sight.'

'Yeah, it's hard, but you gotta remember her baby brother was murdered, how would you feel if it was Noah?'

Michael looked at Rob as though the thought had never occurred to him. 'I suppose, I just don't understand why anyone would want to hurt Uncle Owen though, everyone loved him.'

'What about this girl he was talking to?'

Michael blushed, 'she was pretty, Owen said she was out of his league, but I thought she was a bit…suspect.'

'how so?'

'Every time he suggested Facetiming she always had an excuse, not enough data, poor wifi, her phone was playing up. He thought I was being cynical but I was starting to think that she wasn't real.'

'Your mum said they spoke on the phone.'

'That doesn't mean anything. You can make computers do that these days if you're clever enough.'

'I did a reverse image search and showed him that she wasn't real, the pictures weren't of this Rachel person.'

'How did he take that.'

'He was pissed off, but in the end he told me this was a teachable moment and the opportunity to learn that what someone looks like isn't as important as the emotional connection you make with someone. It was after that he pushed her to meet him for a date. I thought she'd just ghost him, I couldn't believe it when she agreed.'

'What did he tell you about that conversation?'

'That she admitted everything, she was sorry, and she sent him a real picture of herself.' Michael paused, his face pale and his eyes bloodshot 'If she killed him then this is all my fault.'

Rob patted the boy on the back. 'We don't have enough information to know what happened yet and even if it was her then it definitely isn't your fault. It would be great if you could remember what this woman looked like though.'

'I can show you. I have Owen's old phone, so all our photos synced to one another's phones, he joked that it was annoying, but I knew he didn't even care.' Michael already had his phone out scrolling through the photos until he came to one of a woman with dark curly hair, she looked like she was in her late twenties, and with a figure that could be described as curvy.

'Can you let me get a copy of that.'

Michael nodded.

'If you think of anything else you call me,' Rob handed Michael his business card and was just about to stand up when he said, 'you don't happen to know Owen's computer password do you?'

'No sorry,' the boy said.

'Michael come inside,' Diane called from the doorway.

Nancy wondered how long she'd been lurking there.'

She was marching towards them. 'Don't you need a parent present to question him.'

'If we were questioning him, we would need a suitable adult, but for consoling a teenage boy on the loss of his uncle we're good,' Nancy replied, chastising herself for not having enough compassion for the woman.

'Inside Michael now, Noah needs you.' She held out her hand towards him.

Michael stood up and walked towards her brushing off any attempt she gave to touch him.

They stood and watched as the two figures went inside. 'There is something not right there.' Nancy said as she opened the passenger door and got in.

Chapter 9

Nancy would have kept working through the night, but perhaps that had more to do with going back to a dark campsite and a tin of beans for dinner, but she could tell the troops were starting to flag, they'd been up since early and if she wanted them at their best then she needed to let them rest and she didn't want to have the excessive overtime conversation with Cooper too soon into the investigation either.

Her drive home took just under an hour and she spent the time running through scenarios in her mind. Was Grace Abbotts right and there was a connection between the murdered Australian and the death of Owen Fairmile? Their shared marking suggested there was.

The temptation to stop past The Wee Chippy on the way back to her van was immense but if she kept doing that, she'd be the size of a bus in no time and then Chris would think she'd been eating her emotions and was heartbroken rather than lazy. She should be heartbroken, should have cried, but the only feeling she'd managed to muster up was rage.

Then as if her thoughts had conjured the demon himself her phone rang. She rejected the call. He tried again, and again. Perhaps she should've answered but it had been a long day and she was in no mood for his bullshit.

Her car scrunched over the gravel as she pulled onto the campsite and round to her van. She caught site of a figure sitting on the one of the folding deck chairs she kept under the van. In the darkness it was hard to make out who it might be. Nancy was in no mood for company, but it looked like she didn't have a lot of choice. She parked the car and took her police torch out of her bag shining it at the intruder.

'Bloody hell mum, you're blinding me with that thing.'

'Dylan?'

'Obviously, who else were you expecting.'

She thought about the missed calls. She wrapped her arms around the boy, who, though only sixteen made her look short. 'How long have you been sitting here?'

He shrugged, 'a couple of hours. I got the bus.'

'Are you alright?'

'Had a huge fight with dad, and I just wanted to talk to you.'

'You hungry?'

He nodded his head.

'Fancy a chippy?'

'When do I not.'

This was not a conversation to be had over a shared tin of baked beans. 'Right, we can walk down, it's a nice enough evening.'

Nancy passed the walk with pleasantries about school

and the rugby team, whatever was bothering her boy needed to be accompanied by a hot meal and a strong cup of tea.

Once inside the welcoming restaurant and with a double order of Fish, Chips, bread, baked beans and a pot of tea ordered Nancy asked the question she should have asked the moment she'd laid eyes on Dylan.

'So does he know you're here?'

'I told him I was coming to see you, but he doesn't know I'm here, here, because I kept my promise and didn't tell him where you're living.'

'Thanks, we should probably tell him you're safe though, so he doesn't worry.'

'I don't want to talk to him, he's a dickhead.'

Nancy couldn't disagree with that statement, but she also knew it wasn't worth the hassle of not calling Chris. 'Fine let me call him and tell him you're with me and you're staying for a couple of days.'

'Okay.'

Nancy called the number, 'hey it's me, sorry couldn't answer when you called. Dylan is with me, I think it's best he stays here a couple of days.'

Nancy shut her eyes in exasperation, waiting for his response.

'Tell me where you are and I'll come and get him.'

'No. I told you he's staying with me for a couple of days.'

'I'm his father and I'm telling you he's coming home.'

'Doesn't what Dylan want count for anything?'

'You can't just kidnap him, how would it look if I let Cooper know what you're up to.'

'I'm hardly kidnapping him, I'm his parent too remember.'

'No, you're not, he's my son not yours, tell me where you are or…' Nancy hung up the call and turned to Dylan, 'That went about as well as could be expected. You want to tell me what you two were arguing about?'

The conversation was momentarily paused as two steaming plates of food were placed in front of them.

'I told him I wanted to see my mum and he said my mum was dead, and I said you were my mum and he said not anymore, so I told him he was a bellend and that I never wanted to see him again.'

'You will always be my son, and I don't care that there's not the legal paperwork for it or that I don't have the stretch marks to prove it.' Dylan had been 4 years old when she'd moved in with Chris and she'd become mummy within weeks. Not able to have biological children, Dylan was a blessing and the only reason she hadn't left his twat of a father sooner.

He smiled back at her. 'He wants me to move into the small bedroom because Aunt Catherine wants my room for the nursery, she says the new baby needs the space.'

'Charming.'

'Can't I just come live with you?'

'I live in a van Dylan, there's barely room for me never mind the two of us.'

'Could you not get a new place?'

When she'd met Chris she'd had her own flat and for years she'd kept it and rented it out, then three years ago he'd persuaded her to sell it, pay off the mortgage on the house and do an extension. She'd been stupid and not insisted on getting her name on the deeds and now she had nothing. She needed to see a solicitor to see if she had a leg to stand on to get anything back from him.

'I'd like that but it's complicated.'

'I'm sixteen, I don't see why he should have any control over where I live.'

'Let's just deal with tonight first.'

Chapter 10

DAY TWO, TUESDAY

Dylan already had the kettle on before Nancy unzipped her sleeping bag. 'I'll get breakfast ready if you want to go across and get washed.'

'Do you not have school today?'

'No, it's a study day,' he laughed at her, she retaliated by sticking out her tongue. 'I'll be back in about twenty minutes.'

Today she'd deliberately picked out a long sleeved top that wouldn't show the creases like a shirt. The jeans from the previous day had passed the sniff test. Dylan had coffee and a bowl of Coco Pops waiting.

'Remember when you wouldn't let me eat these, you tried to get me to eat sultana bran flakes instead.'

'You've been a bad influence on me,' Nancy said before taking a mouthful. 'What are you going to do today?'

'Thought I'd go for a walk and maybe do some grocery shopping seeing as your fridge is empty.'

'And your dad?'

'What about him?'

'We need to do something.'

'I should at least get to spend the weekends with you.' Dylan said.

'Okay, you're here till Sunday, I'll speak to your dad later and get it sorted out.'

On the way to the station she thought about Michael Bridlington talking about Owen treating him like he was grown and wondering if he'd shared more with his nephew than he'd let on.

Nancy was the first person into the office, relishing the stillness she made herself a coffee and text Rob to ask him to stop by a shop on the way in and get her a sandwich. A breakfast of coco pops can only get you so far.

'Morning boss,' Cal's cheerful voice made her jump.

'Hi Cal. I've got a job for you, I want you to see if you can find the woman who was catfishing Owen, his nephew Michael gave us her picture yesterday, so see what you can do yourself and pass it off to the techs if you need to.'

'No problem,'

'How come you joined the police, surely you'd have a quieter, better paid life working in cyber security.'

'You sound like my dad,' he smiled awkwardly. 'my last year of uni I was attacked, beaten up in and the police were great, it had all been caught on CCTV, but none of them knew what it was like to be beaten up because of how you look. I just thought maybe if I joined up then I could make a difference and you know my tech skills come in handy as well.'

'Why not join the technical forensics side then?'

'I wanted to do a job where I would be seen.'

Nancy was quiet for a few moments, 'I'm sorry that happened to you.'

Cal gave a slight upward nod of his head in acknowledgement.

'Bacon sangers all round.' Rob said bursting through the door. 'Cal I didn't know what you like so you've got bacon, cos I figured it was a safe bet, boss, square sausage and for you,' he turned to Isla who had followed him through the door, 'Egg and bacon, because one filling in your roll is never enough.'

'Thanks.' Nancy bit into the roll. 'Right troops, DC Grace Abbotts with be joining us later today and I'm sure you will make her feel very welcome. Isla can you work with Grace on the cold case, link in with forensics and Dr Clarke on the PM and see if there are any other similarities between our victims disappearance and death. Cal, you can try to find our mystery woman, and then can you look back through both victims online presence and see if you can find anything that overlaps.'

She was interrupted as Rob pulled the ring pull on his energy drink can and took a noisy gulp. He looked at her smiling with a vague apology.

'Rob, you get the pleasure of my company, we're going to go and see where Owen worked, hopefully see his colleague Jake, that Diane said he was at odds with.'

She finished her roll and threw its brown paper bag wrapping in the bin. 'Let's make some progress today folks,' she picked up her jacket, indicating for Rob to follow. 'You drive today.'

'That's two days in a row.'

'uh-huh'

'It's not like you.'

'I need to make a phone call on the way.'

Part of her hoped that Chris didn't answer, then she'd have the freedom to leave him a voice mail.

'Hello, Chris' phone.'

Amazing, Nancy thought, bloody amazing. 'It's Nancy I need to speak to Chris.'

'Oh he's in the shower just now,' her sister giggled, Nancy felt a little bit of sick rise up her throat.'

'Can you tell him I called, and that Dylan is staying with me until the weekend, I'll drop him back on Sunday evening.' She was about to hang up when her sister said…

'You know it's wrong of you to try and take Dylan away from us, he's not your son.'

'Well Chris wasn't your partner and you still fucked him.' Her cheeks were flushed with anger, she could tell Rob was giving her a certain sideways look. 'I've raised Dylan since he was four years old, he's my son and nothing you say or do will ever change that. So just tell Chris that Dylan will be back on Sunday.' Nancy hung up.

'That sounded like it went well,' Rob replied.

'Just drive, I don't want to talk about it.'

The estate agent was situated on East Port in Dunfermline town centre, it was one of several similar businesses all located within a stone's throw of each other. It had probably made sense when this street had housed four banks.

The door made a beep-boop sound as they pushed it open. A pretty young woman behind an oversized desk looked up and smiled. 'Is there anything we can help you with?'

They showed their ID, 'Any chance your boss is in today?

'Um, he's in but, he's not working,' the woman whose name badge identified her as Melissa said.

'We're not interested in buying houses, Melissa, we're here about a very serious police matter.' Rob said.

Melissa glanced nervously at the office directly behind her.

'Is he in there?' Nancy asked already making her way past reception.

Melissa sprang up from her seat, narrowly making it to the office door before them, she knocked quickly and opened the door. Inside the very plain white painted office was a man in his late fifties, blue jeans turned up at the bottom, boating style shoes on the feet that stuck out from under the desk. A pink designer label shirt, top two buttons undone exposing tufts of chest hair.

'Melissa, I said no clients,' he smiled politely towards us, his expression in juxtaposition to the one he shot at the woman.

'I know Mr Andrews, but they're not clients, they're police.' Her cheeks were scarlet and there was a slight tremble in her hands, but she stood her ground.

'How can we help officers?'

'Thank you Melissa,' Nancy said waiting until the woman closed the door and left.

'We're investigating the murder of one of your staff, Owen Fairmile.'

'Owen's dead?'

'Yes.'

'You can't think we would have anything to do with that,' he shifted in his seat. A message pinged up on his phone, just too far away for either Nancy or Rob to see it. Mr Andrews opened the desk drawer and pushed the phone inside.

'No one is saying you did. Has something happened here to make you think his death might be connected to his work?'

'Of course not, we sell houses, we help people achieve their dreams.'

'How did Owen get on here?'

'Good, I liked him, thought he had potential, he was hard working, meticulous, a bit too much in the detail sometimes.'

'How did he get on with his colleagues?'

'Well, he wasn't one for drama.'

'His sister mentioned that he'd had a falling out with someone named Jake?'

'Professional differences, nothing personal.'

'Is Jake in today?' Nancy asked.

'No it's his day off, he worked last Saturday.'

'What did you think when Owen went missing?'

'I was shocked, he didn't seem like the type to walk out on his life without a word to anyone, but when his sister called to see if we'd seen him and said she was worried about him going missing I have to admit I wasn't initially concerned, he's still a young man, I thought the likelihood was that he had found himself a bit of company.'

'But then he didn't come back.'

'No, his sister was very overbearing, I remember thinking she spoke about him like she was his mother and I wondered if he needed some space from her, I wasn't that convinced he was missing, more avoiding her...' the man paused. 'But now you say he's dead, she was right to be worried.'

'What was he doing the last time you saw him?'

'He was visiting someone to do a valuation appointment in the morning then in the afternoon he met a couple to do a viewing.'

'Was that a normal sort of day for him?'

'Not really, he wouldn't normally do the viewings, it was

Jake's appointment, but he phoned in sick that day, so Owen said he'd do it and then he was going to work late to do his paperwork.'

'Do you still have that property on your books?'

'Umm, I can check, but even if we do that was over a week ago, there will have been lots of other viewings and then there's the owners…oh.'

'What is it?' Nancy asked.

'It seems there was a boundary dispute logged on this property the following Monday and until that's resolved we can't sell it.'

'Is anyone living there at the moment?'

'No, looks like it had been an Air BnB but with all the new regulations in Scotland we are seeing more of them coming onto the market.'

'We're going to need the keys. And the viewers details.' Nancy said.

'The keys I can do, but I can't just give you out people's details, besides Owen came back, finished his day and went home, so they can't have had anything to do with what happened to him.'

'We can come back with a warrant.' Rob said.

'Then you do that, I'm sympathetic and I want you to find out who hurt Owen, but if my customers knew that I just gave up their details to the police – well I wouldn't be in business much longer.'

'I see your point…' Nancy gave a disappointed smile. '… but I can't imagine what they will think when they know you don't want to help the police solve a murder,' she stood up. 'Anyway, we'll come back with that warrant.'

Mr Andrews stood behind his desk pondering the quandary he now found himself in. 'I'm sure they'll understand, after all, like you said, you're investigating a murder.'

'Well, if you're sure.' Nancy said staring back at him.

'I'll ask Melissa to get you the keys and the details.'

'Thank you for your co-operation,' Rob said.

Mr Andrews looked back and forth between them. 'Is there anything else,' he looked at his gold wrist watch. 'it's just I need to be getting going, the wife is expecting me.'

'We'll need Jake's home address and contact telephone numbers as well.' Nancy replied.

A few minutes later they were back on the street. 'Right Jake first, you think?' Nancy said.

'He's just down the road in one of the old hospital flats.'

'You want to walk?' Nancy asked.

'No danger, walking down the New Row is one thing but I'm not walking back up it.'

'I thought you were supposed to be training for a triathlon,' Nancy frowned at him.

'I was, but it's a lot of work and it turns out I'm not a fan of swimming in the Forth.'

She laughed at him, 'we're walking, don't be so blooming lazy.'

'It's number 117,' Rob pushed the external door and finding it open, they began to climb the stairs to the first floor flat.

Nancy held her finger on the doorbell for a couple more seconds than polite and was rewarded with the sound of an irritated male voice, shouting that he was coming. With a jingle of keys and a few choice curse words the door opened revealing a man in his late twenties in a pair of boxer shorts and ankle length black socks, his hair dishevelled. The inside of the flat looked like it hadn't seen the sunshine, such that it was, today.

He squinted at them, the light from the hallway dazzling into his face, 'what?'

'Jake Masters?'

'Who's asking?'

Nancy took out her ID, 'DI Nancy Ravenscroft and DS Rob MacDonald, can we come in?'

Jake frowned but moved out of the way. As she passed she was met with the smell of stale alcohol on the mans breath. 'Find your way to the kitchen and make him a coffee would you.' Nancy said to Rob.

In the kitchen Rob unearthed the kettle from under an open box of half-eaten take-out pizza, he leaned in and gave it a sniff, recoiling quickly in disgust. That was not last night's dinner, in fact he couldn't be sure how long it had been sitting in the kitchen, but long enough that he wouldn't have even considered eating it and that was saying something. Rob was proud of his Teflon stomach, but that was pushing it.

The only milk had been left on the work surface and had started to curdle. Rob managed to find a clean mug in one of the cupboards, instant coffee and some slightly worse for wear looking sugar in another. A few moments later he carried the mug through to the living room, which given the state of the kitchen wasn't as bad as he'd expected. He put the mug in front of Jake, not worrying about a coaster on the smoky glass coffee table.

Jake was now wearing a striped burgundy and navy dressing gown and looked more like he'd stepped out of the 80s than 2023.

He took a sip of the coffee and pulled a face, looking accusingly at Rob and said, 'could you not find the milk, mate.'

'Oh, I found it, but I didn't imagine you wanted lumpy coffee.'

Rob sat next to Nancy, both of them opposite Jake. She

knocked his leg with her knee and used her pen to indicate the residue of white powder on the table.

'I've explained to Jake that we're investigating Owen's death,'

'We weren't mates, I thought he was uptight, like he had a pole up his arse, you know?' he looked at them for clarification, their faces remained expressionless. 'He said I cut corners.'

'And did you?'

He shrugged, 'probably, but it's not like it was a big deal, the punters love me, I show them a house and they love it, sale in the bag.'

'You called in sick the last time Owen came into work?'

'Yeah, I had the shits.' Jake put his hand in the dressing gown pocket and took out a packet of cigarettes and a lighter, paused for a moment with one secured between his lips and said, 'I'd ask if you mind, but this is my flat, so I don't give a shit.' Then he lit the cigarette and sucked hard on the filter.

'Do you remember the house you were meant to be showing that day?'

'It was one of those ones in the backend of beyond, I hate those ones, takes sodding ages to get there, you do the viewing, nine times out of ten it's out of the viewers price range anyway and then you have to haul back to town, I could show three places in the time it takes to do one of those.'

'You weren't bothered that Owen did the viewing then?' Rob asked.

He shook his head.

'And on the Monday it was off sale, is that right?' Rob continued.

Jake stood up and walked to the window, curtains now open, his view was over the main road below. 'If you say so.'

'You don't remember finding out about the boundary issue, seems like something someone like you would remember.' Nancy said.

'Well, I don't, alright. Is that everything, it's just I'm needing to make a start to my day.'

'I wonder if your drug use effects your memory. DS MacDonald I think we should get a team in here to see what this white powder is, Jake can come to the station with us whilst we turn his flat upside down making sure there's not anything we should be aware of.'

The colour drained fully out of Jake's face, 'What?'

'Rolled up money, white powder all suggesting cocaine use, do you have a criminal record?'

'No. Look I'm sorry, I want to help, I'm just a bit hung over.' He stubbed out the cigarette in an already full ashtray. He sat back down on the sofa and leant forwards, leaning his elbows on his knees. 'What if something a bit unusual did happen back then?'

'Then we'd stay here talking to you a bit longer.'

'I wasn't sick, I got a message from someone saying they'd pay me to call in sick that day, I thought it was a joke, why would anyone care if I was off my work. Then I came home and there was an envelope through the door – it had 100 quid in it and a note explaining, if I took the day off there was another 100 in it for me, so I called in sick.'

'Did you get the rest of the money?' Rob asked.

He nodded, 'Through the door on the Monday.'

'Did you keep the envelope?'

Jake looked around the living room almost like he was looking into an unfamiliar space, 'hold on a second,' he moved piles of paperwork off the floor and on to the sofa beside him, unceremoniously discarding items back to the carpet when they turned out not to be the thing he wanted. Nancy and Rob exchanged glances but said nothing. A couple of moments later Jake shook crumbs off an A5 brown envelope, 'this is it.' He thrust it towards them. Rob deftly pulled out an evidence bag and managed to get it inside without accidentally touching it.

'See what you can do when you put your mind to it,' Rob said standing ready to leave. Nancy stayed seated.

'What was the boundary issue with the property?'

'The previous owner had built their garage partially over his property line.'

'Isn't that the sort of thing that should have been picked up before the property was put up for sale?'

'Normally yes, but this was a bit of an unusual situation and we didn't know until the report came in on the Monday.' Jake said.

'Where did the report come from?' Nancy asked.

'It was on my desk when I came back into work − I just followed protocol and took it off sale until it was resolved.'

'How long does that type of thing normally take?'

'Never had a case like this, but Mr Andrews was pissed off, because he wasn't going to see any commission out of it anytime soon.'

Nancy stood up, 'try to stay out of trouble, and don't leave the area.'

Jake looked for a moment like he was going to be sick, Rob swore he turned a very distinct lime green as he watched them leave.

Chapter 11

The house was in the middle of nowhere as Jake had described, down a single track road that only led to this house. The surrounding area was farmer's fields, not that there was any sign of tractors today. Nancy was glad of her warm jacket, with nothing to stop it the wind was bitter here. Maybe it would be nice to live somewhere like this, she thought, bet the local chippy is a bit of a way away though, she smiled to herself.

They walked the perimeter of the house together, no sign of any other vehicles. 'That's a bit weird don't you think,' Rob indicated towards the windows, every one of them had the curtains closed.'

'Maybe they don't want the sun to fade the furniture,' Nancy suggested. She took the keys from the envelope the estate agent had provided and turned one in the lock. Immediately hit by an overwhelming scent of bleach she gagged a little, turned and took in a large breath of fresh air before heading inside.

The inside of the property was much more modern

than the grey stone outside had suggested. Rob climbed the stairs as Nancy continued her search of the ground floor. It was empty, and yet she could feel her skin crawl as she went from room to room. She'd had a friend once who believed that buildings absorb the energy that existed within them, happy family homes absorbed joy, this one felt like it had contained something evil.

'Boss, you'd better come up,' Rob called from the top of the stairs. He was standing in the door of the bathroom looking at a badly cleaned bloodbath, literally, there was a ring of dark red around the edge of the old enamel tub. The shower curtain had been torn from the ceiling and lay discarded and stained on the bathroom floor and as he leaned into the room he was certain he could see the remanets of human hair in the plug hole.

'Why bother with the bleach if you weren't at least going to do a decent job,' Nancy said from behind him making him visibly jump.

'When did you get so stealthy?'

'I made plenty of noise, you must have been too focused to hear me. Looks like you found the crime scene. I'll phone and get a forensics team up here to go over the place properly. We should get out before we get shouted at for contaminating everything.'

They sat in the car with the doors open, neither one of them wanting to be confined within the vehicle despite it growing colder.

'It's a bloody long way from here to that recycling bin,' Rob said. 'You need to be pretty ballsy to be alright with driving for forty-five minutes with a dismembered body in your boot.'

'And it would have made quite a mess I would've

thought, unless it was carefully wrapped, that towel wouldn't have done it.'

'Whoever the killer is they were clearly targeting Owen, but why not just kill him when he came out to show the house? Why wait and how did they get him back here?' Rob pondered.

'If they'd done it in the afternoon he would have been reported missing much sooner, and this would have been the first place anyone would have looked. Maybe the person lied and said they'd accidentally left something at the property.' Nancy replied.

'If they lured Owen back how did the keys get back to the estate agent?' Rob asked.

'We should check to see if there were two sets.'

It was starting to get dusky when the forensics team arrived. Daniel Burrows, the crime scene manager, approached them with a scowl, 'I need a note of everywhere you've been and anything you might've touched, then you can go.'

'How very kind of you,' Rob muttered under his breath earning him a glare from Nancy and Daniel.

'If it's any consolation neither of us actually went into the bathroom…' Nancy trailed off taking the clipboard with the piece of paper prepped for them to list their movements.

'We'll let you get on with it then, sorry to ruin your evening.' Nancy said. Rob was already on his way back to the car when Nancy turned to leave.

'I'm sorry about Chris,' Daniel said.

Nancy shrugged her right shoulder, 'not your fault.'

'I just don't want this to be awkward for us at work, I know he's my brother and you're supposed to stick by family, but if you ask me, he's a bloody moron.'

'Thanks Dan, sticking by family is something I'm struggling with a bit at the moment too.'

Daniel blushed, 'sorry...'

'It's okay, honestly, but do me a favour and check in on Dylan, he's staying with me this week but I know Chris would rather keep us apart,' embarrassingly Nancy felt water pooling in the bottom of her eyes, desperate not to cry at a crime scene she turned her face into the bitter wind that had got up enough now that should could pass her tears off as being produced by the elements rather than her emotions.

DC GRACE ABBOTTS had hoped to have been greeted by DI Ravenscroft when she'd joined the team that afternoon, instead she was met by Cal, DS Tung. He took almost twenty minutes to explain to her the work he was doing on reverse image searches before DC Isla Shepherd saved her.

'Hey, the boss wants us to look at the last month of known movements of your victim, Maria, and cross reference them with the movements of our victim, Owen, at the same time and then in the month before he went missing to see if there's any overlap.

'Okay, Maria worked at a place called 'Burns Night' before she went for the interview to be a nanny, it's a club that has fire eating to the backdrop of bagpipes, very niche, very touristy, very popular.' Grace looked through the file on her desktop. She was well liked, hardworking, friendly, the manager said he would have been sorry to lose her but understood she wanted to do something different.

'Let's start there then and see if Owen ever went into Burns Night, I'll check through his bank and credit card records if you check through his and the bar's social media' Isla said.

'Could this be him?' Grace asked a few minutes later. Isla scooted her seat next to her new colleague and looked at the computer screen. 'This is Maria, it would have been the last weekend she was working and that looks like Owen.' The photograph was of Owen looking a little inebriated wearing a t-shirt that said, 'Billy's a Stag' and had a picture of a man's face with antlers on his head.

'I'll call Owen's sister and get details of the stag party, his friends are bound to have taken plenty of photos that night and you can see if you can find any other pictures of Maria and Owen.'

An hour later they'd collated dozens of photographs and managed to contact the attendees from Billy's stag do, most of whom had agreed to come into the station the next day to allow the photographs of that night to be taken into evidence.

Chapter 12

Printed out and stuck to the wall had seemed like the only way to properly examine the pictures in their entirety. 'Can we try to move them around according to their time stamp, so we get an idea of what happened as the night went on.' Nancy said.

'Burns Night said they had a professional photographer in that night as well doing some promo shots for an event they had coming up.' Grace said. 'They didn't answer when I called so I've left a message.'

'Thanks, let me know if they get back in touch.' Nancy said. 'We're pretty confident that this is the only point of commonality for our two victims and whilst we still have to bear in mind they may not be connected it's looking more and more likely that they are. With that in mind DC Abbotts is going to take the floor and get us quickly up to speed with what looks to be the first victim in this case.' Nancy stood back perching on the edge of a desk letting the young detective speak.

'Maria Fisher, age 22, came to Scotland like most

Australians do to see the sights, she had been here for 4 months when she went missing and most of that time she'd worked at Burns Night. From what her colleagues there said Maria wanted to stay in Scotland and wanted a job that was a bit more of a career. She applied for a job as a Nanny, the last communication from Maria was to her mum, saying she was going for the interview. Her mum started to get worried about Maria when she didn't hear back from her.' Grace looked up, her new colleagues had been quieter than expected and she hesitated.

'When did her mum come over?' Nancy asked, encouraging her to continue.

'A couple of days later – she felt that she wasn't being taken seriously over the phone, one of Maria's flat mates had also been into the station to raise concerns, but for whatever reason there wasn't much action taken until Mrs Fisher arrived here. It was just after that the team I was working with got involved.'

'What about the nannying job, was that real?' Rob asked.

'Yes and no, all the information in the ad had been taken from a real advertisement, details of the ages of the children and where it was etc, but the phone number was a burner number, we never found it.'

'Not our burner – I take it we've double checked that?' Rob looked around.

Cal half stood up, 'sorry yes, the number was checked against any on-going cases, and nothing came back.'

Nancy nodded at Grace to carry on.

'All of our leads were dead ends, Maria's body was found ten days after she was last seen, wrapped in a towel in the commercial bins behind a "massage parlour" in Edinburgh. By that time she'd been dead for approximately 72 hours according to the post mortem, her body was discovered when the bins were put our for emptying, whoever had put her there had covered the body in black refuse sacks. The conclusion the lead detective made was that Maria hadn't got the job as a nanny, and too embarrassed to tell anyone she'd become a sex worker, she had fallen foul of one of her clients and he'd killed her. '

'That's one hell of a leap, especially as she presumably had a job to go back to at Burns Night,' Nancy looked at Grace.

'She hadn't given notice at the club, the manager was aware she was looking elsewhere but had no reason to believe she wouldn't turn up for her next scheduled shift, she'd always been a very conscientious employee.' Grace said.

'And what about her flat, surely even if she'd decided to become a sex worker, she would've gone home at some point to collect her belongings at least. And why think she'd have been embarrassed to not get the job?' Nancy asked.

'Mrs Fisher wasn't happy with the theory either, she said her daughter would never have stopped contact with her, and the roommate said all of her belongings were still in the flat, including her passport and other personal items.'

'Did you get any leads as to who her alleged clients were?' Nancy said.

'Unsurprisingly the ladies we spoke to weren't very forthcoming about potential clients, but also no one admitted to having seen Maria before.'

'And what about the branding mark on her, was that looked into at all?' Nancy asked.

'The theory was that it was a mark to show she now belonged to a human trafficker, although when we checked our records there was no information on that sign being used by any group or gang.' Grace said.

'Thank you DC Abbotts,' Nancy stood up and made her way back in front of her team. 'As you know, yesterday afternoon Rob and I found what we believe will turn out to be our crime scene for the murder of Owen Fairmile. The location of Maria Fisher's murder hasn't been discovered, but we do know she wasn't killed where she was found. Both victims were missing for slightly more than a week before their bodies were dumped, both had identical markings, both bodies were found naked wrapped in towels and both went missing after heading out to appointments with people they'd never met before. Have I missed anything?'

Cal raised his hand.

Rob pushed it back down and shook his head, 'you're not at school mate, just shout out.'

'The picture you gave me yesterday, the one of the woman Owen thought he was meeting, also a catfish. It took a bit of finding because it turned out to be an old photograph, I found it in a social media reunion page, with a picture from when they were at uni and one from now. The woman in our photograph is now 55, she was 25 when the photo was taken in 1992. Someone had digitally enhanced it to make it look current though.' Cal said.

'Great work.' Nancy smiled in his direction.

'He was catfished twice,' Rob frowned. 'Why would someone catfish you twice.'

'Because you needed him to agree to go on a date with you, whoever it was realised their original profile had been rumbled so they decided to send this picture to make him believe he was talking to the real person.' Grace said making eye contact with Rob for the first time that morning.

'Have we found any other connection with the woman

in the second photograph and either of our victims?' Nancy asked.

Cal looked at his computer screen for a second, 'haven't had a chance to look yet, it took a while to figure out who the picture was of.'

'Can you check today please. Rob and I are going to see Owen's friend Billy, can we chase up the mobile phone Owen was found with and can we find out where the last tower Owen's actual phoned pinged from.'

The rain battered against the windows of the office making Nancy pause to zip up her jacket before leaving the building.

Billy lived in Pitcorthie, a private housing estate mostly built in the mid 70s, now the houses were popular for their large rooms and the connection to two excellent primary schools. Nancy could see the appeal, even if they did all kind of look the same to her.

'You get a lot of house for your buck here,' Rob said.

'You considering a new career in estate agency,' Nancy laughed.

'I'm just saying, if someday I wanted to have a family then this is the sort of place I could see myself living.'

'I thought you were dedicating your life to being a bachelor,' Nancy quipped.

'Only until the right woman comes along,' Rob laughed.

Since the new Duloch housing estate had been built it had left Pitcorthie showing its age, but Duloch wasn't new anymore and lots of buyers had realised that this estate had a lot to offer. Most of the streets had been named after trees and bushes and Mulberry Drive was no exception. They stopped on the road outside choosing to park by the pavement rather than entering the steep driveway.

Rose bushes lined the steps up to the doorway, trimmed

back now, but in summer they would prove a bit of a thorny gauntlet for the postie. Nancy knocked at the door, Chris had once asked her if they taught that knock at the police academy in Tulliallan, she wished she'd realised then what an obnoxious twat he was and she could have saved herself a lot of effort and money.

The door was opened by a man in his late thirties wearing pale grey tracksuit bottoms with a football top. Nancy introduced herself and Rob, and Billy showed them through to his living room.

It was a much larger room than Nancy had expected, its pale laminate flooring adding the feeling of space. The walls were cream and strewn with pictures from Billy's wedding, where Nancy noticed he looked the part.

'I wasn't sure what time you were coming,' Billy said, standing at the doorway to the living room. Nancy and Rob perched on the edge of a deep burgundy leather sofa, afraid to sit further back in fear of not being able to stand up easily. 'Becca,' Billy called up the stairs. 'It's the police come to talk to us about Owen, could you pop the kettle on,' he turned to face them, 'do you want tea or coffee?'

'Coffee please,' they said in unison.

'Three coffees and whatever you're having.' Billy let the door swing closed and sat on one of the two armchairs. 'Shall we wait till Becca's here to start?'

'Actually, I was thinking we could start by talking about your stag night, if that's okay?' Nancy said.

Billy furrowed his brow, 'you wanted everyone's photos didn't you, I've got mine sorted for you, but honestly I can't see what my stag do has to do with Owen's disappearance, that was months ago.'

'I understand that, however it would be useful to our investigation if we could go back to that night for now.'

'Owen was my best man, we met in the Navy, we just clicked, even though he was a couple of year younger than me, I never felt the age gap, he didn't seem like a boy. Anyway, we left a few years apart but always kept in touch, so I asked him to be my best man. It was him that organised the whole evening. We went for a curry and then to Burns Night, the entertainment there is always spot on and I'm not one for strippers or any of that nonsense.' Billy said.

'Just as well,' Becca said skilfully pushing the door open with her hip whilst holding the tray of drinks steady in her hands, partially balanced on a swollen pregnant belly.

Rob shot up, 'let me get that for you,' he said taking the tray and setting it down on the table in front of them all.

'Thank you,' she blushed. 'I was fine honestly, I keep telling Billy, I'm pregnant, not sick.'

'How far along are you?' Nancy asked.

'Only five months…' Becca started.

'We're having twins.' Billy finished, pride evident in his beaming grin.

'Wow, double trouble,' Rob said.

'We were going to ask Owen to be their Godfather,' Billy's expression had lost its previous glee.

'You were saying, Billy organised the stag do, was he a regular at Burns Night?'

Billy shook his head slowly, 'I wouldn't say that. We'd been there a few times, there was one of the acts he was a bit soft on,' Billy chuckled. 'She was out of his league, but a man can dream.'

Nancy took her phone out of her pocket and clicked on a picture of Maria, 'do you remember seeing this woman when you were there?'

Billy took the phone and examined her face carefully for a moment, 'sorry, I don't.'

'She wasn't the woman Owen fancied, then?'

'God no, no offense but she looks pretty young and that wasn't Owen's thing at all.'

Nancy took the phone back and swiped to reveal the photograph of Owen and Maria together, 'you don't remember this photo being taken?'

'I don't, we took pictures with everyone, it doesn't mean anything. I'm pretty sure he took photos with some American tourists in cowboy hats as well, the place was busy, there was someone with a proper fancy camera, I remember because Owen was trying to arrange with her to get copies of the pictures, but she was quite rude to him.'

'Did you see much of Owen before he disappeared?'

'Not much, with the wedding and the honeymoon and then we bought this place, it's been a bit manic, but we were still texting and talking on the phone when we had a moment.'

'Do you remember the last time you got a message from him?'

'Yeah, it was the Saturday he went missing, I knew he was going on this ridiculous blind date, I sent him a message wishing him luck and saying to let me know how it went.'

'Did you get a reply?' Rob asked.

'A weird one,' hold on. Billy picked up his phone and navigated to the last conversation he'd had with his best mate. 'Here,' he passed the phone to Nancy.

'Been stood up. All my fault. It's time to pay up and leave.' Rob leaned his head towards Nancy so they could read the words together.

Chapter 13

There hadn't been much more to gain from chatting with Billy and Becca, Nancy had thanked them for their time and left.

'Don't you think that reply sounded a bit melodramatic for someone who was stood up by a blind date that he knew was likely a catfish?' Rob asked.

'Yeah, even the way it was typed felt, I don't know, sort of unnatural and when you read back through some of their text exchanges it was much too stiff and formal. To go from calling your mate a bawbag to "it's time to pay up and leave" just feels off.'

'Hopefully we'll get some CCTV from the restaurant tomorrow and we'll be able to tell if he speaks to anyone there.'

Nancy's phone vibrated interrupting their conversation, she answered. 'Hi Isla, you've got me and Rob on speaker.'

'Great, I've had an update from forensics on the towels that Maria and Owen were wrapped in.'

'Okay.'

'They're from the same batch, the fibres match.'

'I think that's the last piece of proof that our victims are connected, good work Isla,' Nancy was about to hang up when Isla continued.

'That's not it all though – the towels are from the mid 70s, apparently you can date them by looking at the dyes and stuff, anyway, these would have been expensive in their day, originally made for John Lewis.'

'You can find out who sold a towel from the fibres?' Rob asked.

'No, you muppet, they were able to reconstruct the label on one of them, the other thing is the forensics say these towels look like they've never been used other than for wrapping dead bodies.' Isla paused. 'I mean who keeps unused towels that long and does this mean our killers are like in their 60s or something.'

'More likely they got the towels from a vintage shop I would have thought,' Nancy said.

'I've heard of vintage clothes, but vintage towels, is there really a market for that.' Rob scoffed.

'Isla, were forensics able to give you any idea of where these towels have been for the last 50 years?'

'Sorry boss, nothing.'

'Right, reach out to any vintage shops in the area, maybe even some of the charity shops, see if they've had anything that matches the description of our towels in.'

'Will do.' The line went dead.

'Great we've got vintage towels, weird markings and dismemberment, I could do without this case getting any stranger to be honest.' Nancy sighed.

Her phone rang again before she had time to put it back in her pocket. 'Lucy what can I do for you?'

'Other than tell your piece of shit ex to delete my telephone number from his directory?'

'You're on speaker with me and Rob.' Nancy said.

'It's not like he doesn't agree with my assessment of the man, I don't know how many times I have to tell him I don't know where you're living and even if I did, I wouldn't tell him.'

'I appreciate the loyalty but was there something else?'

'Yes, the blood found at your crime scene, it doesn't match Owen or Maria, looks like you have a third victim.'

'Bugger,' Nancy disconnected the call. 'The question is, have we missed a body or is there one about to be discovered by some poor unsuspecting sod.'

'Do you think we should put word out to the council refuse workers to keep a watch for anything unusual?' Rob asked.

'You're thinking because the last two victims were found in a bin then the next one might be as well?'

'Just a thought.'

'Maybe.'

They drove in silence, Rob had worked with Nancy for long enough to know when to keep quiet and let her think.

She called Lucy back. 'Me again, any way of telling how long it's been since...' she trailed off thinking about how to pose her question.

'Do you mean since the blood was inside a body instead of the bathtub?'

'Yes,'

'I'll be using the Raman spectroscopy and as long as the

blood is less than two years old, which we know it is thanks to the estate agent's particulars, I'll be able to narrow it down to approximately a two week window. Once I've run the test, I should be able to give you gender and estimated age.'

'How long will it take?'

'I've bumped you to the top of my list, give me a couple of hours and I'll be able to give you something to start with.'

'Thanks.' Nancy hung up.

Rob checked the time, 'you fancy stopping somewhere and getting some lunch?'

'I could eat.' Nancy replied.

Rob pulled into the carpark of a Brewers Fayre pub, where he was content that the food was reliable and reasonably priced, two things that he liked, especially as he had a nagging suspicion that he was going to get stuck with the bill.

They were seated quickly by a girl that looked like she was barely out of high school. 'Can I get you something to drink?' she asked poised with a small notepad and pen.

'Lime and soda,' Nancy smiled.

'Irn Bru, thanks.'

'I'll be back in a couple of minutes to take your food order.'

'No need, I'll have the steak pie, chips and peas and she'll have the macaroni cheese and garlic bread.'

The waitress scribbled down the request. 'Okay everything will be with you shortly.'

'It doesn't look like our killer murders his victims immediately, there seems to be about a week between disappearance and being placed in the deposition site, so where is he keeping them in between.' Nancy said.

'and why not just kill them straight away.' Rob added.

'Logically whoever was killed in that bathroom must've been disposed of already. We know that Owen's body was dumped within hours of him being murdered and the report said it looked like Maria had been killed elsewhere and her body dumped almost immediately after.'

'That would make Owen victim number three…'

The waitress came over with their drinks, Nancy hoped that she'd stopped talking before the girl had come into earshot.

'Do you think he might've already taken his next victim?' Rob asked. 'And do you think the killer was the one that paid Jake to phone in sick because he wanted Owen to go to that house knowing that when he killed his next victim we'd likely think it was Owen?'

'I don't think we can be sure, at the moment all we know is that house wasn't a crime scene the day before Owen disappeared, which means our killer murdered one victim on the same day he took a new one. That feels like an escalation to me, which suggests that his need to kill is growing.' Nancy said.

'Given that Maria and Owen have nothing in common, the victimology seems completely random, it's impossible to predict who might be next.' Rob said.

They both stopped talking when the food arrived. Nancy used the slices of garlic bread to dip into the melted cheese sauce scooping up cheesy pasta onto it before putting the combination into her mouth.

Her phoned buzzed, mouth still full she answered holding it to her ear.

'Sorry boss have I caught you at a bad time?' Isla said.

'No, no I was just having some lunch, what is it?'

'The towels, Grace and I had phoned round a bunch of charity shops and vintage places, most of them wouldn't sell that type of item and then on a whim I called my friend Stella who works at the Top Hat Auction house, they get all sorts of things, and she told me they would sell something like that if it was part of a lot.'

'that's interesting, you should follow that up…'

'One step ahead of you boss, Stella and I go way back to nursery school, so she agreed to check to see if they had sold those particular towels, I sent her a picture, don't worry there was nothing to give away what they'd be used for. Anyway, they photograph every item individually when they come into the warehouse and before they're sorted into lots.'

'And?' Nancy asked poking her food with the next slice of garlic bread. She glanced across the small mahogany table to Rob who had stopped eating, his steak pie almost half gone.

'And they sold them, she's sending over the details of where they came from and who bought them. You have to register on their website to be allowed to bid on anything and pay by credit card, I should have it all in a couple of hours.'

'That's bloody good work, well done Isla.'

Nancy took a few more mouthfuls of her lunch before relaying the news to Rob.

'Buying towels doesn't make you a murderer though,' Rob said.

'True, but in this case, it does make you a suspect.'

As they drove back into the police station carpark a bustle of reporters made their way to the car.

'Is it true you've found Owen Fairmile's body?'

'Was he murdered?'

'Do you think you did enough to try and find him at the time of his disappearance?'

The questions had been fired at Nancy before she even

had the opportunity to get out of the car and close the passenger door.

'I can confirm that we found the body of a man in the early hours of Monday morning. There will be a press conference tomorrow morning when we'll be able to give you a full update.' Nancy said pushing gently past them.

Rob had used the fact their attention had been fixated on his boss to make his way inside without being seen.'

'Thanks for abandoning me out there,' she said shaking her head as she walked past him. 'Can you get the team together so I can brief them on the latest update.'

'Where are you going?'

'To see Cooper.'

The DCI was in his office staring at one of the two computer monitors that faced him, she knocked on the door and entered. He scowled at her as she sat in one of the two chairs on the opposite side of the desk. Nancy waited for her boss to be ready to speak, remembering the first day she'd come to see him in this office, when she'd knocked on the door, waiting politely outside for nearly fifteen minutes before being called in. He'd told her then that if she wanted to succeed as a DI she couldn't afford to be timid or always be waiting on someone else to take action. On reflection he probably hadn't intended that speech to mean please walk into my office without invite any time the notion grabs you either, but as far as Nancy was concerned Cooper only had himself to blame for the current circumstances.

'You have news,' Cooper stated.

'Maria Fisher and Owen Fairmile's deaths are connected, we have the branding, they were both stabbed with a similar object, the fact they were both in the Burns Night club and now we know the towels they were wrapped in came from the same bundle.'

'I thought Maria Fisher had her throat slit.' Cooper said.

'That was done post mortem. Lucy, Dr Clarke, confirmed that she was stabbed and from the looks of the wound she believes by the same implement.'

'Are you sure the towels are from the same batch?' Cooper questioned.

'Forensics have said they're made from identical fibres and we now know that they were sold as a bundle of four unused vintage towels, still in original John Lewis packaging by a local auction house.'

'How's the house to house going?'

'We've been collecting up all the doorbell cam footage from the twenty-four hours prior to Owen's body being discovered and hopefully we'll get something from it. It wouldn't hurt to have a bit more manpower though, especially as we need to be looking for a third victim.'

Cooper's forehead creased, a deep vertical line visible between his eyebrows, 'third?'

'The blood in the bathtub at that house wasn't either of our current victims, Dr Clarke says she'll be able to give us approximate date of death, age, and gender later today.'

'I'll call around and see if I can get some officers down from the surrounding stations in time for your morning brief tomorrow.'

'Thanks boss,' she was about to leave when Cooper continued speaking.

'Chris Burrows called me yesterday, said he intended to make a missing person's report on Dylan, that he thought you'd kidnapped his son.'

Nancy closed her eyes momentarily, in part to conceal her embarrassment, but mostly in an attempt to quell the rage she felt building in the pit of her stomach. 'I'm sorry,

Chris knew Dylan was with me, he was just being a dick. It won't happen again.'

'Indeed, it won't, I reminded him that making a false report of that nature was wasting police resources and I was sure that he didn't want to explain to a judge how he tried to manipulate the police to get back at his ex.'

Nancy could tell her cheeks were a bright shade of red, 'thank you.'

'Isn't Dylan sixteen already?' Cooper asked.

'Yes.'

'Then he doesn't need his father's permission to leave home, might be worth thinking about.' Cooper added.

'Yes sir,' Nancy closed the office door behind her. Chris knew she hated her work life being messy, she'd worked so hard to keep everything compartmentalised, he would be getting a twisted kick out of upsetting her equilibrium like this.

Back with the team she got everyone up to speed, 'Tomorrow we'll have more hands to help but for now I need you, Cal, to go back through the missing persons reports for the two weeks prior to the date Owen disappeared. Working on what we know, he keeps his victims for slightly more than a week before murdering them. It stands to reason our missing victim was murdered some time during the twenty-four hours before Owen went missing.'

'Any idea who I should be looking for?' Cal asked.

'We'll be able to narrow it down further when Dr Clarke has her test results back, until then gather all the information on anyone reported missing in that two-week period.'

'Isla and Grace, I need to know if there is anything else that ties Maria and Owen together, I'm struggling to believe that this can have been one single chance encounter, did they use the same coffee shop, gym, take the same bus route, anything, okay.'

'On it, boss.'

Nancy went back to her office and closed the door, she looked at the bodies of the two victims on her computer screen, both murdered in a gruesome way. It had been overkill, there was no need to dismember Owen, he was dead before it had happened, and Maria was dead before her throat was slit. So why, other than for dramatics?

Mr Andrews, the estate agent, had suggested that Diane was overbearing, acted more like she was Owen's mother than big sister, maybe she didn't want her little brother taking her son away, showing him the world, helping him escape the little bubble she'd created for her family. That would be a motive to kill her brother, perhaps, though surely it would be easier to just say no to the trip. But what reason would she have for killing Maria? Nancy couldn't come up with anything.

She was so deep in thought it took a moment to register that her phone was ringing.

'Hi Lucy, what have you got for me?'

'Your victim was male, approximate age early seventies and the blood in the bathtub is between one to two weeks old.'

'Thanks Lucy.'

Nancy ended the call and made her way across to Cal's desk. 'How are you doing working through the missing persons files?'

'There's more than I expected.' He replied.

'Any of them in their seventies?'

'Two, a woman named Esme, aged 78, last seen at her daughter's home almost seven weeks ago…'

'Nope, next.'

'Donald Stark, 72, went out to get the morning paper, his car was found at the side of the road, keys in the ignition, paper on the seat, no sign of him since, that was around two weeks ago.'

'I'm betting this is our man, what else do we know?'

'His wife Susan phoned the police when he was late returning, it says here that he was like clockwork, every morning he'd take a drive, buy the paper, come home and they'd have a cup of tea and a slice of cake.'

'Any ideas as to what happened?'

Cal shook his head, 'his car was found within an hour of him being reported, there was nothing to suggest there had been any struggle, the layby that he'd driven into was close to a wooded area, which was searched quite extensively, in case he'd caused himself harm, but there was no sign of him at all.'

Chapter 15

Dylan had been disappointed when Nancy had told him she was taking him back to his father's house, but when she explained the call to Cooper, he accepted it on the understanding that it wouldn't be forever and she'd find a way to see him more regularly. Now they were both standing on the doorstep dreading the next ten minutes. Catherine answered the door after a few moments. Nancy tried to keep her eyes away from her sister's belly, despite only being four months pregnant there was no denying she was showing already.

Catherine reached out her hand to Dylan attempting to hug him, he pulled back. 'We were so worried about you, don't do that to us again, alright.'

'Get away from me,' Dylan replied taking a step back and placing Nancy in the middle.

'You really had no right…' Catherine began.

'Stop, I am not having this fight on my own doorstep, you are in no position to talk about rights.'

'Nance, you're my sister we can't keep fighting like this, it's not fair to use Dylan as a weapon against Chris.'

'I mean it, stop acting like you're the one who's been wronged here. This house you're swanning around in, my money paid off the mortgage and you bloody well know it. And I might not have given birth to Dylan, but he sure as hell *is* my son.'

'You know I never meant for any of this to happen.'

'Yes, I know apparently it's my fault for having a fulfilling career and the kindness to take my sister in after she broke up with her boyfriend, silly me. Look Cathy, is Chris here or not?'

'Well yes and no.'

Nancy took a deep breath and tried to release it in a slow and steady way, just like it had shown on the YouTube channel about managing your stress. 'Either he is or he's not, which is it.'

'He's in the bath.'

'Finally,'

'He told me to tell you there won't be a repeat of this, you're not welcome here and you're not to try and contact Dylan.' Catherine at least had the good grace to look at her feet as she spoke the words.

Nancy felt Dylan coil ready to lunge at her sister. She held out her arms to stop him and found herself laughing. 'Well, you tell Chris that Dylan is sixteen and legally he doesn't need anyone's permission to leave home, I'm not here to return Dylan I am here to accompany him whilst he collects more of his possessions.'

'You are?' Dylan asked from behind her.

Catherine looked horrified, 'no you can't.'

'Yes, I can.' Nancy took a step forward to enter the house.

'No, you're not allowed to come in.' She held out her hand as though she was stopping traffic.

'Cathy, the bills for this house are still coming out of my salary so perhaps you should take a step to one side and allow Dylan to come in and collect his belongings.'

'I'll call the police.'

'Go right ahead.' Nancy stepped into the hallway, everything felt the same but utterly different. 'You go get some stuff, whatever you need for school, etc and we'll work the rest out later,' she said to Dylan who practically jogged up the stairs.

Moments later she watched as Chris came down the carpeted stairs dressed in jogging trousers and a t-shirt. He made a point of kissing Catherine in front of her and Nancy wasn't sure which one of them she was more disgusted by.

'Why is she in my house?' He asked Catherine.

'She said Dylan is going to live with her.'

He laughed, 'I don't think so, you want me to call your boss again?' he smirked.

'Feel free, I'm pretty sure Cooper was clear on the ramifications for you if you chose to do that.'

Dylan appeared at the bottom of the stairs. 'I don't know what nonsense she's filled your head with, but you're not going anywhere, now take your stuff and go to your room.'

Dylan glanced at Nancy, she gave him an encouraging smile. 'I'm going with mum.'

Chris grabbed hold of his wrist, gripping it tightly, 'she is not your mother, do as you're told.'

'Let go of me.' Dylan cried.

'Not till you do what you're told.'

'Let go of him, you're hurting him.' Nancy said.

Chris released his grip. 'Why are you doing this,' he said turning his anger on her.

'What am I doing?' he was in her face now, she could smell his breath, garlic prawns. For a second she worried that Catherine might've eaten them too and that was dangerous for the baby, but she realised that he would have been eating whatever suited him, without any thought to his pregnant girlfriend.

'Turning my son against me.'

'You don't need my help, you're doing a fine job of that yourself.'

'You'll never be his mother.'

'Don't do this,' Nancy said, 'don't make this kind of scene in front of Dylan. What you're experiencing is the consequences of your own actions, and it's uncomfortable for you, but is a you problem, not a me problem, and definitely not a Dylan problem.'

Dylan moved across the hallway to Nancy.

'You do this son and there's not going back.'

'Let's go, mum.' Dylan said turning away from his father.

'We'll be back at some point to collect the rest of Dylan's things and they had better be where he left them, do I make myself clear,' Nancy said, she took one last look at her sister, half pity, half disgust before she picked up one of Dylan's bags and left.

'Thanks,' he said when they got into the car, 'I didn't know you'd changed your mind.'

'Neither did I until we got there, and I just couldn't leave you with them. But our living situation isn't ideal for getting you to school for the next couple of weeks, so I need to make some calls and figure a few things out.'

Nancy had known she could phone Rob and he would

open his home to them no questions asked. He came down the stairs and carried their bags up to his flat before ordering a curry.

'You do realise that this is going to get the rumour mill well and truly turning, don't you?' Rob laughed.

'Fuck 'em,' Nancy replied.

Chapter 16

DAY THREE, WEDNESDAY

Rob and Nancy had dropped Dylan at school and headed into the station together. 'We should go and visit Susan Stark this morning, let her know that we believe her husband is dead and see what else we can find out.'

The office was buzzing as they entered, Cooper had done a good job of rallying troops from other places and Nancy was pleased to see some familiar faces.

'Morning everyone,' she called out and the chatter died down in favour of hearing what she had to say.

'You should all have been provided with a file that has everything you need to know about the case so far, please make sure that you are fully up to date with its contents. I am looking for someone to start going through the door cam footage we've managed to collect from the day Owen Fairmile's body was disposed of, that then has to be cross referenced with the footage we have from Burns Night and the surrounding businesses at the time of this photograph.' Nancy pointed to the picture of Owen with his arm wrapped around Maria.

Two hands shot up from the back of the room, 'we worked CCTV for a murder case in Dundee,' one of the uniformed officers said.

'Great then you take that.'

Another hand was raised tentatively on the far left of the room.

'Yes,' Nancy said looking at the man.

'I was reading the file and I don't know if anyone here follows true crime programmes or podcasts,' he looked around the room pleased to see some agreement. 'It's just this case reminds me of something that happened in the states in the mid-seventies, not the victims so much as how they're being killed and where their bodies have been dumped.'

Nancy looked at the man.

'I'm DS John Gibbs, I normally work out of Dundee,' he said answering the unspoken question.

'Thank you John, I'm not a true crime podcast enthusiast so get me up to speed.'

'In 1976 a young prostitute,' John paused, 'sex worker,' he corrected himself, 'was found naked, wrapped in a towel with her throat slit post mortem, her body had been left amongst some garbage bags at the back of an all-night diner that working girls of the area would use to hide from the rain, have a cup of coffee etc. Then a few months later a Catholic Priest was found, his rosary beads wrapped around his neck, body was found in the compost heap, behind the gardens of a local community centre.'

'How old was the priest?' Nancy asked.

'I can't quite remember, but he was definitely an older man. Later the body of one of the prostitute's clients was found in two bin bags outside the door of a thrift store, the final victim was a young police officer, only been on the job a matter of months, legs broken, and skull crushed by a baseball bat. All the victims had been stabbed then additional damage done to the bodies after they'd been killed.'

'The links are tenuous, but I don't like the similarities. DS Gibbs you can work with a couple of officers and you can be in charge of finding out everything you possibly can about the historic case.' Nancy faced back into the room. Isla can you get the details of this podcast from DS Gibbs and follow up with the presenters and producers, see if there's been any communication from any of their fans that would give them cause for concern, obviously be discreet.'

Everyone around her looked like a tightly coiled spring, ready to leap into action, the thing with springs though is to make sure they don't fly off all over the place and cause problems.

'Cal, find a list of all community centres and find out if they have compost heaps and then when you have done that, widen your search and look for anywhere that has a compost heap or bin that could be accessed easily by a member of the public, then get out with a small team and search them. Norman Stark's body is somewhere, and if there's a chance it's been sitting in a compost heap for a couple of weeks, we're losing evidence by the day.'

Nancy went back to her office taking a quiet moment before heading out to see Susan Stark. She Googled the podcast that John Gibbs had mentioned, the crime had been split into four parts titled: The Prostitute, The Priest, The Pervert and The Police. Charming she thought, wondering about a police detective who spent his spare time listening to true crime podcasts, you'd have thought he got enough true crime in his day to day that he wouldn't need it for entertainment. Who was she to judge, she could binge cooking shows for hours but would rarely pick up a saucepan.

Rob knocked on her door, 'we going to see Mrs Stark?' he asked.

Nancy paused, tempted to click on the transcript for 'The Priest' section of the podcast to see what had been divulged, but decided against it.

'Come on then.'

'What do you reckon to this copycat idea?' Rob said as they walked down the stairs.

'Hard to say, for now I'm sceptical, but if we find John Stark's body anywhere near a compost heap or a community hall my mind will be changed.'

Donald and Susan Stark lived in a bungalow in the popular Garvock area of Dunfermline, when Nancy was growing up if you came from Garvock you were seen as a bit posh. She wasn't sure if that was still the case, the houses didn't look that dissimilar to any others of its era, but she was sure long-time residents like the Starks would likely still consider the area a cut above the rest.

A maroon N plate Jaguar was parked in the driveway, the car might have been old, perhaps even now considered a classic, but either way it was in good condition and looked like it was regularly washed and polished. Rob parked on the street outside the house.

The Starks' front door was entirely frosted glass, with the letter box at the very bottom of the aluminium frame. She rang the doorbell noticing that it was the camera kind. A speaker crackled into life.

'We don't buy at the door, and we've already found Jesus and know who we're voting for.' A female voice snapped.

Nancy wasn't sure which of those assumptions about their reason for calling was the most offensive, but campaigning politician had to be the worst. She pressed the button again. Unsure if she would be given the time to respond to the previous statement, this time instead of trying to get a word of explanation in, she held up her badge so it could be clearly seen on the camera.

A couple of moments passed. Nancy was considering ringing again and Rob had begun shuffling his feet behind her when the door opened. A smartly dressed woman, with white hair and glasses opened the door.

'Can I see your badges?'

Nancy and Rob offered their identification to the woman.

'You can't be too careful, you get some terrible scammers these days.'

Nancy noticed that Susan Stark hadn't asked them why they were at her doorstep, perhaps putting off the inevitable or maybe completely oblivious, they were about to find out.

'Could we come in Mrs Stark?'

The woman's hand began to shake, and suddenly she looked frail.

'Are you here about Donald?'

'Yes, would you like us to call someone to sit with you whilst we talk?'

Susan nodded, 'my granddaughter Elizabeth lives just down the road.'

'Why don't you give my Sergeant the address and he will go and fetch her.'

Susan sat stoically at the yellow pine breakfast bar in the kitchen whilst they waited for Rob to return with Elizabeth, Nancy made herself useful putting the kettle on and locating the cups and the tea bags.

Nancy glanced around the kitchen, it was spotlessly clean, it looked like it could have jumped directly out of an

MFI Kitchen catalogue from the early 90s, still why change it to keep up with the times. The front of the refrigerator was covered in brightly coloured magnets, a sandal from Corfu, a volcano from Lanzarote, a cowboy hat from Texas.

'You like to travel?' Nancy said indicating to the magnets.

'We went as often as we could, Donald would have moved abroad,' she paused, 'I didn't want to because of the grandchildren, he used to say, "for God's sake Susan, they can get on a plane and visit." But I wanted to watch them grow up, not just see them on high days and holidays.'

The front door opened, 'Where are you Gran?' a young woman's voice rang out of the hall, moments later she burst through the door and into the room.

'You must be Elizabeth,' Nancy said. 'I think we should all go into the living room. DS MacDonald will make some tea.

She herded the women out of the kitchen into the living room to sit on the cream leather sofa. On the wall behind the three-seater there was a large picture of Susan, Donald, Elizabeth and a younger girl, Elizabeth's younger sister most likely, she had the same blonde hair and blue eyes. There was the logo of cruise company in the bottom right-hand corner.

'Are you here about Granddad?' Elizabeth asked? 'Have you found him?'

Nancy took a breath, this was never an easy conversation to have, but made significantly harder by the absence of Donald's body. Loved ones would gloss over you telling them that all the evidence points towards him being dead and hang on the fraction of a percentage that you might be wrong on the basis of a missing body. She couldn't blame them, juries did the same. Perhaps they'd be right, until she'd got something that could be tested for DNA then the blood in the bathtub could belong to any missing 70 year old man.

'We haven't found him, however we have, unfortunately found some evidence that we believe indicates he has come to harm.'

'What does that even mean?' Elizabeth asked.

Rob came into the room; clearly having failed to find a tray in the kitchen he was holding all the mugs of tea in his hands, a carton of milk tucked under his arm.

'In the course of another investigation we found some blood that we know is from a man of approximately your granddad's age. It would be helpful if there was anything here that we could use to check his DNA against.' Nancy said.

'You can take anything you need,' Susan said quietly.

Nancy nodded to Rob to go and have a look to see what he could find. 'Thank you, my Sergeant will have a look, a toothbrush or hairbrush would be the best.'

'His toothbrush is in the white case on the side in the ensuite,' Susan said. 'I put it in there to stop it getting dusty.' Her voice was thin and wispy. Elizabeth wrapped an arm around her Gran and held her tight.

'What other investigation?' Elizabeth asked.

'I can't discuss that with you…'

'Has it got something to do with that man that was just found dead?' Elizabeth interrupted her.

'I know you're frustrated, and you want to understand what's going on, but the best way you can help us, and more importantly your gran is by answering my questions and helping me learn more about your granddad.'

'Susan, you reported your husband missing when he didn't return from getting the morning papers, is that right?'

'He liked routine, I thought it might've been nice to get the paper delivered, but I think Donald like getting up and about in the morning, a way to start his day.'

'Was anything different about that morning, was Donald worried about anything, had he seemed out of sorts?'

'No, he was his usual cheerful self. We're meant to be going to Canada next month, taking the train journey, have you seen it, they have a glass observation carriage at the end of the train.' Susan looked at Nancy.

'I think I might have on one of those travel programmes.'

'Donald always wanted to do it, and it's our Golden Wedding Anniversary, so we thought we'd treat ourselves.' The old woman frowned. 'He's never coming home, is he?' she whispered.

'You both must've been looking forward to that.' Nancy said trying to avoid the question.

Susan nodded. 'When he went out that morning, he said he'd be back in aboot half an hour,' a smile flit across her face at the memory. 'he was trying to do a Canadian accent, I thought he sounded Australian.'

'What did your husband do for work before he retired?' Nancy asked as Rob returned to the room holding up a clear plastic evidence bag containing Donald Stark's electric toothbrush head.

'He was a teacher.'

'What subject?'

'RE, Religious Education, although I don't think they call it that now.'

Chapter 17

Nancy and Rob exchanged looks. 'And was he a particularly religious man?'

Susan laughed, 'no, not at all. My Father-in-Law was a vicar and he wanted Donald to follow in his footsteps, but Donald had suffered through all of his father's sanctimonious sermons without any desire for that to be his life. But it was a subject he knew a great deal about, he wanted to be a lawyer, but his father wouldn't hear of if it. He used to say get a classroom full of young people together to talk about religion and you'll have more arguments and debates than you'll have in any courtroom.'

Nancy noticed Elizabeth smiling as her Gran recounted the memory.

'You were close with your Granddad?' she asked.

'Our parents run their own business, they worked long hours so me and my little sister Mandy spent a lot of time here after school and in the holidays.'

'Now you see why I wanted to stay close.' Susan added.

'And when was the last time you saw your Granddad?' Nancy asked.

'The Saturday of the previous week. I'd normally see him through the week, but I was away for work, so…' she trailed off in the realisation that the trip had cost her precious last moments with him.

Nancy waited, hoping that Elizabeth might have something more to share about her last interaction with her Granddad.

Elizabeth's cheeks reddened, 'I was out for a hen do in the evening, we'd ordered a taxi to pick us up and take us home, but when it came the driver said that Maxine, the bride-to-be was too drunk, and he wasn't prepared to drive us in case she was sick in the car. I didn't want to get in some random cab, you hear all sorts of things, so I called Granddad.'

'What time of night was that?' Rob asked.

'Hmm, about two in the morning, it was kicking out time at the club.'

'And he didn't mind you waking him at that time of night to play taxi to you and your friends?'

'Not at all, he would have been so angry if I'd not, he always told us that he'd rather get a call in the middle of the night than a knock on the door from you lot the next day.' Elizabeth gasped, the words giving way to a cascade of tears and sobbing.

Nancy handed her a paper handkerchief from the box on the coffee table. 'So, he came to pick you up, and everyone got home safe and sound?'

'I came here and slept in the spare room, but all my friends got home fine.'

'What club were you at?' Rob asked.

'Burns Night, it's that place in town where they do the fire breathing, it's pretty cool, have you been?'

Under different circumstances Nancy would've laughed, the idea of Rob, the man with two left feet and absolutely no rhythm dancing was ridiculous.

'Do you have any photos from that night?'

'On my phone,' Elizabeth took out her mobile and began scrolling. 'I don't know what good they'll be though, it was the following weekend that he went missing.'

'That's okay, it's really helpful for us to build up a picture of the full week before.'

Elizabeth handed over the phone, Nancy took a moment to flick through them, her eyes darting over them for any glimpse of Owen. 'Do you mind if we take a copy of these away with us?'

'If you think it might help.' Elizabeth said. Nancy handed the phone to Rob to sort the pictures out.

'In the week before he went missing did Donald say he thought anyone might be following him or had he noticed anything unusual?'

'Not that he mentioned to me.' Susan said.

'What about you, anything at all, Even it was someone coming to the door.'

Susan frowned for a moment, 'a man came to the door asking if I wanted a quote for carpet cleaning. I told him no thank you and he left, but that sort of thing isn't that unusual.'

'Did he leave a leaflet or a card?'

She shook her head.

'Do you remember what he looked like?'

'No, but he'll be on the door cam footage I suspect, normally I wouldn't have answered the door, but I was expecting a package to be delivered that day and I had wrongly assumed that was it arriving.'

'Can you send me a copy of the footage and we'll take a look. I'll let you know as soon as we've done the DNA test.'

Susan nodded.

'I'll see you out,' Elizabeth said walking them to the door. With the living room door closed and her Gran out of earshot she said, 'if the DNA matches is there any chance,' she looked past them unable to hold eye contact and ask the question. 'Is there any chance that he's not dead?'

'I'm really sorry, but it would be very unlikely.'

She wiped her eyes with the cuff of her sleeve, the yellow material now streaked with black make-up.

Nancy was quiet on the drive back to the station, Maria wasn't a prostitute, Owen wasn't a pervert and Donald wasn't a priest, if you wanted to re-enact a crime, why not do it properly. Perhaps a lazy copycat would be more careless? Whoever they were they'd managed to kill three people without drawing attention to themselves and if they were a copycat there would be one more in their sights.

The office was busy when they got back, Nancy felt energised by the throng of people working hard, focused on their own tasks. She walked across to where CCTV was being trawled through. 'How are you getting on?'

'Door-cam footage has picked up an image of a man with a large wheely case twelve hours before the body was discovered.' Nancy waited whilst the officer loaded the film. 'You'll notice that as he takes the case past he's walking backwards pulling the handle with both hands. Then twenty minutes later the same person comes back pulling the case behind him.'

'Do we get any other sightings?'

'No that was the only one, the house we took that from is on the corner of the street so it's a bit more sensitive.'

'Good work. I'm not sure that suitcase is big enough to fit both parts of the body in.'

'We'll keep looking to see if we can see anything similar.'

'Great, let me know if you find anything else.' Nancy said leaving them to it.

Back in her office she opened the internet file on the historic case, the sex worker had been the first victim, nineteen-year-old Betty Louise Randal, she'd travelled to New York to audition for a Broadway show from somewhere more rural, didn't get the part, didn't want to go home, found herself down on her luck and working the corner of a street in a less nice neighbourhood. When her body was found in a dumpster behind a diner the police it seems had done very little investigation. Nancy could imagine what they would've said, a victimless crime, as if being a sex worker made you less than human. According to this article it had taken almost eighteen months before someone thought to notify the girl's parents.

Imagine going all that time not knowing where your daughter was, only to discover she'd been murdered. Nancy looked at the newspaper archive site she was subscribed to, the killing hadn't even made the papers.

There had been no actual evidence that Maria had been a sex worker and yet that had been the immediate conclusion the lead detective in the case had made. That case had gone nowhere either. Grace had intimated that the investigation had only gained any impetus when they discovered that Maria's mother was speaking to the press.

Alan Schwartz, the man convicted of all four murders in 1977, was only captured after he murdered a policewoman, very publicly displaying her naked body, wrapped only in a towel, against a statue. He'd taken time to score abusive words into her body before he stabbed her to death. Alan was seen running away from the dump site by an off-duty policeman, who'd chased him down.

In court Alan said that the voices in his head had told him to do it, they had picked his victims and he was powerless. He was sectioned and sent to a secure mental facility where he died only three weeks later.

'You look annoyed,' Rob said from her doorway, 'I got you a sandwich by the way, it's ham and cheese.' He put the packet on her desk, sat down in the seat opposite her's and pulled open his own packaging taking a bite of the triangle of cut bread. He chewed and waited for a response.

'I'm just looking at an article from the case that John mentioned in the briefing.'

'Okay.' Rob placed his sandwich packaging on the edge of her desk, reached into his jacket pocket and produced a can of energy juice, the ring pull made a crunch followed by a burst of fizz as he opened it, two large gulps later and it was done.

'Betty Randal's murder didn't even make the papers, it wasn't just that it wasn't front page news, it wasn't news at all. And I know I shouldn't be shocked, it was the 70s etc, but sometimes I worry we haven't actually come that far at all.'

'You can't fix it all so you might as well focus on what you can, and essentially it doesn't really matter if our killer got inspiration for their crimes from this case because we're not going to solve it by focussing on something that happened almost fifty years ago on the other side of the world.'

'I hate it when you're right.' Nancy replied. 'Based on

what we do know, Maria was well liked by her co-workers, flat mates and had a good circle of friends, she just wanted to change her job. I think it would be worthwhile bringing the flat mate in for a chat, you know in case they've remembered something now. And I'd like to reinterview the staff who worked with her at Burns Night.'

'It does feel like that club is at the centre of this case.' Rob replied.

'There is one thing that's bothering me, though,' Nancy said. 'If we believe that the victims are being picked to fit into the pattern of the 1970s case, I can see how, very loosely, someone might pick Maria to fill the position of Prostitute and Owen as pervert, but if everything links to Burns Night how on earth would anyone have known that Donald Stark was a retired religious education teacher?'

Chapter 18

Burns Night didn't officially open until 7pm and even then it didn't get busy until around 10pm. Nancy had noted that in the original investigation into Maria's disappearance and subsequent murder the owner of the club had been described as resistant, sometimes hostile. She wasn't sure how they'd respond to her turning up this afternoon and frankly at this point she didn't care.

'This club has been here since 2016 and I've never been.' Nancy said as Rob pulled the car to a stop at the kerb outside.

'I just about remember when this used to be the cinema,' Rob said. 'I remember my dad bringing me for my birthday, I was allowed to bring one pal and then we went to get a burger after, I thought I was the business.'

Nancy laughed, 'The closest I got to going to the cinema was when my dad got the projector out.' A momentary memory filled her head, her and Cathy sitting bundled up together, sharing sweeties. She pressed the buzzer.

'Deliveries are round the back please.' A man's voice stated.

'It's the Police,' she said back.

They waited until a side door opened revealing a man in black jeans and a white shirt. Nancy introduced them as they entered. 'Is the manager or owner here?' she asked.

Dave Pickering had a nice office, the only part of the building that gave away its history as a cinema, it might've been Nancy's imagination but it even vaguely smelt of popcorn.

'I assure you all my licences are up to date, we've had the place inspected, we meet the fire regulations, so what can I do for you?'

So far Nancy would describe him as irritable, not hostile, but that could all change. 'Good for you Mr Pickering but we're not here about that. We're here about the deaths of three people which are all linked your establishment.'

He frowned, 'some kind of drug overdose situation, because we do our best, if we catch people using, they're kicked out and barred, if they're selling, we call you lot. It's not worth putting our performers at risk.'

'Not drugs – murder.'

'Murder,' he was shaking his head.

'You remember Maria Fisher,' Rob said showing him a photograph of the young Australian.

'Of course, that was a bloody shame, but it didn't happen here and again I had no idea she was on the game, I said that to the bloke who came round here at the time.'

'Was it a shock to you when it was suggested that Maria was a sex worker?' Rob continued.

'Yes.'

'Why?' Rob pressed.

'Because she was sweet, some girls,' Dave glanced at Nancy and saw a look of disapproval. 'women,' he corrected himself, 'they come across as sexy, flirty and even though I would never, because I'm happily married, you could imagine them in a more intimate way.'

'But not Maria?' Nancy said.

'No, she was sweet like I said, I mean she wanted to leave here and go work as a nanny and to be honest that seemed like it would be a career that suited her.'

'Do you think that she was likely to get taken advantage of?' Rob asked.

'No, she was lovely, but she didn't tolerate anyone getting handsy with her, not that we have a lot of issues with that here, but we do get a lot of stag dos and they can get a bit stupid with too much drink,' then looking directly at Nancy, 'not that the woman are much better, in fact it's more often them I have to tell to leave our male performers alone.'

'Had she handed her notice in before she went missing?' Nancy asked.

'No, I knew she was looking for something else, we open at lunchtime on Saturdays so she'd asked me if it was okay to come in late one time when she was away at a first aid course.'

'Other than sweet, what was she like?'

'Hard working, she'd been with us a while, she was always here on time, didn't take too much time off sick. Honestly, I don't know the waiting staff that well, the nature of the job is that we have a higher staff turnover than I'd like, so I don't generally waste my time.' He sighed.

'Anyone that might have known her well?'

'I think she was quite close to one of our angle grinders,

Natalie, they were both from Australia, so I think they bonded over that.'

'Sorry, what's an angle grinder?' Rob asked.

'Someone that wears something metal and then they use the angle grinder against them to create sparks.' Dave replied. 'They're very popular.'

Rob opened his mouth to speak but Nancy interrupted him. 'Is Natalie still working for you?'

'Yes,' he looked at his watch. 'All performers are required to be in by 5.30 for rehearsal and safety checks so she should be in the dressing rooms by now. I'll take you along.'

Dave got up out of his chair and began walking down a side corridor, Nancy and Rob followed. Two doors led off the corridor, Dave stopped and knocked on one, before opening the door a fraction and calling out, 'is everyone decent.' When he knew it was okay he opened the door fully and cast his eyes around the room. 'Has anyone seen Natalie?'

'She's popped to the toilet.'

'Are you happy to wait here for her by yourselves or do you need me to stick around and do the introductions, it's just that I've got things I could be getting on with.'

'We'll be fine,' Nancy confirmed.

They stood in the doorway conscious of not wanting to get in anyone's way, a few moments later they saw a dark haired woman approaching the door.

'Are you Natalie?' Nancy asked.

'Yes, who are you?'

Nancy introduced them, 'is there anywhere quieter we can go and talk?'

'Hold on, let me grab my coat and we can go out back and at least that way I can have a quick vape.'

They followed her outside to a small courtyard, not visible from the street and clearly designed to house dustbins discreetly. She pulled her vape out of her pocket and soon the air was heavy with clouds of candy floss smoke that Nancy knew would stick to her hair and clothes for days.

'What can I do for you?' Natalie asked between inhalations.

'We wanted to talk to you about Maria, Dave said you were close?'

She took a puff and then noticing Rob's face said, 'I started this because I wanted to give up smoking, but I'm not convinced it's any better for you, but there you are, sometimes I think about going back to the ciggies.'

'Have you ever tried the patches? Rob asked.

Rob had beaten his twenty a day habit over a year ago, crediting it to the use of nicotine patches rather than his own will power.

'No, maybe I should,'

'So Maria, you two were friends?' Nancy said desperate to get the conversation back on track.

'Yeah, she was a nice girl, we're from the same town in Australia, small world isn't it. Anyway, we would hang out sometimes, I thought she might enjoy doing something like this, the pay is decent and when I'm not working here, I'm picking up other gigs, but for some reason she had her heart set on being a nanny.'

'Do you remember anything strange or unusual happening on the run up to Maria's disappearance.'

Natalie was quiet for a moment puffing on her vape releasing so much smoke she could've been mistaken for a steam train. 'There was this one thing, but it was a couple of weeks before she disappeared.'

'What happened?' Nancy asked.

'It was a Friday night, we'd been busy. I was taking a break at the bar, we're not allowed to go outside or drink alcohol whilst we're performing – you know for safety reasons, but it's hot work and I get thirsty, so I always get some ice water and lemon in my breaks. Maria was busy doing her thing, I waved to her and then this woman came over to her screaming about her being a slut and a tart. The woman was with a couple of her friends and Maria was completely outnumbered, I didn't think that was fair so I went over to make sure she was okay.'

'Why was the woman so pissed off?' Rob asked.

'It was hard to figure out at first she was just screaming like a banshee, but it turned out that she'd found a photograph of her boyfriend with Maria on his phone, and she was accusing Maria of trying to steal him, saying that she was sleeping with her bloke.'

'Don't you have security to deal with that kind of outburst?' Rob asked.

'Normally, but they were breaking up a fight in the gents' toilets.'

'What happened with the woman?'

'She full on expected Maria to go outside and fist fight her, poor Maria, I don't think she'd ever been in a fight in her life. Anyway, I took that daft bint across to the photo wall and showed her all the pictures we have of people with our staff, it's just a thing we do.'

'Did she calm down?'

'Eventually, I think one of her friends managed to pull her away and then I called Maggie, the bar manager, over and she chucked them out, I think she barred the one that caused the drama.'

'Were there any repercussions after that?'

'Like what?'

'Did she try to contact Maria again, or wait outside the club for her?'

'No, and Maria would have mentioned it if she had.' Natalie said.

'How was she after the fight?' Nancy asked.

'A bit shaken up, Maggie sent her out the back to have a break, offered to let her go home, but she didn't let it bother her and came back out about ten minutes later like nothing had happened?'

'Any chance what this woman was saying was true?' Rob asked.

'No danger,' Natalie laughed. 'Sorry, I know this is going to sound mean, but the bloke was one of those skinny, missing teeth type that you can't imagine anyone fighting over and Maria was so far out of his league, but she was a sweetheart and she always stopped for photos, you kind of get used to it here, we have a professional in most weekends taking pictures.'

'What did you think when it was suggested that Maria had become a sex worker?'

'That was utter bullshit, there was just no way in hell. I knew something bad had happened to her as soon as she went missing.'

'How could you have known that?' Rob asked.

'Because she was the type that spoke to her family every day, she never skipped out on a shift, there was no way that she just walked away from all her stuff and her life and became a hooker, I'd never heard something so bloody ridiculous. Anyway, why are you asking all these questions about Maria now?'

'I've reopened the investigation into Maria's death, and we believe it might be connected to the death of this man, Owen Fairmile,' Nancy brought the photo of Owen and

Maria up on her phone and showed it to Natalie. 'Do you recognise him?'

She looked at the photo for a while. 'Yeah, we dated for a bit, he was nice. I didn't know he was dead.' Tears had begun rolling down her pale cheeks. Rob took a clean, folded, fabric handkerchief out of his pocket and handed it to Natalie.

'I'm sorry, we didn't know that you'd dated,' Nancy said.

Natalie lent back against the grey stone wall, 'what happened, was he murdered too?'

There was no easy way to break it to her. 'Yes, his body was discovered a few days ago.'

Natalie began to slowly collapse down the wall, her legs no longer able to hold her upright until she was sitting on the ground hugging her knees and sobbing uncontrollably.

Chapter 19

Nancy hadn't been prepared for the outpouring of grief, if Owen and Natalie had only dated for a bit this seemed excessive, but then who was she to judge. She waited for the sobbing to slow and then lowered herself to the ground so that she was sitting opposite Natalie.

'Can you tell me about your relationship with Owen? Did you meet him here, at the club?'

'No, I met him in Costa, he was looking for somewhere to sit, the place was mobbed, and he asked if he could sit with me. I wasn't sure at first, but he was really nice ,and we got talking. I could tell he wasn't going to ask me out, so I asked him, I'm not one of those the man has to do the asking types.'

'How many times did you go out?'

'We dated for about six months, he'd come into the club to watch me perform sometimes.'

'Who ended it?' Rob asked.

'Me,' Natalie was shaking her head as she said the word.

'How come?' Nancy asked.

'I thought he was getting too serious.'

'What made you think that?'

'I told him I was going back to Australia in the summer, and I wasn't sure when or if I was going to come back to Scotland. Then he told me he'd cleared his calendar and he was coming to Australia, it freaked me out. He said he was going to bring his nephew but that if he liked it, they might stay.'

'Owen would stay, or they would both stay?'

'Both, he was living with his sister, that's why we could never go back to his, she had strictly forbidden him to bring anyone back, I suppose I understand she had two sons, didn't want them picking up any bad habits, but…'

'But what?' Nancy asked.

'She wouldn't even let me in the house, I came by to pick him up and she answered the door, face like fizz, she called Owen like he was her child, I could hear her going on at him from outside, about how he hadn't told her was going out, that it was inconsiderate, how dare he have me come to the door. I don't think she really understood what I do, she referred to me as an "adult performer" which I thought was odd.'

It was the second time someone had described Diane as over protective of Owen, motherlike and controlling.

'So why did he stay living there?' Rob asked, it was a good question, Owen was making decent money as an estate agent he could have afforded somewhere of his own.

'For Michael, his nephew. Before Owen moved in Michael had run away a few times to Owen's flat and then Diane would come and drag him back, accused Owen of trying to turn the boy against her. I was surprised that she had agreed to the trip to Australia, I can't imagine she thought there was any chance her boy might not come back though otherwise hell would have frozen over before she'd given her blessing.'

'How did Owen take it when you ended the relationship?' Nancy asked.

'Not great, I could see he was really sad, and I was too I like…liked Owen, I was just scared, what if this man follows me halfway across the world, gives up his job and everything here and then it doesn't work out, it felt like a lot of pressure to be putting on us, on me.'

'The day he went missing he was meant to be going on a date with someone he met on a dating app, do you know anything about that?'

Natalie shook her head. 'We weren't really talking by then and the only reason I knew he was missing was because Michael turned up here looking for me because he thought I might know where his uncle was.'

'Would Owen and Maria have known each other through you?' Rob asked.

'Yeah, I guess that's why she looked so comfortable in that picture, she normally hated getting her photo taken with the customers, if you go inside and look at the wall, you'll see she looks totally different.' Natalie put her hand out to Rob, 'give us a hand up, I need to get myself sorted to go on stage, Dave will have a fit if I miss the safety briefing, even though it'll be exactly the same as all the others.'

Whilst Rob helped Natalie to her feet Nancy made her own way back to standing up.

'Thanks for your help this evening, and I'm sorry for your loss.' Nancy said.

'Can you let me know when the funeral is?' Natalie asked.

'Of course,' Nancy said, thinking about Diane's reaction to seeing the woman at her brother's funeral.

Natalie led them back inside the club and out to the main door.

'I think we should go back and talk to Diane, there was obviously something a bit off about her relationship with her brother.' Nancy said getting into the passenger side of the car.

'She seemed devastated when we told her Owen was dead do you really think she might have something to do with her brother's death.'

'I don't know, I just think their living situation wasn't as cordial as she made out and that warrants a few more questions. I'd quite like to question Michael as well.'

'I can't see Diane agreeing to that.'

'I'm happy to arrange for a responsible adult to be present, just not her.'

Diane was carrying shopping in from her car when they pulled up outside the sandstone house.

'I wasn't expecting to see you again so soon.'

'We have a few follow up questions, if that's okay?' Nancy asked whilst Rob walked over to the boot of Diane's car and lifted out the three remaining shopping bags.

'I'll take these for you,' he said. They followed her through the front door past the living room where they'd sat the time before and into the kitchen. 'Do you want a hand putting these things away?' Rob asked.

'No thank you,' she filled the kettle and set in on its base to boil as she got out cups and tea bags, without saying anything to her guests she walked out of the kitchen and stood at the base of the stairs. 'Michael, come down I need you to put the groceries away.' She waited, Nancy could see her through the open kitchen door, the woman's arms tightly crossed, her neck strained to look up the stairs.

'Michael do not make me come up,' her words harsh and angry.

A moment later there was the sound of a door being slammed and the thud of teenage footsteps on the stairs. He appeared in the kitchen, a scowl on his face, looking like he was ready for a confrontation when he saw them, his expression immediately morphing into compliant politeness.

'Sorry I had my headphones on, I mustn't have heard you the first time.'

Diane was stirring the coffee, the metal spoon clanking off the sides of the mugs. She put them on the breakfast bar near where Nancy and Rob were standing, taking a moment to observe her son in his task.

'You told us Owen came to live with you because his flat was being sold and he wasn't sure about buying?' Nancy asked thinking that if she didn't start the conversation they could be stood in a silent showdown for hours.

'Yes.' Diane replied.

'And did the two of you get on well?'

'Mostly, like I said it was nice to have an adult conversation,' she looked at her son as though it was his fault that he wasn't mature enough to talk to.

'How did you get on when you were kids?' Nancy asked.

'Fine, he was my little brother and I thought he was annoying, normal sibling stuff.'

'Are your parents still alive?' Nancy asked.

'Yes, mum got early onset dementia, she's been in a home for years, doesn't recognise any of us anymore, we don't visit, it only upsets her.'

'I'm sorry, that must be very difficult, what about your father?'

'He spends most of the year living in Spain, they always

planned to retire out there and dad decided that he would honour their plans.' Diane said.

'Have you told him about Owen?' Rob asked.

She nodded, 'he's coming back next week.'

'Will he stay with you?' Rob asked.

'No, he's staying with friends, dad and I rather clash, and we didn't think it would do anyone any good.' Diane replied.

Michael was putting the groceries away slowly, Nancy could see he had his head very slightly cocked to one side trying to listen in to as much of the conversation as he could.

'Owen's boss described you as overprotective towards your brother, maybe even a little controlling, what do you think about that?' Nancy asked.

Michael snorted and then quickly began coughing as a cover, Diane glared in his direction. The boy didn't turn around.

'Perhaps he doesn't have any siblings, I don't know, all I know is that Owen could be a bit impetuous, he didn't always make the best decisions, someone had to keep an eye on him.' Diane retorted.

'Owen was a grown man, why did you feel like you should be involved in his decision making?' Rob said.

'I told him if he wanted to live under my roof then he would have to follow my rules, that's all.' Diane said.

'Like a child.' Rob said. 'You were treating him like one of your sons and not an equal.'

'Is that why you felt like it was your right to get involved in his love life?' Nancy asked.

'If you're talking about that tart from the club, then I have no regrets, she was clearly using him and of course I knew what he saw in her, men only think with what's inside their pants.' Diane was looking at her son as she spoke.

'Were you angry with him that he was going on a date the day he disappeared?'

Nancy asked.

Diane threw her untouched cup of coffee down the sink, 'I'd like you to leave now.' She proceeded to take the half-drunk mug out of Rob's hands.

'Did you argue?' Nancy asked ignoring the request and the scene Diane was making.

'No, we did not.' She shrieked.

'Liar,' Michael said quietly from inside the open fridge.

'What did you fight about?' Nancy pushed.

'I told him we should be enough, he had his nephews to thinks about and that he was setting a bad example going out, meeting women and not coming home at night.' Diane had given up trying to prise the mug away from Rob. Defeated she sat down on one of the stools. 'I just wanted someone to put us first for a change.'

'He was your brother, not your husband, you can't have expected him to live a celibate life and stay as the father figure in this mock family you'd invented in your mind.' Nancy said.

Diane began to cry, not loud sobs like Natalie, but quiet tears. 'Don't you think I know that. I'm going to have to live with the knowledge that the last conversation I had with my baby brother was an argument.' Diane got up from the stool and left the kitchen, they watched as she climbed the stairs.

'I'm sorry about mum,' Michael said closing the fridge door, 'she's been a bit like this since dad left.'

'That's okay, nothing to apologise for, we'll leave you to get on and remember you've got my card if you need to talk.' Rob said.

Chapter 20

'I feel sorry for the boy,' Rob said as they drove off. 'I can see why the uncle stuck around, probably thought Michael would never get away to live his own life.'

Nancy thought about Dylan, the two boys were pretty much the same age, how would she have felt if he had turned his back on her. Heartbroken was the answer, but she'd never given him any reason to do so. Michael on the other hand was expected to fill the role of man of the house, father to his younger brother and emotional support to his mother.

'Arrange for him to come into the station, you can do the interview, I think he likes you.' Nancy said.

Their conversation was interrupted by Nancy's phone ringing.

'What's up Isla?'

'You said you wanted to speak to the podcast hosts of that true crime show, turns out they're local, well Dundee. They said they're happy to come down tomorrow morning and bring all their research on the case and any correspondence they've received…' the pause went on long enough that Nancy got the sense that she wasn't going to like the next thing Isla had to say. 'But in exchange they were hoping they could interview you, you know as a guest on the show.'

Nancy sighed, 'did you tell them requests like that need to go through the proper channels?'

'Of course, but they were quite insistent that there was something in it for them to make the trip.'

'It's thirty-five miles, it's hardly an arduous journey, was the pleasure of doing their civic duty not enough for them. Never mind just get them to fill in the form and hopefully it'll get lost somewhere.'

There was a moment of silence again, 'the thing is,' Isla continued. 'They were really insistent about it, so I spoke to the DCI, and he signed it off.'

'Fine, what time are they coming in?'

'They said they'll be here by 10am.'

'And when am I supposed to be doing this interview?'

'I told them it wouldn't be until after this case was wrapped up so it's not like they're expecting it tomorrow.' Isla replied.

'Good work for getting them to come in, let's hope it's worth it. See you later.' Nancy hung up then thumped the back of her head on to the car head rest.

'Hey, my car has done nothing wrong here,' Rob sniggered. 'Do you think it's significant that Maria and Owen actually knew each other?

'It's hard to say, but it feels like an awfully big coincidence, and if was only the two of them then I'd say let's lean into that angle, but now there's Donald Stark and the only thing that ties him to them is that he picked up his granddaughter from Burns Night.'

'But then until this afternoon we didn't know that Owen and Maria were connected beyond the club, maybe we haven't found the thing that ties them together.' Rob countered.

'Argh! We wouldn't be agonising over this if it wasn't for this bloody true crime podcast copycat thing.'

'We don't even know that the blood in that house belonged to Donald Stark yet,' Rob replied.

'What, you're suggesting there's another seventy something year old man that's missing and dead that we don't know about yet?' she paused. 'Did Lucy say when she'd get back to us with the DNA test?'

'She said she'll mark it as urgent, but it probably won't be until tomorrow.' Rob said as they pulled into the station carpark.

Nancy hadn't made it to her office before she was stopped by Isla, 'DCI Cooper said to tell you to come and see him as soon as you got back.'

Nancy considered ignoring the request, all she wanted was ten minutes peace and quiet in her office with the door closed so she could think about this case without anyone interrupting. It was no use putting it off, she had a good relationship with Cooper, but he wouldn't appreciate her dodging his orders. She spun on her heel heading back out the door and up the flight of stairs to his office. The stairwell reminded her of an 80s high school or probably every council building of that era.

'You wanted to see me,' she said walking into his office. She didn't sit down hoping that staying standing would somehow make this a quicker process.

'Close the door and sit down,' Cooper said without taking his eyes off the computer screen.

Now it felt even more like high school, where she'd seen

the inside of the headmaster's office more times than she'd care to admit.

'You know, of course that if you enter into a romantic or,' Cooper paused and pulled a face with his nose wrinkled slightly, 'sexual relationship with someone of a lower grade or that is under your command that you're meant to report that, fill in the appropriate paperwork.' He looked at her as if he wanted to be having this conversation about as much as her.

'I do.'

'Good, and if you were in a relationship with someone you work with you would have the good sense and common courtesy to tell me?'

It was Nancy's turn to frown and screw her nose up. 'I would, why are we having this chat, sir?'

'It was brought to my attention today that you were seen coming out of DS MacDonald's apartment this morning and that it appeared you had stayed the night. Care to comment?'

'I did stay the night at Rob's apartment, we are not in a relationship though and it might have added some context if the person who'd shared this titbit with you hadn't forgotten to mention that I also had Dylan with me, and I don't know how other people conduct themselves but I'm not planning to take my sixteen year old son with me to any future hook ups.'

Cooper smiled, 'well that's a relief. But why are you staying with DS MacDonald?'

'Because Dylan is living with me and my current accommodation isn't really...' she stopped for a moment thinking about her camper and how much she had enjoyed living in it. '...practical for two people, Rob has a spare room and is closer to the school, so he offered to let us stay there until I get something more permanent organised.'

'Ah, good, well that's all then.' Cooper looked back at his computer screen.

'You going to tell me who the rat is then?'

'I am not.' Cooper said.

'Was it DI Penman surely she's not still pissed that I'm borrowing Grace?' Nancy said crossing her arms.

'Haven't you got a murder to look into,' Cooper said shooing her towards the door.

Nancy made it to her office this time without being interrupted, she had a strong urge to slam her door, but that would likely only encourage someone to disturb her and honestly, she wasn't sure the door would survive it.

Instead, she closed it firmly turning to rest her back against it like a human barricade. The cold of the glass felt nice against the warmth of her back, she closed her eyes, ignoring the gentle buzzing of the phone in her pocket. Maria knew Owen, and someone accused Maria of sleeping with their boyfriend, what if someone mistakenly thought Owen and Maria were sleeping together, but who would that matter to? They hadn't found any possessive, jealous exes in Owen's closet, only his sister.

Could Diane be described as possessive and jealous? Natalie had said that she treated Owen like he was a child, trying to control his movements. At a stretch she could see Diane killing Natalie, but not Maria, she doubted Diane even knew Maria existed.

Rob wrapped his knuckles against the outside of his boss's door, Nancy jumped moving out of the way and letting him come in. 'Everything okay?'

She considered for a moment telling him about her conversation with Cooper, but decided against it, he would find it too funny and use every opportunity to continue the spread of the rumour for his own amusement. It would be lost on him that things like this could haunt a female detective's career.

'All good, I was thinking.'

'Did it make you deaf?'

She frowned.

'Dr Clarke called, she said she tried your mobile twice and you weren't picking up?'

Nancy took her phone out of her pocket and looked at the screen, 'Oh, like I said I was thinking, is everything alright?'

'DNA results are back.' Rob said.

'That was bloody quick,' Nancy replied.

'I imagine Dr Clarke can be pretty persuasive when required, anyway she thought you'd want to know. The blood in the bathtub, it was Donald Stark's.'

'There are six community centres within a few miles radius of Dunfermline, three of them have gardens, all of which have their own compost heap or bin,' Cal said.

'That shouldn't take much searching then,' Nancy replied.

'I was coming to that, I got uniform to go out to each of them to do a preliminary search and there was no sign of any human remains.'

'We're back at square one, then?'

'Not exactly, there are also allotments to consider. Whilst they don't have a communal compost heap, a lot of the allotments have their own one, but I ruled them out on the basis that they're highly populated, a body would be hard to hide in a smaller heap and also I think it would have been discovered by now.'

'Any other thoughts?'

'There are schools and nurseries with gardens and compost heaps, but again I think it would have been found by now. But there's one nursery that's been closed for the last couple of months, due to asbestos being discovered in the leaking roof. It's a day care style nursery, not a council one and they've moved to a temporary location whilst they're waiting to find out what's happening with the building. No one's allowed on the premises, it's been cordoned off, which means the nursery garden and compost bin has been left unattended since about a fortnight before Dr Clarke thinks Mr Stark was murdered.'

'Excellent work Cal, call forensics and have them meet us up there, Rob let's go and find out if we've located Donald Stark's remains.'

The nursery was protected by Herras fencing all the way around the perimeter of the building and grounds. Nancy and Rob waited for the forensic team to show up. In the old days detectives would have gone on ahead, but too much could be lost in forensic evidence to risk it and besides Daniel Burrows, the crime scene manager was not someone she planned to get on the wrong side of, despite being her brother in law he would have no qualms about bringing her down a notch if she degraded the crime scene by impatience.

Daniel arrived ahead of his team, 'you've not been in?' He asked.

'No, we're just waiting for your guys to show up, we'll wait around to see if you find anything.'

Nancy hated sitting on the side lines watching, now there were six people in white crime scene suits. Large floodlights had been set up along with a designated walkway to the potential crime scene. She was impressed by the speed everything was set up.

Rob leant into his car and took a can of energy drink out of the passenger side door pocket, 'You want one?'

Nancy looked at him, frowning as she did some mental

maths, 'That must be about your fourth one of those today. Is that all you drink?'

'Nope I've also had two coffees and a litre of water.' Rob smiled unapologetically. 'You didn't answer my question.'

'No thanks, it tastes like cough syrup.'

'It's an acquired taste,' he grinned. 'Don't you hate the waiting though,' he said tipping his head towards where Daniel and his team were at work.

'Yeah,' it was a macabre feeling, standing watching, where best case scenario was finding a dead body.

They didn't need to wait long until they saw Daniel walking back from the compost area at the back of the garden along the designated path created from white plastic panels. Nancy walked towards the gap in the Herras fencing followed by Rob.

She waited expectantly for him to speak.

'We have human remains, the body has been there a while, and given the environment it's been in there's not a lot of soft tissue left. Luckily the teeth are still intact so if nothing else you'll be able to get a dental record match.' Daniel said.

'How long's a while?' Nancy asked.

'Over a week, less than two, there's a lot of insect activity and the site is designed to aid decomposition, so getting an exact time on a deposition site like this will be difficult.' Daniel replied.

'How long till you've recovered the remains?' Nancy asked aware that it was getting towards the end of the day, and they still might not have a positive ID.

'We're going to be here a while. I'm just about to call for some additional support, we're going to need to take the whole compost heap away with us to sift through it for evidence and remains.' He glanced from Nancy to Rob. 'No point you two standing about watching, there's nothing you can do here, might as well get yourselves back to the station, I'll let you know when everything is back at the lab.'

'Okay thanks, have you given Dr Clarke the heads up that another body will be coming her way?' Nancy asked.

'She knows, though there's not much left to do a post mortem, I'll get the soft tissue to her as soon as I can.'

'Thanks Daniel, I'll arrange for some uniformed officers to stand around and keep you company and ward off any curious passers by.'

When Nancy called the station, she was pleased to hear the familiar voice of the desk sergeant. 'Jed it's Nancy I have a crime scene that needs some eyes on it while Daniel and his team work.'

'Text me the address and I'll send a couple of constables over.' The Irish lilt in his voice had never faded despite living in Scotland since his early twenties.

'Thank you.' Nancy hung up. 'Right, back to the station for a debrief and then home I guess.'

'Talking of home,' Rob said as he opened his car door, 'do you want to take seperate cars this evening or are you alright with me giving you a lift?'

'Why wouldn't I be alright with a lift?'

'I wouldn't want to do anything to tarnish your reputation, that's all.'

They got into the car, 'you've heard then, who do you think got that rumour going round the building.'

'Who knows, I'd ask who you'd pissed off at the station but that could be a long list,' he smiled. 'You're not upset about it?'

'I think it's ridiculous, I might get you a black cap and sit in the back so everyone can see I'm just using you for your chauffeur skills.' She laughed. Nancy wasn't thrilled that someone had seen fit to start gossip about them, but it could be worse, having the station talking about Chris getting Cathy pregnant would be intolerable, although she knew that it was inevitable.

Back at the station she gathered the team, updating them on the scene. 'Good work Cal for identifying the location and whilst we don't know for certain that it's Donald Stark, I think we can say it's very likely.' She paused thinking about Susan Stark and telling her about finding her husband's remains. 'Tomorrow, thanks to Isla and Grace, we have the hosts of the true crime podcast coming in at 10, so John, I want everything we know about the episodes that covered this crime on my desk by 8.30 and Isla, everything about the hosts.'

There was a round of no problem boss from all parties.

'Rob, I want you to get Michael Bridlington in, and interview him without his mother present.' She looked around the room for the officers who'd been looking at the CCTV. 'I'd like a rundown of all the CCTV material tomorrow morning as well please.'

Nancy paused running through everything in her mind. 'Cal I've got a new job for you, I want you to find out everything you can about Donald Stark, no stone unturned, alright?'

Cal nodded.

'At the moment we're working on two theories, one that this is some loose copycat of the podcast crime, the other being that they're connected to Burns Night in some way. I specifically want to know if Donald had any other interactions with the club and if this is a copycat then who would know that he was a retired RE teacher.'

They'd been late leaving the station and stopped by the Chinese take away on the way home. Back in the flat and sitting around Rob's too small table, Dylan was scooping up sweet and sour sauce-soaked rice with a prawn cracker.

'Dad came to the school today.' He said.

'Why?' Nancy asked.

'He went to the head to tell him that they weren't to send any correspondence to you and to ask them to give him the address you'd left with them. They didn't though, don't worry.'

'It's your gran's address anyway so it's not like it would have been any use to him, what did they say about the other stuff?'

'They called me in to the office and I said that I'd chosen to live with you, and they said I was sixteen and I could make decisions for myself.'

'I bet that went down well.' Rob said.

'He went mental, screaming about how he was my father, and he would pull me out of school if they didn't treat him with having authority over me. The head had to threaten to call the police before he calmed down and left.'

'I'm sorry he's behaving like this, hopefully in the future he'll calm down and realise how hard all this is for you and then the two of you can repair your relationship.' Nancy said.

'I don't want anything to do with him, ever.'

Nancy knew that was likely untrue, Dylan was angry that his father had behaved in a way that upended his life, removed me from it and in a five months was going to give him a baby sister. Her mum had tried to get her to go the gender reveal party, but she'd declined. Nancy had seen the pictures on her mum's social media.

'We should arrange to pick up the rest of your stuff soon,' Nancy said.

'There's not much left.'

'Still better to pick it up, depending on how this case goes we'll do it at the weekend.'

Dylan was staying in Rob's spare room and although their host had tried to insist Nancy took his room and let him sleep on the sofa bed Nancy wouldn't hear of it. She was pleased that Dylan had his own space here, she knew he needed to be able to go into the room, shut the door and play video games to give him time to process how he was feeling.

With Dylan safely out of earshot she felt comfortable looking at the text she'd just received from Daniel. 'That's the scene of crimes all finished up on site and everything back at the lab, he has sent some pictures.' She opened them on her phone, sharing the small screen with Rob.

Rob wrinkled his nose, 'rather them than me, that looks grim.'

Nancy had taken the opportunity to take a trip to a

body farm at the University of Tennessee in the US when there was a cross Atlantic initiative. She'd seen bodies in various stages of decomposition and thought she would never be rid of the smell that had seemed to line her nostrils for the week she was there. But even so, looking at the remains of what was surely Donald Stark was still stomach churning.

'If we're dealing with a copycat killer, are you not a bit concerned that the last victim will be a female officer?' Rob asked.

'I'm hoping that we find them before we come to that.'

'I was just thinking that if Burns Night is the centre of this then the only female officer that's been there is you.'

Nancy smiled, 'on duty, but we've no idea how many of our female officers might have gone there recreationally and if the pattern holds then it wouldn't be an actual police officer, but someone linked loosely to the police.'

'Did you see the DCI on the news earlier, he got a proper roasting from the press.' Rob changed the subject.

'Hardly surprising, murder will do that, at least they don't know there's a connection between Maria and Owen yet, but I think he'll need to be sharing that information soon, especially when we get the DNA results back for the remains found tonight.'

Chapter 23

DAY FOUR, THURSDAY

Nancy slept fitfully thinking about the case and the next morning as she entered the office she was fuelled mainly on caffeine and sugar. She made a mental note to find something more substantial to eat than the half a Snickers bar she'd had this morning.

As instructed, DS John Gibbs had left a file on her desk with information on the 1976 case. Nancy opened it pleased to find that John had separated the information shared on the pod cast to information he'd taken from other sources. It had been a four-part show, using information taken from public record mostly, with some social history commentary added in.

She closed the file and opened the one Isla and Grace had provided on the two hosts, Kayleigh McGuire and Lucas Martin. Kayleigh, 32, was from Dundee, she'd done a degree in journalism and worked for a number of local and national papers before starting the podcast. Her co-host Lucas, 39, was American and he had a degree in history and a postgraduate in Criminology. They'd started the podcast two years ago and it had, what looked to Nancy, a lot of subscribers.

The pair had covered well known cases like Jack the Ripper and the Boston Strangler, jumping around across the globe and through the decades. They'd won a couple of awards for their work and had even been invited to talk at a seminar at a university in the US.

Not ghoul seeking hacks it would appear then, and possibly not a huge leap from either of their previous careers to this, but why this case, why now. That was Nancy's first question. Just after 9am she wandered out of her office to get a cup of coffee, maybe she should leave the building, pick up a sandwich and a coffee that would actually taste of coffee.

'Are you alright, DI Ravenscroft?' Cooper asked. It was rare for him to address her this way, she shook herself and looked up.

DCI Cooper was standing next to her and behind him was the Chief Superintendent.

'Sorry sir, I was deep in thought about the case.' She smiled at him and nodded a quick tip of the head to the superior officers.

'And where are we with that?' the Chief Super asked.

'Gathering evidence at the moment, seeing where our victims lives intersect and creating a working theory on why they were selected.'

'And are you any closer to discovering who the killer is?'

Nancy wanted to say that it was Thursday morning and the first victim had been discovered in the early hours of Monday and therefore the fact they had collated as much information as they had was a bloody miracle. But where was the point in making yourself stand out as a troublemaker, even if the man must know what he was asking was bordering on ridiculous.

'Sadly not as yet, we're hoping that studying the victimology will lead us to the person responsible.' Nancy smiled, Cooper caught her eye, clearly relieved that she'd opted for the appropriate response and no doubt expecting that she would tell him her actual thoughts later on in the privacy of one of their offices.

'The sooner we have someone arrested the better, DCI Cooper will be holding a press conference later today when we have confirmation on the third victim. A serial killer at large is very unsettling for the community.' The Chief Super said.

'Absolutely, as soon as we have a viable suspect we'll make the appropriate arrest, I assure you.'

'Good work Inspector, I hope to hear you've made progress soon.'

The two men walked away, smile and nod she thought, reminding herself that for the most part she was left in peace to conduct investigations and follow the evidence, but it was no surprise that this case would be catching the attention of the most senior officers, especially as it involved reopening the death of an international woman. Having got that case so wrong there would be pressure not to make mistakes this time. Talking of which she needed to phone Maria's mother.

'Cal,' she called across the room to where the man was engrossed in his computer screen.

He looked up blinking, casting a gaze around the room trying to locate the origin of the voice. Realising it was his boss he stood up quickly sending his chair wheeling backwards into Isla's legs as she made her way to her own desk. He fumbled an apology and then walked across the room, his long legs appearing to catch on every desk leg and chair wheel in the process.

'Yes boss.'

'How are you getting on with Donald Stark's life?'

'It's not very interesting, lots of holiday pictures but hopefully I'll discover more as I dig a bit deeper.'

'Good, well take a break and go out to the catering van in the retail park and get me a coffee and a roll of some sort and whilst you're there get something for yourself,' she glanced around the room, 'and something for this lot. Wait there,' she went back into her office and came back handing Cal £30. 'That should cover it.'

'They're contactless only,' he said looking at the money in his hand as though she'd asked him to pay with refrigerator drawings.

'Then use your card and consider this me paying you back, but in advance.' Nancy didn't wait for a response, instead she walked back to her office and closed the door.

He stood for another thirty seconds in the middle of the office before he left in pursuit of Nancy's food order.

Nancy's heartbeat quickened as the phone rang, she'd rather have this conversation face to face, in the absence of that she'd rather not need to leave a message asking Mrs Fisher to call her back.

'Hello?' the Australian accent was strong.

'Mrs Fisher?' Nancy asked.

'Yes, who is this?'

'My name is Detective Inspector Nancy Ravenscroft, we've not met, but I'm calling about your daughter, Maria.'

There was a moments silence. Whatever Mrs Fisher had been doing in what was her evening she hadn't expected it to be shattered by a call about her murdered child.

'What about Maria?' she asked.

'I'm reopening the investigation into her death, and I wanted you to know before it is reported in the media.'

'Why, why are you reopening the investigation?' She asked, her voice breaking, a hard intake of breath the only give away that the woman was undoubtedly crying.

'Maria's death has been linked to the death of someone else, a man named Owen Fairmile.'

'Are you going to tell me that my daughter was murdered because she was a prostitute?'

'No, I'm not. Nothing in my investigation to date has led to me believing that to be accurate.' Nancy answered.

Silence again, the woman was weighing her up, trying to decide if she trusted this detective. Nancy understood her hesitation, she'd felt let down, betrayed even, by the police the first time her daughter's death was investigated, why would she believe that Nancy would do a better job.

'Should I book a plane ticket and come over?'

'That's not something that's necessary at the moment, but you are welcome to do so if that's what's best for you.'

'When I came before the detective then didn't want to hear anything I had to say about Maria, he'd made up his mind and that was that. Made me feel like Maria had brought it all on herself.'

Nancy was appalled that there were still detectives out there who thought that sex workers brought harm on themselves, and even if Maria had been a prostitute, she deserved a proper and thorough investigation into her murder and not a lazy attempt.

'I don't think that anyone brings murder on themselves. I want you to know that I'll be investigating Maria's death thoroughly and I might have more questions in the future if you'd be willing to do that. And if there's anything you'd like to ask me I wanted to make sure that you have my direct line.'

'You'll excuse me if I don't have a high expectation of the police.'

'Of course, I completely understand why you feel that way, I hope that I can bring you some closure.'

'Thank you.' Mrs Fisher replied.

'In the meantime if you're contacted by journalists I'd ask you not to share your story with them at this stage. I'm not trying to suppress you I just don't want their focus taken away from us finding a murderer.'

'I aways send them away, they pretend to care about you but they're nothing but vultures using your pain to sell the papers.'

Chapter 24

'Thank you for coming in today,' Nancy said as she sat down opposite Kayleigh and Lucas.

'Always happy to help the police.' Kayleigh smiled. Her red hair was contained in a messy bun on the back of her head and she was dressed in an ankle length skirt, with black top and oversized woollen cardigan giving her the appearance of primary school teacher rather than a journalist.

Nancy wanted to say *for a price*, because after all they'd wanted something in return for their gracious help. 'How do you pick the true crime cases you cover on the podcast?' She asked instead.

'We typically look at older cases, things that aren't going to be in people's memories as readily and we try to cover the globe, we find that our listeners enjoy the geographical variances.' Lucas said.

He was tall with blonde hair and blue eyes, he might've been handsome if his skin wasn't pock marked all over his cheeks. A cruel scar of what was likely a serious case of adolescent acne.

'And we like to be able to comment on the social history and compare it to the modern day or look at the language used in the media when they describe people,' Kayleigh continued. 'For example, a fifteen-year-old girl that's the victim of a crime is a "child" but if the girl was the criminal then she'd be a "youth" or a "young adult" the language is used to evoke the response the writer wants their audience to feel.'

Nancy had been given media training and after conducting thousands of interviews she knew only too well the power of language, but she'd let Kayleigh continue as though she was sharing something new.

'And what sort of language do you use when you write your scripts?' Nancy had spent the preceding hour listening to the podcast, she knew the language they used was often disparaging of the police force.

'We try to be honest,' Lucas said. 'We give our opinion and we're clear that's all it is.'

'What made you pick this case to review?'

'Honestly the fact that it was already referred to as The Prostitute, The Priest, The Pervert and The Police made it stand out.' Kayleigh said. 'It makes it really easy to separate it out into segments and make sure that each victim gets an equal amount of airtime.'

'Do you do much research into the victims and their families?'

'Sometimes we're able to find out more than others, some cases have a lot of data, like the Jack the Ripper case, there's a decent amount that you can look through, but other than distant relatives you don't need to worry about how family will take it. We did pull the plug on one case last year, the murder of a schoolgirl in Sweden in 1985, after we contacted the family they made it very clear they didn't want us to talk about it, we respected that.' Lucas said.

'You talked about how language elicits a reaction out of people, did you think about it when you talked about Anna Taylor, the sex worker? What emotion were you trying to get when you discussed her?' Nancy asked.

'It's interesting that you say that, because we did have some serious conversations about it because I really don't like the word prostitute, but in the end, we thought that it only highlighted how attitudes had stagnated over the years. In this case like so many before it, the police didn't take much in the way of action after the first victim's body was discovered. We discussed how the police took the view that being murdered was an occupational hazard.' Kayleigh replied.

Reluctantly Nancy knew she agreed with the woman, and to give them their due they'd referred to Anna Taylor as a sex worker throughout their conversation. 'Were you able to contact any of Anna's family?'

'To be honest, of all the victims, the least is known about Anna. Not surprising with attitudes being what they were in the 70s, it wasn't uncommon for family members to distance themselves. They would have known that if the press of the day came knocking at their door, they wouldn't have come off favourably, so best to pretend she never existed.' Lucas said.

'And the other victims?' Nancy asked.

'The priest had no family, the "pervert" had been disowned by his family long before he was murdered and the policewoman was an only child, parents now deceased. I know it might be hard to accept, but it is never our intention to hurt the relatives of victims. How crime is dealt with really speaks to how society views different facets of the population and that's what we focus on, we're not about making light of someone's suffering.' Kayleigh replied.

They were saying all the right things and it was hard for Nancy to believe that this was an act. 'Tell me more about the third victim in the case.' Nancy said.

'The pervert, as he was dubbed, was called that because he'd been arrested for soliciting multiple times, he was in possession of a large collection of pornographic magazines, some of which would raise eyebrows even today.' Kayleigh said.

'Did he know Anna? Had he been her client?' Nancy asked.

Kayleigh shrugged, 'it's possible, we'll never really know, it wasn't till the connection was made to the priest's murder that the investigation really took off, a sex worker and a pervert didn't really motivate the law enforcement of the time, plus as bad as it sounds, the level of public outrage at their murders was practically non-existent. In part because Anna's murder didn't even feature in the media, and Bradley, "the pervert "only featured in an "at least that's more scum off the streets" kind of a way.'

'But the priest upset people?'

'Father Michael was in his late sixties and was well liked in his community. He was a, "my church door is always open" kind of a man, when his body was found that got boots on the ground.' Lucas said. 'Fascinating that there was an immediate assumption that he was a good man, there was no attempt made to look into his life and life choices to back this up, it was merely "this man is a man of God and therefore is good", which when we consider what we now know about the behaviour of some religious leaders of that time might make you wonder if that in fact was the truth, or could it be that the killer knew something more sinister about the man.'

Kayleigh frowned at her co-host, 'it's also important to note that there were never any allegations against Father Michael, either during his life or after his death and as history has also taught us, when someone dies is often the time that their victims feel empowered to speak out.'

Lucas had clearly veered from the co-hosts planned script and now Kayleigh was invested in getting them back on track. Did that mean they had something to hide or was it merely that Kayleigh didn't like being caught off guard.

'What made anyone connect the deaths?' Nancy asked.

'All the bodies were found naked and wrapped in identical towels, not killed where their bodies were left and each one had a Jesus fish scored into their skin. Not something that's easy to ignore.' Lucas continued. 'Of course, everyone cared that Anna and Bradley had been murdered when they discovered that Father Michael had been targeted by the same person. Then there was public outrage at how little had been done to find the perpetrator.'

'And how were they caught?' Nancy asked.

'Alan Schwartz was a homeless man, he'd regularly attended Father Michael's church, had even been fed by the man's soup kitchen. When he disposed of Doreen O'Sullivan's body it was done very publicly. He left his fingerprints on the scene. Then it transpired that he'd been caught on a film talking to Doreen the day she disappeared. There had been a community soccer game for charity. One of the sponsors was an electrical appliance store owner who'd brought along a little Cinemax camera to record the game. Later when he looked at the footage, he realised he'd not stopped recording when he'd been speaking to some of the other sponsors. The footage caught Alan and Doreen having a disagreement, he was trying to grab hold of her arm, and she was seen to be shaking him off and trying to walk away from him. Alan followed her shouting at her'

'The footage was good enough to identify him?'

'It wasn't great, but when Alan was arrested it was decided that it was a good enough likeness that it would substantiate the police's case that Doreen was killed because Alan had a personal vendetta against her.' Kayleigh said.

'What reason did Alan give for killing his victims?' Nancy asked, she'd read up on the case and knew what was publicly documented, but she was keen to know if the pair had uncovered any new information.

'Alan Schwartz was likely a schizophrenic, he'd been in and out of prison and been committed once but wasn't on any medication at the time of his arrest. He simply said that he was told who to pick, what to carve on the bodies and where to leave them.' Kayleigh said.

'What about the towels, that's an oddly specific detail.' Nancy said.

'A month or so before the killings began Alan was arrested on suspicion of shoplifting, there was no proof it was him and he was released. One of the things stolen from the department store was a pack of four bath towels.' Kayleigh replied.

'There's no proof that he was mentally ill either though, he died three weeks after being committed to an asylum and there were some very dubious circumstances surrounding his death, it was ruled accidental, because according to the investigation he was stock piling medication and taking it erratically, but there's nothing to say that he wasn't intentionally incorrectly medicated.' Lucas said.

'And how was his death reported in the media?' Nancy asked.

'Like a victory, his death was seen as just, many people of the time thought that he should've been tried and convicted without any consideration to his mental condition, he would of course have been sentenced to death if he'd been found guilty.' Lucas said. 'We'll never truly know, as he was denied the ability to properly tell his story.'

'You sound like you feel sorry for him.' Nancy said.

'Not at all, I was just musing over the fact that we'll never know any more about his motives because he didn't live long enough to be interviewed by properly trained medical professionals.' Lucas replied.

'Tell me about the response to the series.' Nancy said.

Kayleigh and Lucas looked at each other, 'because this case wasn't famous before, it split our audience a little bit. We got emails saying they thought Alan was set up, that he had been exploited because of his undiagnosed disorder, we received a bit of criticism that we were continuing the false belief that all unmedicated schizophrenics were dangerous to others. There was also long discussion on our comments about whether or not modern-day forensics meant that they would have been discovered immediately and others arguing that we still live in a society where the death of a sex worker wouldn't be investigated in the same way the murder of a priest would be.'

Nancy thought for a moment, the cynics had been right, Maria's death had not been investigated as vigorously as it should have been.

'Did any of the participants of this conversation stand out to you as off?' Nancy asked.

'The thing with true crime podcasting...,' Lucas said standing up and walking towards the back of the small room.

Nancy rolled her eyes, she was about to be lectured at.

Looking a Lucas now, his chest looked puffed up, reminding her of a bird trying to impose its dominance.

'…It attracts multiple different types of people, our audience is made up of approximately 85% women and often they feel an affinity to the victim because the patriarchal society we live in forces them into that role on a regular basis, they understand the terrifying tightrope they walk, and that wrong place, wrong time can make victims of any one of them.'

Nancy wondered if she could gag him and claim she was rebalancing society, instead she looked at him with a half-smile feigning interest. Kayleigh caught Nancy's eye and struggled to suppress a quiet giggle.

'I understand that,' she interrupted as soon as Lucas paused for breath or affect, she wasn't sure which he was going for, maybe both. 'but in amongst "the down with the patriarchy" and "the police are shit stuff" that you normally experience, did anyone stand out as being too interested in the finer details or seemed excited by the murders?' Nancy asked.

A slightly deflated Lucas made his way back to his seat, reminiscent of a sulking teenager you've told to sit down a dozen times but now claims they're going to sit but only because they want to.

'I printed out all the conversations for you, with usernames etc and if your IT people need access to the actual feed, just let us know,' Kayleigh said. 'Honestly there was nothing that worried me when I was moderating them, I always make sure they're checked for anything inappropriate, then I remove the comment, but I keep those too, because if it happens too frequently, we'll block and ban that person, like I said we're not about the glorification of murder.'

'Anything like that on this occasion?'

'A few things, we blocked one person, he'd been warned, but anytime we have a series where a sex worker is killed, he comments on the fact they deserve it, that they're parasites. He's also said that women don't own sex and that a man isn't wrong for expecting it if he buys someone dinner etc, just really gross stuff. And before you ask, I already made my concerns known to the police, I went into the station in Dundee and gave them all the information.' Kayleigh said.

'Were all the details of the case already public record?' Nancy asked.

'We had to do a bit of research to pull everything together, I think the lesser-known fact was that the victims were held captive for about a week before they were murdered.' Lucas said. 'That and the carving of the Jesus fish on the body, it's well known that he carved words into Doreen O'Sullivan, but the police of the day had been cagey around the fact that all the victims were marked, probably because that would have added fuel to the fire that their lack of action early on lead to more deaths.'

'Any idea where Alan was keeping his victims or what he was doing to them?' Nancy asked.

'Alan Schwartz came from quite a wealthy family, that only came out after he was dead. They had a cabin in some woods that they owned, it was near a lake, rarely used by the family, but was well known as one of Alan's favourite places to go during his childhood. The family stopped using it after Alan's younger brother drowned in the lake. He and Alan were out swimming together, allegedly the younger brother got cramp and drowned. Alan, who wasn't a competent swimmer, tried to get to his brother but didn't get there quickly enough.' Lucas replied.

'Any suggestion that's not what happened and that perhaps Alan was involved in some way?'

'No, nothing like that,' Kayleigh said. 'The parents refused to be interviewed after Alan's arrest and death, but years later they did talk about it a bit more freely.

'Any evidence to show the victims were killed there?'

'None, no sign of blood or even that anyone had been held captive there to be honest,' Kayleigh said. 'I think the police decided it must've been the place because logically and logistically it made sense.'

Nancy sat in the interview room alone for ten minutes after Kayleigh and Lucas left, reading the comments from their podcast. You could never underestimate the second-hand rage felt by people on the mishandling of a murder. Not that she could blame people for expecting the police to investigate thoroughly no matter who the victim. But Kayleigh had been right, there was nothing there that obviously stood out.

Nancy had questions, and much like the 1976 investigation, right near the top of her list was where had Maria, Owen and Donald been kept in the week preceding their murder.

Cal knocked on the door, 'sorry to disturb you, boss, I've got all that data you were looking for on Donald Stark.' He looked at her sitting alone in the interview room and wondered how long she'd been there and what she'd been doing. He had no intention of letting her know, but he was so eager to make a good impression and make up for the mess he made of their first meeting that he'd come in at

5am to start looking into Donald. This morning when he'd said that he was just getting started he had already been through the man's social media history and used that to track down all the places he liked to go.

'Anything interesting?' She asked.

'A few things,' Cal said, still holding out the cardboard folder waiting for her to notice and take it from him.

'Do you want to give me the highlights?'

He placed the folder on the table, 'there's a few interesting things,' Cal began.

Nancy opened the file, 'you have been busy,' she commented.

Cal tried to suppress a smile. 'it's taken a bit of work to pull together, but as I was saying…' his confidence was growing when Rob knocked on the door and joined them. Cal sighed, the moment stolen from him.

'Rob, what can I do you for?' Nancy asked.

'DNA results are in, the human remains uncovered at the nursery gardens are that of Donald Stark.'

Nancy nodded her head, 'we expected as much,' then she smiled at Cal, ' just as well otherwise you getting here at 5am to get started on this would have been such a waste of time.'

How did she know? Cal thought, the desk sergeant must have told her. He smiled back awkwardly, 'I wanted to get ahead, I know these searches can take time. '

'Well now we know it's him I think it's best if we head back up to the team and you can go over your findings with everyone.' Nancy said. 'Didn't I send you to get me food earlier?'

'Yes, but when I came back, you'd already left.' Cal said.

'Does that mean my coffee's gone cold, bugger.'

'I can put it in the microwave for you, if you'd like.' Cal said.

'Cal you're a Detective Sergeant not my maid, I very much appreciate you stepping out to pick me up refreshments, but please be assured I can microwave my own coffee, or if he's very lucky I'll ask Rob here do it for me.' She smiled at them both.

With a microwaved coffee in one hand and a cold sausage roll in the other she gathered the team. 'We've had confirmation that the remains discovered yesterday are those of Donald Stark. Working on the theory that our killer is some sort of copycat then Donald would fill the role of Priest as he was a retired Religious Education teacher. Cal has been looking into his life and is going to share his findings with us all now.' She looked at the young man, 'The floor's all yours.' Was it cruel to put him on the spot like that. She worried for a moment it was, but the lad was a sergeant, and he should be able to command the whole room.

Cal took a deep breath, start at the beginning he quietly told himself. 'Donald Stark retired from teaching twelve years ago, his last position was at Dunfermline High School, where he was the Religious, Moral and Philosophical Studies teacher or RMPS as it's more commonly known,' then as an aside he turned to Nancy and said, 'they haven't called it Religious Education for a while.'

Rob choked momentarily on his coffee as he tried to swallow a laugh and a mouthful of liquid simultaneously.

'The interesting thing about that was that he taught Owen Fairmile and his sister Diane Bridlington. I contacted the school and whilst they weren't keen to give me too many details without a warrant, they were able to confirm that. I can't find any connections between him and Maria, other than the Burns Night sighting, but as she was Australian and hadn't been in the UK for her schooling that makes sense.' Cal said.

'I want to make sure I'm clear, Donald Stark actually taught Owen and Diane? Or was he just a teacher at the same time as they went to school?' Nancy asked.

'He taught them both, Diane took RMPS for her exams, Owen didn't so he stopped taking his classes when he was around fourteen. One of the questions we have is if Donald was selected as a victim when he was seen collecting his granddaughter and her friends from Burns Night, how the killer knew that he had anything to do with religion at all. Whilst it might merely be that he met the right age profile, I wanted to make sure there wasn't anything we were missing. Donald was a regular member of the congregation of his local Methodist church. I phoned the vicar there and asked him about Donald and he told me that last November Donald helped to set up a gift and foodbank for those in need over the winter period, people who couldn't afford to buy gifts for their kids etc.'

Nancy remembered seeing the photograph on the wall in Dave Pickering's office when they went to speak to Natalie at the club. The man had been holding a huge display cheque and there had been shopping trolleys in the background filled with food and presents.

'The event was sponsored by a number of local businesses, including Burns Night who provided a space for people to come and collect what they needed. Mr Pickering, the manager, also put on a meet Santa event for the families who were struggling and in addition to the gifts that were donated by the general public, Mr Pickering paid for one gift for every child who met Santa. It was a huge photo-op and when I looked on Burns Night's website there are a number of pictures of the event including several of Donald Stark. It was also featured in the local news.' Cal said. 'In both the newspaper article and on Burns Night's website it says Donald Stark is a retired RMPS teacher.'

'That's excellent work,' Nancy said standing up and walking across to him.

'Actually, there was one other thing,' Cal said.

Nancy stood beside him, she didn't want to walk back to her chair and sit down, leaving her standing there next to him as the only option. She clasped her hands together and waited.

I asked the manager at Burns Night if he could send me all the pictures from the event, including any taken by staff and in one of the ones he took on his phone you can see a woman organising the food table, assisted by a teenage boy. The woman is Diane Bridlington.'

Nancy pivoted to face him. 'Owen's sister was there helping with the event?'

'I asked Mr Pickering about her. He said he vaguely remembers her face but the church and the photographer brought along people to help out.'

Dave hadn't struck her as the philanthropist sort, so throwing a food and gift drive for local under privileged families seemed wildly out of character. 'Did Mr Pickering say why he wanted to be involved in the project?' Nancy asked.

'He said that he needed to build bridges with the community, apparently they had "misunderstood his establishment".' Cal used air quotes around the words to make sure everyone listening knew they weren't his. 'He also said that charity work is good for the accounts.'

Nancy dismissed the team, thanking Cal for his hard

work, then she found the two constables that had offered to go through all the CCTV they'd collected.

'How are you getting on with CCTV, anything from the restaurant the night Owen went missing?' She asked hopefully.

'The restaurant doesn't have any CCTV out front or in the customer side of the building, only in the back and in the secure room. Owen took a taxi to the venue, we have reports from the taxi company. We followed up with the waiting staff from the restaurant. They remember Owen coming in, he ordered a drink, waited about half an hour, took a phone call, paid up and left. They said it looked like he'd been stood up, according to the woman that served him he looked pretty dejected when he was leaving. We know he did order a taxi and he isn't picked up on any CCTV in that street at the time he left the restaurant. If we knew what we were looking for then we could trace it, other than that it's a dead end.' One of the PCs said.

Nancy sighed, 'Great work getting all that chased down, doesn't help us figure out who he was meeting but at least we know what time he was last seen at, thanks.'

Nancy headed to her office with Rob in tow. 'How did you get on with Michael Bridlington?' She asked.

'He didn't come in, his mum called to say he was sick with the flu and couldn't.'

'Well that's bullshit. First, she refuses to have a family liaison officer and now this.' Nancy replied. She sipped the coffee, it was still hot but bitter, she reeled back from the disposable paper cup. 'That's nasty.' She pushed the cup to the edge of the desk as if its proximity to her was offensive.

'I know, but short of going to her house and collecting him, what do you want me to do?'

Nancy sat back in her chair trying to find an acceptable

reason for Diane to be this bloody annoying. Why didn't the woman want to help them investigate her brother's death? She reported him missing and now that his body had been found it felt like she was no longer interested.

'Actually yes, that is what I want you to do. I want Michael Bridlington brought into the station, he's a material witness in this case and I will not have his mother playing silly buggers with my investigation. Go to the house, politely tell her that we need to interview Michael with an appropriate adult that is not her, and that if she protests then arrest him on suspicion of withholding evidence.' Nancy said.

'Okay, and if I get there and the boy is actually sick?' Rob asked.

'Then you say you were just checking up on his welfare, see Michael and then leave.'

'If that's what you want I'll go now.'

'Take Isla with you.' Nancy instructed, she'd been tempted to suggest that he took Grace, but she'd reminded herself she was sleeping on his sofa bed and decided not to rock that particular boat.

Chapter 26

In Rob's absence Nancy decided to take DC Grace Abbotts with her to talk to Susan Stark.

'Do you ever get used to doing this?' Grace asked as they approached the front door.

'No and I don't think you should either, it helps to remind you that we're dealing with real people and it's our job to find out what happened to them,' Nancy replied before Susan opened the door.

She looked at them on the doorstep, tears already forming in the corners of her eyes, moments later she was joined by her granddaughter and they all went through to the living room. Nancy declined coffee this time.

'I'm really sorry to have to tell you that we have now found your husband's body,' Nancy said choosing not to use the word remains in describing him.

Elizabeth gasped and began to cry a loud breathless sob.

'I'm so sorry for your loss.'

'What happened, how did he die?' Susan asked.

'At this stage we're still trying to determine the cause of death, but we do believe he was murdered.' Nancy said.

Grace had moved to the sofa to sit next to Elizabeth, her arm wrapped around the young woman helping her to control her body wrenching sobs.

'But how…how can you know he was murdered but not know what killed him?' Susan asked.

'Your husband's body had been exposed to the elements for some time and that makes it more challenging for us to determine these things immediately.'

'What do you mean exposed to the elements, what does that even mean,' Susan half yelled.

'Donald's body was discovered in a compost heap behind a disused building.' Nancy replied trying to be as tactful as she could.

Susan covered her mouth with both her hands. 'Can I see him.'

Nancy thought about the pictures Daniel had sent her, the skin and flesh on Donald's face in a stage of decomposition. 'That won't be possible.'

'I need to say goodbye to him, I need to see his face so I can be sure it's him.' Susan insisted.

'I am so sorry, but I can't do that. I can assure you it is Donald, we have completed a DNA test. It's really important that you remember him the way he was, like this,' Nancy pointed at the large picture on the wall.

Elizabeth had regained her composure and seemed to have understood what Nancy was trying not to say. 'Gran you can't see him,'

Susan turned to face her granddaughter, 'why do people keep telling me what I can and can't do. I want to see my husband's body, I want to see his face.' She was belligerent now.

'No Gran,' Elizabeth tried again.

Susan slapped her across the face. Grace stood up in shock and instinctively went to intervene, Nancy shook her head. The woman had just been given the worst news of her life and she was sure Elizabeth could deal with the situation.

The young woman took hold of her Gran's wrists, a scarlet handprint now welting on her cheek. 'Gran, I love you, but you can't see Granddad's face because it's gone, he's been outside, they needed to do the DNA to know who he was. He's gone and it's okay to be upset, but the detective is right, you cannot see him – do you understand me.' Susan's shoulders slumped and she became limp. Elizabeth let go of the woman's wrists and wrapped her arms around her. Then facing Nancy said, 'I'm going to put her to bed, I'll get the doctor to come out if I need to, he's old school so I know he will if I call.'

'Thank you, we'll see ourselves out. This is my card, we will need to come back and ask some more questions, but we'll leave you in peace for now, can you let me know when your Gran might be up to it.'

Elizabeth took the card and put it in her jeans pocket. 'I will.'

Nancy ushered Grace out of the living room towards the front door.

'That was intense,' Grace said outside.

Nancy nodded, 'she's lucky to have family nearby.' Then she looked at her mobile phone, 'Bugger.'

'What is it, boss?' Grace asked.

'Missed call from Rob.' Nancy noticed as Grace pulled an involuntary face. 'You can drive,' Nancy said, handing her the keys to the pool car. 'And when this is all over you're going to tell me what happened between you and

Rob and why you pull that face every time you hear his name.'

Nancy didn't give the other woman the chance to respond before getting into the passenger seat and calling Rob back.

'You called?'

'Yeah, a bit of a problem here. No sign of Diane or the boys, knocked on a few neighbour's doors, found one who shared with me that he'd seen them getting into a taxi first thing this morning loaded up with suitcases, he asked them where they were off to, and she said Tenerife. He had no idea that Owen was dead either.'

'Bloody hell. Any chance the neighbour remembered which taxi firm it was?'

'I asked but, no, he wasn't paying attention to it.' Rob said.

'Okay head back to the station and find out what flights have already left for Tenerife from Edinburgh, Glasgow and Newcastle airports, get Cal calling around all the local taxi firms to see if we can find out where they dropped them off, just because she told the neighbour that's where she was heading doesn't mean she was telling the truth.' Nancy replied.

Nancy thought about phoning Cooper to ask about getting a warrant to search Diane's house, but these conversations were always easier in person. As soon as she was back in the station she went to his office.

'That is not a good news face,' Cooper said.

'Michael Bridlington, Owen's nephew, was supposed to be coming in this morning to be interviewed by DS MacDonald, we believe he could know more about what happened to his uncle than he's been able to tell us, his mother is very overbearing. This morning his mother,

Diane, called to say Michael couldn't come in as he had the flu. It didn't ring true for me, so I sent DS MacDonald and DC Shepherd to pay the family a visit and if Michael was not ill to bring him in. When they got there the house was empty and they had been seen getting into a taxi early this morning.' Nancy said.

'Do we have any idea where they're headlining?'

'Diane told the neighbour Tenerife, but other than that, no. I need a search warrant for her house, gardens and all outbuildings.' Nancy replied.

'Do you really think she had something to do with her own brother's murder?' Cooper asked.

'I've no idea, I didn't think so, but everyone we've spoken to has described her as having a very controlling relationship with him and now she's done a runner on the day her son was supposed to come in and see us. I have to assume she's hiding something.'

'Even if you could show a motive for Owen's death, what motive would she have for killing Maria and Donald?'

'Donald Stark was once her teacher, maybe something happened when she was at school.'

'And Maria?' Cooper asked.

'There's nothing to link Diane to Maria at the moment, but it could be we simply haven't found the connection yet.' Nancy said.

'It sounds like we're clutching at straws trying to find motivation for this woman to be our killer.' Cooper said.

'Maybe, who knows, or maybe she always intended murdering her brother and she saw this as an opportunity to do it without casting suspicion on herself.' Nancy suggested.

'I'll get you your search warrant, but if you really think this woman is our serial killer you are going to need to get all your evidence sorted out if you want to persuade the Procurator Fiscal that you have enough to charge her.'

Chapter 27

There was a throng of activity as Nancy re-joined her team. 'Any joy?' she asked Cal as she passed by his desk.

'I'm working my way through the list, but I've not found out which firm picked her up yet,' he replied.

'How are you getting on with passenger lists from the airlines?'

'As usual they are about as helpful as a wet paper bag. I've managed to agree with one of the low-cost airlines that now that I've given them the names they'll check against flights purchased that leave today from the three airports in question. I'm on hold whilst they do that.' Isla said.

'Deep breaths and keep pushing if they get shirty with you.'

Isla stuck her thumb up as Nancy walked towards her office. She sat down at her desk and put her head in her hands rubbing the palms of her hands across her face. Did she really think Diane was the type of person to kill two innocent people to facilitate killing her brother. Did she even truly believe that Diane would want to kill Owen?

There was nothing she could do about Diane right now, instead she decided to read through the printed transcripts from the podcast forum one more time. At first glance Kayleigh had been right, there was nothing out of the ordinary, but she would have a linguistics expert look over it to see if anything stood out.

Rob knocked on Nancy's door. 'Can I come in?'

She gave a slight nod of her head.

He closed the door behind him and sat down opposite her, 'sorry, I should've headed straight over there when Diane phoned to say Michael wasn't coming in.'

'I doubt she was even still at the house when she made that call if the neighbour has remembered the time of their interaction correctly.'

'Still…' Rob trailed off.

'Still what? We couldn't have possibly known she was going to do a runner, I didn't have her down as a flight risk either. In the meantime, we need to keep investigating this case, God knows what's going on with Diane, for all we know it has nothing to do with the murder of her brother.'

'It looks suspicious, why run if you have nothing to hide.' Rob said.

'Having something to hide doesn't equal guilty of murder.' Nancy replied, aware that she was now having the same conversation with Rob that she had been silently having with herself. We have to hope that when we get inside the house, she's left us something to go off. And you moping around feeling sorry for yourself in my office isn't getting us anywhere, shake yourself off and pull it together and use your frustration as fuel to find her and find out what happened to these people.'

She ushered him back out her office and was about to go and find Cal when her phone rang.

'Lucy, what can I do for you?'

'I've been looking at Donald Stark's remains, and I know you always prefer me to phone if we discover anything unusual.'

Nancy stood still, 'what have you found?'

'A couple of things, first although there is limited soft tissue on the remains, damage to the rib cage indicates that he was stabbed in or around his heart, I'd feel comfortable in confirming that as the cause of death.'

'What about the murder weapon?'

'It's very hard to be completely sure but given the damage to the bone I would say it's the same as the instrument used to stab both Maria and Owen.'

'Any idea what that is yet?'

'An ice pick, the kind that's used for smashing up ice for parties, not the kind you use for ice climbing.'

'Doesn't ice come in cubes?'

Lucy laughed, 'that depends where you're drinking, they still use ice picks in some of the gentlemen's clubs and when I say that I'm not being coy and talking about strip clubs I actually mean the smoking jacket, read my paper whilst someone brings me a drink and I feel superior to the rest of humanity style clubs.'

'I think you and I run in very different social circles,' Nancy laughed. 'you said you had a couple of things – what else was there.'

'Yeah, I think you'll find this very interesting, Donald Stark's hands and feet were severed, post mortem thankfully, but definitely before he was placed in the compost heap. It seems likely that it was done in the bathroom of that house you visited.'

'Given the state of the place that makes sense, but why go to all the effort and then leave them with the body?'

'That's not a question I can answer, but there is one other thing. His left foot was discovered in a plastic box, near the compost heap…'

'Wait, what?' Nancy interrupted.

'I thought you'd find that interesting, the good thing about that was it was protected from the level of decomposition that the rest of the body experienced, although obviously being in a box also creates its own environmental issues. But now I'm getting to the good part, on the ankle was a branding mark, exactly like the others.' Lucy said.

'The killer wanted the foot to be preserved. They wanted us to know that he was part of the pattern.'

Chapter 28

'Cal did you manage to get a list from the estate agents of who had access to that property we found Donald Stark's blood in?'

Cal jumped, 'I thought you wanted me to call around the taxi firms to look for Diane Bridlington and her sons.'

'That's what you should be doing right now, but on Tuesday I asked you to contact the estate agent and get a list of people who had access to that property, please tell me that you remembered to do that.' Nancy said.

'Tuesday?' Cal said.

'Yes.'

'Um, hold on a minute.'

Nancy watched as Cal brought up an online diary file filled with colour coded notes.

'Tuesday, yes, I've got it here. Mr Andrews said there were two sets of keys originally. The other set was given to the photographer for the pictures to be taken for the sales particulars.'

'And where is that set now?'

'The photographer said she has them at home as she had a sick relative so hadn't been able to drop them back off. Mr Andrews said they've been using the same woman for the last four years and he trusted her and with the property off the market he hadn't seen the rush in getting the keys back.' Cal said.

'Does this photographer have a name?' Nancy asked.

'Um,' Cal looked intently at the screen. 'Yes, her name is Cheryl Wilson, she's 46 and a freelance photographer. I sent uniform round to pick up the keys so that no one had access to the crime scene though, so she doesn't have them anymore.'

'At least that's something, did you run any background checks on her?'

'No-o-o,' Cal said the word in a slow elongated fashion as though he was trying to extend the time between the word ending and Nancy replying.

Nancy rolled her head from side to side allowing it to crack slightly. 'If we went to pick up keys, I assume we'd have her address?'

'Yes, I can text it to you so you have it for later. Do you want me to run background checks on her now?'

'Please, see if she has any cross over points with any of our victims or Burns Night.' Nancy had begun to walk away from Cal's desk.

'Do you still want me to call the taxi companies?' He called out after her.

'Yes, Diane Bridlington got into a taxi, we need to know which one and where she went, as soon as possible.' Nancy replied without turning back.

Cheryl Wilson's new built terrace house was part of the Eastern expansion of Dunfermline. Over the last decade rows of terrace houses had sprung up, with their pastel-coloured doors and identical squares of grass out the front.

'I looked at one of these,' Rob announced as he undid his seat belt.

'Instead of your flat?' Nancy asked.

'Yeah, I'd started to wonder if I'd outgrown living in a flat, my downstairs neighbour had got a bit out of control with a broom handle on his ceiling, thought I was being a prick when I was working nightshift.'

'Only then, that's not bad.' Nancy smiled.

'I thought a house might be better, so I looked at one of these and it felt small compared to the flat, that's the benefit of being in an older building, high ceilings, larger rooms.'

'So, you decided against moving?'

'I went and saw the bloke, old fella, I explained why I was coming in at weird times, he was alright really, I fixed a couple of things about the place for him and now we're solid.'

'Good to know.' Nancy said. 'Let's go and have a chat with our photographer.'

It was late afternoon and it was getting cold again, the wind blustered against them as they stood waiting on the doorstep.

A woman answered the door wearing black leggings and a bright pink oversized jumper. 'Can I help you?' She asked, pulling the door into her sizeable body.

'Hi, my name is Detective Inspector Ravenscroft, and this is Detective Sergeant MacDonald, could we come in?'

'Why?' Cheryl asked.

'We'd like to ask you some questions about a case we're investigating, it really would be better if we could come inside.' Nancy said. 'I'm sure you don't want your neighbours listening in to everything, in a place like this it'll be all over the street WhatsApp group.'

The last statement seemed to do the trick, Cheryl stepped back and let them in. The living room door was on the right just as you came into the hall. Nancy could hear voices coming from the kitchen. At first, she thought they'd interrupted Cheryl having company and then as she listened, she recognised them, it was Kayleigh and Lucas. Cheryl was listening to the Death Amongst Us podcast.

'I'll go turn that off, I like to listen whilst I'm editing photographs, give me a moment.' Cheryl walked up the hallway and into the kitchen leaving Nancy and Rob standing in the small living room containing one two-seater sofa and one large armchair.

'You can sit down.' Cheryl said. 'I'd offer you tea or coffee, but I don't have either, I'm waiting on my shopping being delivered.'

Nancy and Rob sat down on the two-seater that was in reality not much wider than the armchair which left them sitting awkwardly close to one another, Nancy's arm brushed against Rob's sleeve as she took her notebook out from her pocket.

'That's not a problem, I'm sure I've already consumed my week's allowance of coffee today.'

Cheryl gave her a half smile and perched on the edge of the armchair. 'You said you had some questions?'

'Yes, we're investigating the murders of Maria Fisher, Owen Fairmile and Donald Stark,' Nancy said, she noticed a slight twitch in Cheryl's face as she'd said Maria's name. 'Do any of those names ring a bell with you?'

She shook her head, 'no sorry, should I know who they are?'

'Not necessarily. Can I show you some photographs, see

if that jogs your memory.' Nancy took out the picture of Donald Stark first and handed it to Cheryl.

She took it and examined it carefully. 'Honestly, he does look a little familiar, but I can't say where from. It's an occupational hazard as a photographer, I look at a lot of faces, so they seem familiar even when they're not really.'

'Okay,' Nancy took the picture back and replaced it with the one of Owen and Maria together in Burns Night. 'That's Owen and Maria,' she said.

Cheryl looked up quickly, 'I suppose I should know who they are…' she started.

'Why's that?' Rob asked.

'Because I took that photo, I do all the promo photography for Burns Night, they're my best client.'

Chapter 29

'You do all the photography, but you don't know anyone's name?' Rob asked.

Cheryl frowned, 'do you know how many staff that place goes through?'

'How long have you been doing the photography for Burns Night?' Nancy asked.

'Just over a year, it started as a one off and then after a couple of events they asked if they could keep me on as their official photographer. I'm still freelance, but I get a monthly retainer on top on my standard charges.'

'You must've seen Maria several times during that period.' Nancy said.

'I suppose. They don't talk to me, I reckon they think I'm a pain in their arse, always wanting them to stop for photographs, especially girls like this Maria, the waiting staff, men want their pictures with them, it's good for business so sometimes I have to be a bit bossy about it.'

'I saw the board at the club, Maria was in a lot of

photos, are you sure you don't remember anything about her?'

Cheryl lifted her right shoulder in a shrug, 'I recognise her face, but I couldn't have put a name to it. She was… standoffish, like she thought she was too good for the place. Girls like that they act like they don't want attention from men, but she's wearing tiny shorts and a crop top.'

'Isn't that the same as every other girl in there?' Rob asked.

'It's their uniform, but they know that before they take the job, they know they'll be strutting around in next to nothing and they could have the pick of the men, but then they have an attitude problem if one of them is a little bit too friendly.' Cheryl rearranged her top, trying to cover the extra roll of fat that she wished would go away.

Rob opened his mouth to reply when Nancy gave a barely visible shake of her head.'How did that make you feel?' Nancy said.

'Frumpy and old, look I know I'm not the slimmest, sexiest woman, but those girls laughed at me, they laughed at my clothes, at my make-up, you think it's bad that I don't know their names, but I bet not one of them could tell you mine. They look at me and don't think I'm worth getting to know.'

'That must have been hard.' Nancy said. 'You were in the club most weekends, and behind a camera is the perfect place to observe everything, can you think of a time when someone was a bit too pushy with Maria?'

'Not particularly. I didn't like the girl, but she didn't deserve to die.'

It was an emotionless statement, Nancy wondered if Cheryl had only said it because she realised in all the vitriol, she'd forgotten to show compassion for Maria as a victim of murder.

'Have you ever given someone else the keys to one of the properties you've photographed for Mr Andrews?' Nancy asked.

The change of topic seemed to throw Cheryl completely. 'Um what…no…of course not.'

'You don't seem too sure about that.' Rob interjected.

'Mr Andrews trusts me, I pick up the keys, I photograph the house, I return the keys.'

'You didn't return the keys for one of the properties.'

'I was going to and then when I called the office to tell them I was down with a bug they said to just hang on to them, something to do with a land dispute meaning the property had to come off the market.'

'I thought you didn't return the keys because you were looking after a sick relative,' Nancy said.

'No it was me who was ill, vomiting, I couldn't even keep water down.' Cheryl replied.

'Then why did Mr Andrews tell us you had said you were caring for a sick relative?'

'I don't know, perhaps he got muddled up, he's been acting weird lately.'

'What do you mean, weird?' Nancy asked.

'Well the other day he called me and tells me one of your lot is going to be coming round to collect the keys and I'm to hand them over. He was very cloak and dagger about it. Kept asking if I'd been back to the house since I took the pictures.'

'And had you?' Rob asked.

'No.' Cheryl said quickly, her bright red cheeks betraying her.

'Look Cheryl,' Nancy said. 'It's really important you tell

us the truth. We now know that someone was murdered at that address and if you aren't honest with me, I'm going to have to consider why you would need to lie.'

'Murdered.' Cheryl repeated. Her scarlet cheeks now pale.

'Yes.'

'Who?'

'I'm not able to share that information. Were you in the house after you photographed it?'

'Oh God,' Cheryl buried her face in her hands, the sound of her hyperventilating still audible.

'Cheryl, I need you to take some deep breaths, pull yourself together and talk to me.' Nancy said.

Cheryl looked up. 'I need a glass of water.'

'Sergeant MacDonald will get you one.'

Rob left the room and reappeared a couple of minutes later with a glass of tap water. Cheryl took three large gulps before setting the glass down on the floor next to her foot.

'Yes, I went back there.' Her voice quiet and timid.

'Why?' Nancy asked.

I've been seeing this man, we met on the internet, and I really liked him,' Cheryl said.

'Tell me about him.' Nancy said.

'He was really interested in me. Asked me lots of questions about what I did for work, even looked at my photographs for hours. He said I was really talented.'

'And you took him to this house?'

'Yes…and a couple of others.' Cheryl looked at her knees.

'Whose idea was it to go to the empty houses?' Nancy asked.

'His, he said it would spice things up between us.'

'You went there to have sex?' Nancy asked.

Cheryl nodded, 'he got really turned on by it, I wasn't sure at first, but he was so passionate,' she closed her eyes. 'Oh God, I can't believe I'm telling you this.'

'How many houses did you take him to?' Nancy asked.

'Five or six, most of the time when a house is up for sale someone still lives in it, but then occasionally you get properties where the owner died, or has gone into a home, or it's an ex-rental, that kind of thing. I know it was wrong, but he was right, it was exciting.'

Nancy could see that Rob had raised his eyebrows in judgement of the woman's actions.

'Did you give him the keys to any of these properties?'

'No. Absolutely not, it was one thing to keep them an extra day or two, but something else to give them to him.'

'Does this man have a name?' Rob asked

'Graham Smyth.'

'You'll need to give us his contact details.' Rob said.

'You can't think he would have done anything bad.'

'Are you still…dating him?' Nancy asked taking time to choose her words carefully.

'We broke up.'

'When?' Asked Nancy.

'A couple of weeks ago.'

'Who broke up with who?'

'He broke up with me. He said I was a prude.'

Now it was Nancy's turn to raise her eyebrows, 'what made him say that?'

'He wanted us to have sex in the graveyard, said there was a particular grave he wanted to do it on, that was too much for me.' Cheryl said.

Nancy didn't think having sex in a graveyard was too outrageous really, in her uniformed days she'd removed dozens of people in compromising positions and various stages of undress from a number of graveyards, but on a particular grave seemed very odd.

'You'll need to give us his contact number.'

'He's not answering it. Recently I was having second thoughts,' Cheryl paused. 'I mean it's not like I've got men banging down my door, I thought maybe sex in a graveyard would be fine. I got drunk and called him a bunch of times, but he didn't pick up and then in the morning I was glad I hadn't left a message.' She shook her head at the memory. 'I was a bit embarrassed of myself, hoped that he wouldn't call back and he didn't.'

'Sounds like you had a lucky escape, and I'm sure there's someone out there for you,' Nancy said offering the woman some kindness after she'd sat in her living room and recounted her sexual exploits. It only felt fair.

'One last thing,' Rob said as Nancy had begun making her way to the door. 'What did Graham look like?'

Cheryl smiled wistfully, 'Tall, blonde, blue eyes that just looked right into your soul, a kind face, really handsome too.'

'Did you take his photo?' Rob continued.

'No, well I did once, I took one of the two of us together, but he got really pissed off about it and made me delete it.'

'Thanks, we'll see ourselves out.' Rob said.

Cheryl watched them from the living room window as they made their way down the short path to the pavement and then into their car.

'What was that all about? The final question.' Nancy asked.

'I recognised the telephone number,' Rob replied. It's for the phone that we found with Owen Fairmile's body.'

Chapter 30

Had Cheryl Wilson just played her for a fool, could it be that she was actually a serial killer? She'd struck Nancy as more of a keyboard warrior, she could imagine Cheryl on forums giving her opinion freely, but stab someone with an ice pick and then dismember them, it seemed unlikely. Yet there was a connection between her and the murderer.

'You think maybe Cheryl and Graham were in it together?' Rob asked.

'Perhaps, more likely Graham manipulated Cheryl, probably with some story that seemed innocent enough to her at the time, all the while he knew that all he had to do was dump the phone with Owen's body and then it wouldn't be that hard to link it back to Cheryl and she would become our main suspect.'

'Seems plausible.'

'Or Cheryl is our killer and she's made up this Graham Smyth to cover her tracks.' Nancy said.

'She didn't strike me as clever enough for that.' Rob said.

'I don't know about clever, but she did seem as though she was the sort of person who would let her emotions get the better of her.'

'Do you want me to bring her in?' Rob asked.

'I don't think we've got enough evidence yet, the phone isn't enough, we should keep an eye on her movements though.' Nancy said.

'She has to be involved, I mean I know coincidences do happen, but she's connected to Burns Night and the houses.'

He was right of course, one coincidence would be fine, but here we have a woman who's a regular feature at Burns Night, a place all our victims went to in the days preceding their disappearances, she also had keys for the property that we know Donald Stark was murdered at, we also know that she routinely took her fancy man to empty properties for sex, including our crime scene, Nancy thought.

'What do you want to do then?' Rob continued.

'I'll get Isla to see if she can find this Graham Smyth, and then we can bring him in for questioning.'

'If he exists,' Rob replied. 'What if the whole weird story is just her way of creating an alibi for herself?'

'I thought about that too, and maybe if we were only looking at Maria's murder I could see it, but why would she kill Owen and Donald.'

'Maybe her and Diane Bridlington were in it together,' Rob suggested. 'Maybe it was one of those things where Diane killed Maria for Cheryl and Cheryl killed Owen for Diane.'

'Then who killed Donald? On that basis there would need to be four participants to this crime, Cheryl and Diane, like you described, then someone to kill Donald and someone else to kill an as yet unknown policewoman. Or if this case follows a pattern, someone who's not a police-woman but does a job vaguely similar or could be construed as someone in a similar position.' Nancy said. 'the only thing that scenario would clear up is the reason why Diane took her kids on the run.'

By the time they got back to the station Nancy felt like she'd already put in a full shift but it would be a while before she'd be home. Not that Rob's flat was home, she needed to go and check on her van soon, she didn't like leaving it parked up but the site owner had assured her that she would keep an eye on it and Cellardyke is a low crime area.

Cal stood up as soon as she entered the room, making his way quickly towards her. His long legs put her in mind of a spider.

'Everything okay?'

'Diane Bridlington called a taxi firm based in Oakley, that's why it took me a while to get to it. They didn't take her to an airport though, she and her boys were dropped off at Inverkeithing railway station. She tipped the driver fifty quid to not say anything if anyone asked about her. I had to threaten him with arrest for him to give the details up.' Cal said.

'Excellent work, the good news is we can stop looking for them at airports then, but the bad news is we have no idea where she might have gone. From Inverkeithing she'll most likely have gone to Edinburgh and then from there she could have taken a train literally anywhere in the county.' Nancy said.

'I should have the CCTV from the station by tomorrow, so we'll at least be able to see what platform she got on a train and that'll give us an idea of the direction she was heading in.' Cal said.

'Have we been able to trace their phones at all?' Nancy said.

'They've been switched off since first thing this morning.'

'We have our warrants now,' Nancy said, the email had pinged on her phone about thirty seconds before Cal had accosted her. 'Which means we can get all of her phone data. Rob and Isla you're with me on the search of Diane's house. Grace and Cal, I want you to find out everything you can about Cheryl Wilson and Graham Smyth. Rob will quickly fill you in with everything we know and then I need you to fact check it and see what else you can find out.'

She made her way to Cooper's office. 'Hey boss, thanks for sorting the warrants out, we're just about to head over there, do you want to come?'

'Do you need me to come?' He asked looking up from his computer screen.

'Nope, but technically you're the SIO,' Nancy smiled.

'You go do all the leg work, I'll take all the glory later.' He grinned at her.

DCI Cooper never took all the glory, no matter how hard the Super tried to get him to. Nancy smiled back, 'standard then. I'll let you know if anything interesting turns up.'

Rob and Isla were waiting for her in the carpark, 'What took you so long,' Rob asked as she came outside.

'Checking in with Cooper.'

'You're lucky, DC Shepherd here tried to call shotgun on the passenger seat, but don't worry I put her in her place.' Rob laughed.

Isla looked at her colleague and shook her head, 'you're a knob.'

They were met by five uniformed officers at Diane's

home. 'Afternoon Sergeant West,' Nancy said, 'are you here to do the honours and get the door open for me?'

The man nodded, 'we'll get you in and then we'll station one at the front of the property and one at the back, just in case there's anyone around that shouldn't be. Then the rest of us will help you with the search inside.'

'And they know what we're looking for? Anything that might tell us where the family have gone, or looks out of place, obviously anything blood stained. I'm also looking for an ice pick, the drinks type.' Nancy asked.

'They've been briefed.' Sergeant West confirmed.

'Fantastic, then give your guys the go ahead whilst we get our shoe protectors on.' Nancy said. She watched for a moment as with one swift batter of the door opener the front door swung open into Diane's hall.

'Rob, can you pay particular attention to the boy's rooms please.' Nancy said as she walked through the front door.

She would have preferred Diane to be present for the search, seeing how she reacted would have been an interesting way to gauge her character. Nancy knew it was an invasive process, one she didn't carry out lightly. Finding Diane and her sons was their primary focus and if this could help then she was happy to do it. But today was in contrast to carrying out a search warrant where you were almost certain the person was guilty of something.

Nancy walked from room to room watching the other officers search through drawers and under sofa cushions. In the kitchen every drawer had been opened by one of the uniformed officers.

'There's plenty of fresh food in the fridge, ma'am,' he said. 'It doesn't look like they were planning on going anywhere when they did their shopping. Dirty dishes in the dishwasher look like they're from this morning's breakfast, three bowls and spoons, a couple of glasses and a mug,' he continued.

'If they had time to load the dishwasher then it doesn't seem like they left in a rush, she must've planned it at some point between going to the grocery shops and this morning.' Nancy thought back to her second visit to see the family, Diane had been bringing shopping in from her car, Rob had helped to carry the bags inside.

'No sign of an ice pick in your searches, most likely would've been with an ice bucket or cocktail making equipment?' Nancy said.

'No sign of any of those things, I don't think your woman was a big drinker either. There's no alcohol in the house and no sign of any empty bottles or cans in the rubbish.'

'Good work,' Nancy said before leaving the room. Diane had been described as a control freak, could that be why there was no drinking or was she just concerned that having it in the house would be a temptation to Michael?

She looked back into the living room where Sergeant West was supervising, he shook his head, and she proceeded up the stairs and into Diane's bedroom. 'Anything?' She said to the female uniformed officer.

'It doesn't look like there's a lot of clothes missing, but there were some cardboard boxes in the bottom of the wardrobe that were empty with their lids off.' She opened the wardrobe to show Nancy what she meant.

Nancy moved closer. 'Now what would someone keep in there.'

'Could have been keepsakes, something important that she couldn't let herself leave behind.' The officer paused.

'Of course, it could equally be incriminating evidence you don't want anyone to find.'

'I've got something.' Rob called from Michael's room.

Nancy joined him in the teenager's bedroom.

'It's Michael's phone,' Rob held it up in his gloved hand. 'His mum must've made him leave it behind. I turned it on, it's passcode protected and then I found a folded piece of paper next to it with a four digit number so I gave it a go and it got me in. Michael was part the way through typing me a message. I'm guessing he didn't have time to complete it or send it before she interrupted him.' Rob said.

'What does the message say?' Nancy asked.

Rob held up the phone. 'You said I could contact you if I needed anything, I really need your help. There's something wrong with mum. She says she made a mistake and now someone wants to kill us all, she's afraid of a man called…'

'Called what?' Nancy asked.

'That's where it ends, like I said his mother must have interrupted him.'

'Now at least we know she's running scared and not from us though, I suppose,' Nancy said.

'I knew she wasn't telling us everything when we interviewed her. I thought they'd done a runner because we were bringing Michael in, but it had nothing to do with it.' Rob said.

'Doesn't mean she wasn't involved in her brother's death though. She could have paid someone to kill Owen and now for some reason they've fallen out.'

'That would make sense if it was only Owen who was dead, but you don't normally pay for a serial killer, especially not one copycatting a fifty year old murder.' Rob replied.

'I wish she'd come to us instead of going on the run.' Nancy said. 'bag the phone, it doesn't look like there's anything else useful to be gleaned from the house. But we can leave Sergeant West and his team to finish up.'

Cal was once again poised for Nancy's return to the office. 'Hey boss, you asked about Graham Smyth. Well, he doesn't exist, at least not the man that Cheryl Wilson was dating, I checked all of the data she gave us against all the Graham Smyth's I could find, and my conclusion is that he gave her a fake name.'

'That doesn't surprise me,' Nancy replied.

'Rob was right, the number that Cheryl gave us for Graham is the same as the one we found with Owen's body. I checked the incoming calls and all the times she said she was calling Graham she was using the number that's attached to the social media accounts in the name of Rachel Howgate, so I think it's safe to say that she is Rachel. I've had a look to see if I can see any other links between Cheryl and Rachel, and the only thing I can find is that all the photos on Rachel's accounts have been altered and we know that Cheryl would have the skills needed to do that.'

'Good work, anything else on Cheryl?'

'Nothing much, we'd need a warrant for all her social media accounts, but I went on to her business pages. She got into a bit of an argument with a woman who gave her a one star review. The woman had hired Cheryl to do the photography at her engagement party. She complained that Cheryl had been unprofessional and had made several snide comments about the bride to be and her friends throughout the evening, that she'd helped herself to the wine that was for guests only and got a bit drunk.'

'How did Cheryl respond to that?'

'Not well, she said that she had been lied to about the

size of the party and that it was typical of people like her, she called the woman a bridezilla and a princess and said she had provided her with beautiful photographs.'

'The woman said some of the photographs were lovely, but others were out of focus because Cheryl had been too drunk to do her job and she'd still been paid in full so had nothing to complain about.'

'Cheryl responded with a couple of racist slurs, the bride to be is of mixed ethnicity, the woman threatened to go to the police if Cheryl continued to harass her, after that Cheryl didn't directly respond but there were two other comments from other people slagging the bride to be off and my guess would be if I do some additional checks they'd turn out to be accounts Cheryl made herself so she could continue to respond.'

'Okay, keep digging and see if you can find anything.'

Nancy made her way back to her office, sat down at her desk and looked at the list of addresses Cheryl had given them of the houses she'd taken Graham to. Any one of these could be a crime scene, the killer hadn't done a great job of cleaning up Donald's blood but perhaps they'd been more vigilant in other locations.

A quick call to the estate agent confirmed that three had been sold and the sales completed meaning they had new owners and three were still for sale. Two had been viewed in the last couple of weeks and one hadn't been viewed in the last three weeks and as far as Mr Andrews knew, no one was going to the property on a regular basis, the sellers were overseas and the solicitor was handling everything.

The estate agent had protested most vehemently when Nancy had told him she would need to send a forensics team to each address as they were all possible crime scenes. He'd complained that the new owners would have noticed and that there might be legal action against his firm if they turned out to be living in a crime scene. When Nancy wasn't moved by his pleas, he had to be satisfied with being allowed to contact the new owners and let them know the police would be visiting, however she warned him that if he gave them any details of the investigation she would happily arrest him.

Chapter 31

DAY FIVE, FRIDAY

'This is Professor Laing at the University of St Andrews, linguistics department. You sent over some transcripts for me to look at.' Professor Ewan Laing sounded a good thirty years younger than Nancy had expected.

Nancy quickly swallowed her toast, cursing the fact that she'd decided to try and eat breakfast before going into the station this morning.

'Yes, thank you, I wasn't expecting to hear back from you so soon.' Nancy took a quick sip of coffee, trying to rinse away the crumbs she'd left lodged in her throat.

'I try and respond swiftly when I get a request from the police, so I've looked at everything you sent over to me, and I wonder if you might be free for us to meet up, I want to go through my findings and it generally works better if I can do that face to face.'

Nancy paused for a moment, deciding if she could justify the time away from the station to make the round trip to St Andrews. 'Yes of course, are you at the university today?'

'I'll be in my office there this afternoon, or you can come to my home this morning, I'm only in Aberdour, if that's more convenient.' Professor Laing replied.

'This morning would be brilliant thank you, are you able to text me your address?'

'I'll do that right away, can we say half an hour?'

Nancy looked at her watch, if she had Rob drop her at the station she could pick up her own car and make it to the Professor with time to spare as long as she didn't actually go inside the building.

'Sounds perfect.' Nancy said.

She'd only just hung up when she remembered that she was meant to be dropping Dylan off at school. The teenager had been in the kitchen eating a large bowl of Coco Pops when she'd taken the call.

'I'll get the bus,' he said before she had the opportunity to speak.

'Are you sure, I'm really sorry.' Nancy replied.

'Honestly mum, I'm sixteen, I think I can cope with getting the bus to school, it's what I've been doing for years.'

'I know, but not normally from here.' Nancy said.

'Oh no, I need to get on the bus at a different stop, how ever will I manage,' Dylan mocked her.

Nancy stuck her tongue out at him.

'Go do your job, figure out who the bad guy is and get them locked up and then maybe we could go house hunting?' Dylan asked.

'We'll see,' Nancy responded. It wasn't that she didn't want a house, it was just going to be harder than it should be. 'Right, I'll see you later.'

'Do I get any say in what's going on?' Rob asked.

She looked at his half-eaten breakfast without remorse,

'I'll give you a fiver to get yourself a sausage roll from the van, I'm sure you'll manage.'

'Well, when you put it like that,' Rob smiled at her.

Nancy got Rob to stop next to her car and then left him to get parked and in to the team. It had been several days since she'd driven anywhere, there was little point her and Rob taking separate vehicles to and fro work.

Professor Laing lived in an old stone built house up a farm road, it wasn't properly in Aberdour itself, more on the outskirts. The grounds were beautifully maintained with an old Victorian style greenhouse against one of the stone walls that encompassed the property.

Nancy knocked on the large red wooden door and stood back. The professor was in his late forties, handsome with a head of thick dark hair, he wore jeans and a checked shirt. She expected brown cord trousers with a cardigan with leather patches for elbows. She smiled at herself for the notion.

'You must be Detective Inspector Ravenscroft,' he said.

'You can call me Nancy.'

'Come in I've got a pot of coffee on the stove,' he looked at her for a moment. 'I hope I've not been sucked into a horrible "police drink lots of coffee stereotype", I do have tea as well if you'd prefer.'

'Coffee is good, especially one that's been brewed on a stove top,' It was rare that she had the time to make herself anything other than instant so this would be a treat.

'Excellent, do you want to take a seat in my study, and I'll bring it through,' he directed her to the room off to the left of the hall just as you entered the home. It had a large bay window that housed his desk, two walls were completely given over to glass fronted bookshelves and in the only remaining corner stood a slightly worn tweed armchair.

There was a spare chair near the desk which looked like it didn't belong in the room, she assumed that the professor had brought it in for her to sit on.

'Do you take cream and sugar?' he called from the kitchen.

Nancy couldn't remember the last time someone had offered her cream for her coffee, she was looking forward to the luxury. 'Cream please, no sugar.'

Moments later the professor appeared, a blue glazed pottery mug in each had. 'Here we go, now we've got refreshments we can get down to business.' He put his mug down on his desk. 'Sorry about the nasty plastic chair, It's the spare I keep in here. I really should look into getting something better though.'

'It's fine, I've sat in a lot worse,' Nancy smiled. 'I'm keen to hear your thoughts on the transcripts Professor.' In truth she felt like she could have happily sat all morning with him drinking coffee and chatting, but that wasn't going to help her solve this case.

'Please call me Ewan. It's very interesting actually, not all of it of course, but there are sections that jump out at you as soon as you see them.'

Nancy had speed read through the document before she'd sent him a copy and she couldn't remember anything jumping out at her.

'Much of it, as I'm sure you'd have picked up, is standard chat, people making comments on the presenting style of the podcast and about the subject matter. A few people are a little more enthusiastic about the murder than you might expect from your average citizen, but not alarmingly so. Now, where it gets interesting is on these pages.' Ewan separated out four pages from the centre of the document.

Nancy took a sip of her coffee and it was every bit as

delightful as she'd anticipated, then leaned in to look at the sections he'd highlighted.

'You'll see here that the conversation seems to be flowing between these two user IDs, it continues on for a few pages in fact.' He looked up at Nancy before continuing. 'It's one of the longest conversations between any two users. This is where I noticed it, User ID Dignity1985 says when men aren't decent respectable people and letch over girls there's never any consequences for them. She goes on to say that in this case when the "pervert" is murdered that at least he suffered the same fate as the "prostitute".

'I see,' Nancy said, without really knowing where he was going with it.

'Then User ID Omnipotent001 says 'in that case justice is served'. Now at first glance it might appear like what he's saying is that in this murder case justice was served, but if I go over the whole conversation this stands out as being linguistically inconsistent.'

'What does that mean?' Nancy asked.

'It could be one of two things. One, someone else wrote that line and Omnipotent001 is not one person but several different people, however if that were true then I would expect to see similar inconsistencies throughout their conversation, which I didn't.'

'What's the other reason?' Nancy asked.

'Part of the conversation is missing. Can I double check how you got the transcripts.'

'They were provided to me by the podcast hosts.' Nancy replied before properly considering if she should be sharing that information outside her team.

'In that case they've either deliberately redacted part of this conversation or it was deleted from the forum before they had the opportunity to print it out.'

'Why do that and then offer to let us have access to the forum directly.'

'I'd hate to tell you how to do your job,' Ewan smiled and took a sip of his coffee, 'but it would seem to me that the only reason to remove part of this conversation and piece it back together like this to make it look, to the untrained eye, like it was a continuous stream of chat. They might also have been trying to buy time to allow them to doctor the digital version as well.'

'You're sure that it's not the full conversation?' Nancy asked.

'I'm sure. It's not linguistically consistent with the rest of their conversation, also I checked through all of the chats with a fine tooth comb and there are several chats between these two users, in fact Omnipotent001 doesn't engage with any other user and if someone else joins their conversation he leaves it.' Ewan said.

Nancy finished her coffee, disappointed to come to the end of the drink. 'But it could have been deleted on the site before the hosts printed it out, I suppose.'

'You'd have to check what the parameters of the forum are and what users can and can't do, all I can tell you is this conversation has been altered.'

'What were these two talking about that they didn't want us to see?' Nancy questioned out loud.

'I'm afraid I can't shed any light on that for you, but, if you were to get the full conversation, I'd be happy to analyse it for you, help you understand if there were any hidden meanings in the interaction.' Ewan said passing her the documents.

'Thank you, I really appreciate it.' Nancy stood up. 'I'd better get back but thank you for giving up your time to look at this for me, and for the coffee, it's been a long time since I've had such a good cup.'

'You're welcome and you know if you fancy dropping by sometime for another cup of coffee then here's my card, it's got my mobile number on it.'

Nancy took the card, was he suggesting a date? Or had she been out of the single life so long she couldn't distinguish between someone being politely friendly and someone asking her out. 'Great, thanks.' She pushed the card into her jacket pocket and made her way back to the front door.

Ewan stood in his doorway and watched her drive away, waving as she left. Nancy had thought about calling Kayleigh from the car and asking her to give them access to the forum moderating feature, instead she decided that it would be better to ask Ewan to do it. If Kayleigh or Lucas were responsible for deleting content, they'd be much less likely to feel threatened by Ewan's friendly persona and right now she wanted to ensure they still felt like they were being helpful and not that they were under suspicion.

She could see why they might have been motivated to delete parts of conversations, if it in some way made them or the podcast look bad, the last thing they'd want is to be linked to a current murder investigation. Then Nancy remembered that Kayleigh had said that as moderator she'd had to remove content from time to time if she thought it wasn't appropriate or didn't meet the forums community guidelines. Could it be as simple as them looking after their community members? But Ewan had said it had been doctored to appear like nothing was missing and that felt like a much more deliberate act.

Chapter 32

DCI Cooper intercepted Nancy on the way into the station, 'The very person, let's have a catch up in my office.'

Nancy followed him along the corridor and sat down in the spare chair, maybe one day she'd come in and sit herself down in his chair just to mess with him, but not today, not in the middle of a multiple murder investigation.

'Where are we?' Cooper asked.

'No fixed suspects yet I'm afraid, I'm following up some inconsistencies with the data we got from the podcast hosts. We think Diane is on the run from someone she's afraid of and I believe Cheryl Wilson, the photographer, gave the killer the keys to the house Donald Stark was murdered in. Now she either did that willingly or she was completely duped by this man she was dating. He used her for access to empty properties so he could scope them out as suitable locations. We now know that the phone we found with Owen Fairmile belonged to the same man Cheryl was in a relationship with and that it was her calling him that alerted Sylvia to the clothes bin in the first place.' Nancy explained. 'We also know that the same number is linked to the profile that catfished Owen.'

'Do you think Cheryl is complicit in the murders?' Cooper asked.

'Hard to say. At the moment I think she's been taken in, she was so infatuated with this man I think he would have found it very easy to manipulate her without her knowing what she was involved in. In fact I suspect that he would have enjoyed knowing that he was playing puppet master to her.'

'And are you ruling the sister out as a suspect?' Cooper asked.

'Not at this stage, we're hoping to find her and her sons, especially if they are in danger and then we can investigate further, but there was nothing suspicious or incriminating when we searched her home.'

'And now you want a search warrant for Cheryl Wilson's online activity, is that right?'

'Yes, we know that she's somewhat of a troll, but without looking into everything, we can't get the full picture of her actions. I believe we'll find that she's happy to go online, argue, comment and spread unpleasantness, but given that Professor Laing has just finished telling me that the transcripts from the 'Dead Amongst Us' chat forum have been altered, it would be good to see if we can tie her to the conversation. Also, with a big enough sample of her online activity, he'll be able to tell us whether she has been on the podcast forum under an alias and what conversations are hers.'

'As far as finding one person with a motive to murder all three victims, we're no further forward?' Cooper asked.

'No sir, I'm aware that there's a lot of attention on this

case, I saw you on the news last night, good job fielding all those question by the way.' Nancy replied.

'Hmm, I have a meeting with the Chief Super tomorrow for an update on our progress, I would really like to tell him there has been some, especially as we reach the end of the first week of investigation.'

'Understood.' Nancy recognised that as the end of the conversation and her cue to leave.

She was nearly knocked over by Rob as he exited their office, phone pressed to his ear, Isla hot on his heels.

'What's the rush?'

Isla stopped. 'Rob's just got a call from Michael Bridlington, he slipped away from his mum and called from the house phone at the B & B he's staying at, we're on our way to pick him up before his mum finds out what he's done.'

'I'm coming with you, have we called for uniformed support in case Diane does something stupid?'

'Yes, we've got a marked car and two officers tagging along.'

The two women were taking the stairs two at a time trying to catch up with Rob. He was already in his car and on the way out of the carpark when they caught up, he braked and rolled down his window, but Nancy ushered for him to just go.

'I hope you got the address,' Nancy said as she and Isla got into her car.

'It's not far, just up the coast in Burntisland.' Isla replied.

'Under our nose the whole time. That's clever, so they took the train to Edinburgh to try and fool us and then doubled back on themselves.'

The coastal road to Burntisland didn't afford much room for overtaking. They'd been lucky that the road coming the other way had been relatively clear and so far, they hadn't encountered any tractors. Still Rob arrived a good five minutes before them.

Pulling into the carpark of what essentially looked like a large mid-century bungalow he already had Michael Bridlington in the back of his car.

'How is he?' Nancy asked as she walked over to Rob.

'Shaken, frightened. He said he called me because he didn't know what else to do. His mum's been acting weird, she never lets them skip school and she wouldn't even call and let the teachers know they weren't coming in. She's been talking about taking them overseas.' Rob said.

'Brave lad. Where's Diane now?'

'She's barricaded herself and Noah into their room. The landlady gave us a spare key, but she must have something up against the door because we couldn't get it open and obviously, we don't know where they are in the room so wanted to avoid forcing the door in case someone got hurt.' Rob continued his update of the situation.

'Have you tried talking to her?' Isla asked.

'Only in so much as to say we're the police, that Michael is safe with us and to ask her to voluntarily open the door.' Rob said.

'Did she reply?' Nancy asked.

'Told us to go away and that we were going to get Michael killed, but she wouldn't elaborate. Do you want me to see if there's a negotiator anywhere in the area, I know there's one in Dundee but not sure of his availability.' Rob asked.

'We'll see, let me go and talk to her.' Nancy said.

Rob and Isla exchanged looks. 'Are you sure boss?' Rob asked.

Nancy ignored the question. 'Where abouts is her bedroom?'

'Top of the stairs on the left, at the end of the hallway.' Rob explained.

'Great, can you clear the rest of the building, it's very unlikely she's armed, but let's not take any risks.' Nancy said before heading to the door of the house, leaving her colleagues to co-ordinate with the uniformed officers.

Chapter 33

Nancy sat on the ground on the hallway side of the door and rapped against the wood gently with her knuckles. 'Diane, it's Detective Inspector Nancy Ravenscroft, do you remember me?'

There was a pause, 'of course I remember you, I'm not an imbecile.'

'I wasn't suggesting you were, how's Noah, is he okay?'

'I'm keeping him safe.' Diane replied.

'It sounds like you've been having a tough time, do you want to tell me what's been going on?' Nancy said.

'Where's Michael?'

'He's with my Sergeant, he's safe.' Nancy confirmed.

'You can't keep him safe, you've no idea what you're up against.'

'Why don't you tell me, then we can keep Michael safe together.' Nancy said.

'You wouldn't understand.' Diane replied.

'Try me.'

"

'I can do without being judged by someone like you.' Diane said, her tone hostile.

'I'm not going to judge you, I might look like I've got my shit together, but honestly my personal life is a mess.' Nancy shared.

'I've seen this kind of thing before, you lie to me so I think you're my friend and get me to open the door, then you have officers barge in here and take my son and stick me in handcuffs.' Diane said.

'I don't want that to happen, and I'm not trying to be your friend, just one woman to another telling you that my personal life is an absolute disaster. My partner of twelve years got my sister pregnant and I had to move out, then I was living in a camper van, but my sixteen year old stepson wanted to stay with me, so now I'm sleeping on the coach of a colleague so that he can have a room of his own.'

'My husband left me when I found out he was having half a dozen online relationships, sexting I think they call it, sending each other dirty pictures, paying to see videos of them. It was disgusting. He was spending almost a thousand pounds a month on various women. It had been going on for years. One day I needed to do something and my laptop was dead, he was out playing golf, so I thought I'd just use his and I saw it all, he wasn't trying to hide it, there was no password or anything.'

'That's awful,' Nancy said. 'What happened when you confronted him?'

'He said I was frigid, that he needed to get affection from these women because I emasculated him, didn't treat him like the head of the house and a whole pile of other vile nonsense.'

'Did you throw him out?'

'I told him that I'd tell everyone what he was doing, or

he could leave. He agreed limited contact with the boys and then he met some woman who fell for his horseshit, and they moved to London. I couldn't have that around my sons. I didn't want them growing up thinking that was how you behaved as a real man.'

'I get that, it's hard with sons, isn't it.' Nancy said.

'Who were you angrier at, him or your sister? Be honest.' Diane said.

Nancy didn't answer straight away. She did wonder how she'd got to a place where she was discussing the shitshow that was her personal life through a door with a woman who for all Nancy knew was a murderer. 'I don't know, I guess it's a different kind of betrayal. When I look at him, I'm disgusted, when I look at her, I'm heart broken.'

'You wouldn't want your son looking up to him and thinking that was an okay way to behave.' Diane replied.

'No, I wouldn't.'

'I worried about the boys you know, that they grow up to be good people, good men. I thought Owen was going to be a good influence on them, but then he started dating that Natalie woman, and I didn't approve of her. And then there were the dating apps, I didn't like that either, talking to five or six women at a time doesn't seem right to me.' Diane said.

Nancy wasn't sure whether to reply, she didn't want to cut her off if she was in the flow of talking. But she had questions.

'If women do what men do, they're sluts and whores and considered damaged goods.' Diane continued and Nancy was glad she'd remained quiet. 'That's not okay is it. I listen to these true crime podcasts you know, I hear how everyone treats female victims, it wasn't so long ago that the police considered the murder of a prostitute as a victimless crime, couldn't even be bothered investigating. But it's supply and demand isn't it. And it's not women kerb crawling and paying for sex, but the police never hold the men accountable.'

Diane was silent for too long this time.

'And you think they should be?' Nancy asked.

'Don't you? Shouldn't we all be held to the same standard? If one of these men who pay for prostitutes gets killed, the media talks about him being a family man or respected in the community, his dirty little secret gets to die with him.'

'That's true,' Nancy replied. 'Who are you afraid of Diane?'

'All I wanted to do was blow off some steam, that's all. I wanted to have a bit of a moan and feel better, have complete strangers tell me I was right, and they agreed with me.' Diane said.

Nancy could feel her heartbeat quickening in anticipation of what Diane might reveal in her next sentence. She almost had her fingers crossed that Diane wasn't about to admit to murder.

'We all need that from time to time.' Nancy said.

'I listened to that podcast, you know, The Prostitute, The Priest, The Pervert and The Policewoman. I didn't want anything to happen to Owen, he was a good man and a good brother.'

'Did you meet someone on the forum that you got talking to?' Nancy asked.

'I spoke to a few people. One woman really seemed to understand me, she said she had kids, and she didn't want them to have bad influences in their lives. I told her about Owen and the dating apps, that he was going on another blind date. You have to understand, not once did I say I wanted anything bad to happen to my brother, I said that one of these days he was going to get himself into bother, that's all.' Diane said.

'What did you mean when you said that?' Nancy asked.

'Just that he was going to find someone he really liked but that he'd have messed her around so much that she wouldn't be interested, or that he'd end up with a drink being tipped over his head. Not that someone would kidnap him and murder him.' It was clear that Diane was crying now.

'Hey Diane, do you think you could open the door and let me in?' Nancy asked softly.

There was no reply, but Nancy heard something scrape along the wooden bedroom floor.

'It's open.' Diane said.

'Thank you, before I come in can you tell me if you are armed?'

'No I'm not.' Diane replied.

Nancy stood up and slowly opened the bedroom door, glaring at the uniformed officers to stay back. Diane was sitting on the edge of one of the beds, red eyed and pale, tears streaming down her face now soaking into the neck of her top.

'How about we let Noah go downstairs and sit with Michael whilst we talk.' Nancy suggested, the boy looked genuinely alarmed by his mother's conversation.

'Okay.' Diane replied.

'Come on Noah, you go out the door and you'll see one of my officers and they'll take you to your brother, okay.'

The boy nodded, opened the bedroom door, pausing to look at his mum, before walking through and closing it behind him. From the corridor they could hear the muffled voices of him being met by the uniformed officers. Nancy was confident that once downstairs Rob would reunite the brothers.

'It's just you and me now Diane and I need you to tell me what's going on.' Nancy said.

'When Owen didn't come home that first night, I was genuinely angry, I thought he's going to waltz in here full of himself after having a one night stand and Michael looks up to him so much. Then he didn't come home that day or the next. I phoned him over and over. I knew something was wrong because he had plans with Michael on the Sunday, and he absolutely would never let him down. I thought there must have been an accident, I started calling around hospitals and nothing. I went to the police and reported him missing, I know they thought I was overreacting, but turns out I was right to worry.' Diane said looking down at the hem of the grey fine wool cardigan she was wearing. She rubbed the fabric between her fingers holding it in both hands.

'You were right to report him missing.' Nancy said.

Diane looked up at Nancy. 'And you were right when you accused me of treating Owen like a child, being too involved in his business. I know he stayed with us for the sake of the boys. I think he thought I was heading for some sort of breakdown, maybe I was. Maybe I'm having it right now.'

'Then I came to your home and told you he was dead.' Nancy said.

'I'd expected it, the knock at the door. It seems dreadful to say it, but it was almost a relief because at least I knew. He was gone and I could grieve. But I felt so alone. I was on all these forums at all times of the night, because I couldn't sleep and that's when the private messages started to happen, someone from the podcast forum wanting to talk to me about it, asking me if I'd heard that Owen was part of a copycat killing of that crime.' Diane said.

'Do you know who it was?' Nancy asked. The theory of Owen's death being anything to do with a copycat had never been made public, even now she knew that the Chief Superintendent was very keen to keep that detail under wraps.

'He called himself Graham, but he knew details of conversations that I'd only had with that one woman and we'd taken those away from the forum into a private chat and I started to think maybe this Graham person pretended to be a woman to lure me in and then he used what I said about Owen to pick him as his next victim.' Diane said.

'Did you confront him with your theory?' Nancy asked.

'I was going to but then he said, now Michael and Noah could grow up without any bad influences and I mustn't be afraid because no one could ever prove what I'd done. That's when I knew we had to run, I'd never mentioned my boy's names online, I never do, I'm really strict about that sort of thing.' Diane said.

Nancy believed her, Diane was a control freak, there was no way that she would put her personal information out there for the world to see. She was the polar opposite of Cheryl Wilson.

'What do you think he meant when he said that no one could prove what you'd done?' Nancy asked.

'He was implying that somehow I'd engineered Owen's death. That I was responsible…' she looked out the window for a moment. 'I think I was, I didn't mean to be, I was weak, and I overshared and because of me Owen is dead.'

'No. Not because of you.' Nancy said. 'You didn't do this, whatever you said about your brother, I guarantee sisters all over the world have said worse, blowing off steam doesn't equate to murder.'

'You're not going to arrest me?' Diane asked, her eyes wide.

'No, other than being a pain in my arse, you've not committed any crimes, and I'm sure the landlady here will be understanding and settle for you covering any damages. But I do need you to come with me and make an official statement and give us access to all the conversations you had with Graham.' Nancy said.

Diane nodded. 'Okay and then what, how do I keep us all safe?'

'We can get you moved somewhere secure, somewhere we can have some officers on hand to protect you on the rare chance this man finds you. Although I think he's trying to scare you into being quiet more than anything.' Nancy said.

'But if he finds out I've told you everything then he might kill us in retaliation.' Diane said.

'I know you're scared, and I get it, but you have to do this, you have to be brave for your sons and you need to show them what doing the right thing looks like and you need to do this in honour of Owen.' Nancy replied.

Diane got up, still crying but more resolute than before. 'I'll do it as long as Michael and Noah are safe, that's all I care about.'

'We'll look after you.' She walked Diane down the stairs and out into the driveway.

Michael got out of the back of Rob's car and rushed over to his mum. 'I'm so sorry, I didn't want to get you into trouble, but I didn't know what else to do.'

Diane pulled the boy into an embrace. Despite being as

tall as her, Michael looked childlike as he pressed his face affectionately against her shoulder.

Rob looked to Nancy for answers.

'Detective Sergeant MacDonald will take you and your sons to the police station, we'll take your statement and organise somewhere for you to stay. I'll arrange to have your belongings packed up from the guesthouse and brought to the station and if anyone needs anything else from the house, one of my officers will collect it for you.' Nancy paused for a moment thinking about the Bridlington house and how upset Diane would be if she knew it had been searched, but now was not the time to open this particular can of worm.

Chapter 34

The kitchen of the upstairs flat lit up like Christmas when Daniel turned the ultraviolet light on. The killer had done a better job of cleaning the blood up at this scene, but not good enough. Now his team were unscrewing cupboard doors and lifting lino off the floor.

Nancy had left Isla to take Diane Bridlington's statement after she received the call from Daniel. Now, waiting outside with Rob, she wondered which one of the victims took their last breaths in this building.

'I can see why this place met our killer's criteria, not remote like the house, but above a closed bank branch with only commercial properties as neighbours, gives him confidence that he won't be accidentally discovered.' Rob said.

'Do you think he keeps his victim here the whole time that he has them hostage?' Nancy asked.

Rob shook his head, 'would be risky I would think, the property is for sale, the risk of someone coming and checking on the place, let alone having no idea if viewings are scheduled, too many variables outside his control.'

'How long has this one been on the market?' Nancy said.

'The week before Owen's body was found Cheryl Wilson said she brought Graham here on two occasions, first on the Monday of that week in the afternoon, then on the Friday morning. From her statement it seems like they spent time together at least twice in all of the empty house locations.' Rob said.

'First time to scope the place out and decide if it was quiet enough for him to bring a victim, the second to take a copy of the keys, she said she never gave him keys, but I'm still not sure that I believe her.' Nancy said.

The empty flat was only a mile or so away from the clothes donation bin Owen's body had been found in. There would be no one much around in the middle of the night to see someone leave with a suitcase full of bits of a person.

A door opened at the top of the stairs shedding light on the stairwell, Daniel Burrows pulled the white hood from his head and joined them.

'Well?' Nancy asked.

'There's significant blood spatter in the kitchen, someone tried to clean it up, but not well enough, the thing with blood is it gets everywhere, and in this case, it seeped under the linoleum and down the back of the skirting boards. We've got a lot of samples that haven't been degraded by cleaning products. We'll run a DNA test against Maria and Owen to see if it's a match.'

'Thanks, don't suppose there's any chance you found the murder weapon whilst you were in there.' Nancy said.

'Afraid not, we've dusted for prints and we'll need to know who to exclude but the door handle of the kitchen has been wiped down, I'd be surprised if we found the killers fingerprints.' Daniel said.

'How much longer are your guys going to need?' Nancy asked.

'A few hours to be honest, we need to take apart most of the kitchen units to see if there's anything useful behind them.'

'Alright, I'll leave you with uniform and you can give me a call if anything else comes up.'

They left the forensic team to their work and headed back to the police station. Nancy rested her head against the passenger door window, watching the world go by as Rob drove, he could have been talking, she didn't really know. Right now she was trying to pin things together in her mind.

'1,000 phone calls in the days since Cooper told the press that we believe we have a serial killer on our hands, and that's before he's even mentioned the copycat element, the press are going to go wild for that,' Rob was saying as Nancy zoned back into the conversation.

'I'm just glad we're not the ones answering the calls anymore.' Nancy said. She and Rob had done a stint on the hotline when they were in uniform many years ago, they'd both been so pumped to have been drafted in to work on a murder case. Twelve hours later they were holding their heads in their hands wishing that someone would send them out to direct traffic.

'I know, it's frustrating that there might be a genuinely important piece of the puzzle being reported but it could get lost in all the other junk that comes in.' Rob said.

'By and large people just want to help,' Nancy smiled.

'But why is there always that one guy who claims to have seen aliens or that something supernatural has been involved.' Rob replied.

Nancy laughed.

'Good job with Diane Bridlington earlier by the way. How did you get her to talk?'

'I was honest and told her about my life, I think she felt better when I told her I'd been living in a campervan and then on your sofa.

'You still haven't got round to telling me exactly why you were living in a campervan in the first place.' Rob said.

'When I left Chris I took my camper up to Cellerdyke, it made sense, gave me somewhere to live, I can move around, it has everything I need. Which worked until Dylan said he wanted to stay with me.'

'Why not rent somewhere in the first place and then you wouldn't need to be sofa surfing, not that I mind.' Rob said.

'I was going to,' that was a lie, in truth the only thing she'd thought about was getting the hell out of that house and away from the people who'd hurt her. 'But then this case came in and I just haven't had time.'

'Or you could buy something, I'm assuming you guys are going to have to sell the house now.' Rob said.

'It's not my house, he never put my name on the deeds,' Nancy said, wishing she could go back to silently looking out of the window.

'Yeah, but you put the money from the sale of your flat into it, I remember you telling me you paid off the mortgage and then did the extension.'

Nancy could feel her cheeks becoming flushed, she'd been so incredibly stupid and now she was going to have to admit that out loud and probably repeatedly. 'Yeah, but it's not my house so I'm not entitled to anything.'

'Did Mr Charming tell you that? I can't believe that's true. I'm going to give you the number for my Uncle Lloyd, he's a lawyer, he'll help you out.' Rob said.

'I don't want to dwell on it, I just want to move on with

my life.' Nancy said hoping that it would put an end to the conversation.

'Oh no, absolutely not, there's a difference between moving on with your life and letting this man take you for a fool, I am not going to let that happen and if not for yourself then for Dylan.' Rob said.

'Jesus, fine I'll speak to your Uncle Lloyd and see if there's anything I can do, now can we please stop talking about my personal life and concentrate on this case.' Nancy replied.

It started to rain as they pulled into the station carpark, the sort of rain that comes down in a fine mist and lures you into believing it's not that bad but in the time it takes you to walk from your car to the building your clothes are soaked and your hair is covered in hundreds of tiny droplets just waiting to burst so they can roll down your forehead into your eyes, or down the back of your neck and under your collar.

They ran from the car to the station door. Nancy pulled her jacket up to cover her head, Rob used his leather document case as a makeshift umbrella. Indoors Nancy shook her jacket, sending the droplets flying into the air and down on the ground making the floor damp. 'I don't mind the cold, I just wish it would stop with this bloody rain,' she said as she half ran up the stairs.

In the office she made a bee line for the coffee machine and took a mug back to her desk. One sip and she grimaced, spoilt by the professor's coffee this morning, her normal drink seemed substandard, but she persevered with drinking it anyway.

Isla had taken Diane Bridlington's statement and had left a copy on her desk. There weren't any additional details in it that she hadn't heard from Diane herself. She's never met Graham, they'd only ever spoken over messenger. Isla had attached a transcript of the online conversations between Diane and Graham and the ones when Diane had thought she'd been talking to a woman.

Nancy called the professor. 'Hi Ewan.' She blushed saying his name, what the hell was wrong with her. 'I'm sorry to bother you again.'

'No bother detective,' he replied. 'Have you managed to get the full conversation for me to look at?' he asked.

'No, this is something else I need your help with. I have a series of conversations I'd like you to look at. We know who one of the participants is, I want your opinion on whether the other people in the conversations could be just one person.'

'Of course, send them over to my email and I'll look at them this evening. Do you want me to run an analysis of them alongside the participants in the conversation I've already looked at?' he asked.

'Yes that would be great.' Nancy said.

'Okay, I'll get on it as soon as I receive them, I don't have any lectures today, I'm doing office hours for my PhD students, but I'll have plenty of time.'

'Great, I've sent them over whilst we've been chatting.'

'Once I'm done, I'll give you a call, and I'll get the pot on for you coming over.' Ewan said.

Nancy ended the call wondering if she was more seduced by the coffee or the professor.

Chapter 35

'Where's Grace?' Nancy asked Isla as she took her mug over to the sink to rinse it out. Soaking it in some hot water and washing up liquid now would at least stop the brown coffee ring around the inside from worsening.

'She's following up on one of the hotline leads,' Isla said pulling a yellow square Post-It note from her pocket. 'A woman said she saw a man in the vicinity of the compost heap a few weeks ago. The timeline correlates with when we suspect Donald Stark was murdered. She was out walking her dog and saw him, said she called out to him to tell him he wasn't supposed to be in there and he told her he was looking for his dog, it had taken a fright and run off. She offered to stay and to help him look but he declined. Grace said she would pop over and take the woman's statement, see if she got a look at him, and then we could compare it to the description Cheryl Wilson gave of Graham.' Isla explained.

Nancy looked at her watch, it was getting late.

'She said it was on her way home, that's why she said she would go.' Isla said as if reading her boss's mind.

'Brilliant, right well you take yourself off home as well and we can all start again in the morning.' Nancy said.

Once she had dismissed the rest of the team she gathered up some paperwork and went to find Rob. 'I've had a text form Dylan saying your cupboards are bare so he's suggesting curry, what do you think, I'll buy.' Nancy said.

On the way to the flat Nancy received a text from the professor, 'looking through everything now, am noticing some interesting sentence structures and some similarities between these users and the one we discussed this morning. Thought you might want to know, speak soon.'

'I take it that was good news then?' Rob said.

'Just Professor Laing letting me know his preliminary thoughts on the conversations between Diane and Graham and Diane and the user that claimed to be a woman, he should have a report ready for us in the morning.'

'Hmm,' Rob replied but said nothing more.

'What did you get me?' Dylan asked as Nancy and Rob entered the flat.

'Butter Chicken, of course,' Nancy smiled.

They sat around Rob's dining room table chatting and laughing for a while. Nancy felt a pang of sadness that her relationship with Chris had become so broken, the possibility of them even being friends had been shattered by the pregnancy announcement. Truthfully, she wouldn't have held it against him for having an affair, she knew they'd been living separate lives for a long time. If only it hadn't been with her sister.

Dylan left them to go play on his Playstation and Rob excused himself to meet some mates in the pub, leaving

Nancy sitting on the living room floor looking at documents, which was where she woke up a few hours later, her neck stiff. She rubbed at her aching shoulders.

Chapter 36

DAY SIX, SATURDAY

'You know you're actually supposed to lie down to sleep right, not just face plant the floor with exhaustion.' Dylan said handing her a mug of coffee and a Danish pastry.

'I thought you said there was no food in this place.' Nancy said, eyeing the pastry suspiciously.

'There isn't, which is why I got up this morning and went to the bakers round the corner and got a few things.'

She kissed him on the cheek, 'you're a saint.'

'Mind you remind her she said that the first time you come home drunk and vomit kebab up your bedroom wall,' Rob said, standing in the kitchen doorway.

Revived by food and caffeine, Nancy took a quick shower before they headed into the station.

'Morning everyone.' She looked around the room at the already tired faces looking back at her. 'As you know we have now found Diane Bridlington and her sons, and she is no longer a suspect. As of right now our main suspect is a man who used the name Graham Smyth when he interacted with both Diane and Cheryl Wilson.' Nancy said.

Isla raised her hand, 'are we sure that Diane wasn't having a sexual relationship with Graham?'

'Yes, I'm confident that she only ever interacted with him online, the working theory is that he got her to open up to him about her frustrations regarding her brother's behaviour towards women. It's possible that he'd already selected Owen Fairmile as his next victim and he saw an opportunity to blame Diane if he ever got caught. We know that "Graham" liked to look at Cheryl's photographs, he will likely have seen the one of Maria and Owen together.' Nancy continued.

'Are you saying that he deliberately went looking for Diane to trick her into saying something about her brother or was that an added bonus?' Cal asked from near the back of the room.

'That's a good question. We know from Owen's work colleague Jake, that he was paid to call in sick, the killer wanted to be sure that Owen would go to the house he intended to kill Donald Stark in. That leads me to think that he'd been stalking Owen for some time, I think he was also stalking Diane and when he saw her views on her brother's behaviour, he saw an opportunity to implicate her. Diane told us he knew her sons' names and she'd never revealed them to him.' Nancy replied.

'What about Maria?' Isla asked.

'We know that Cheryl didn't have a good word to say about her, in fact she was the only person we spoke to that didn't have anything nice to say about her. It wouldn't be much of a stretch to think that the idea of her as the 'prostitute' came from all of Cheryl's rants.' Nancy replied.

'What about Donald Stark?' Rob asked. 'Have we picked up any chatter about him on any of the forums?'

Nancy shook her head. 'Nothing, I had Susan Stark's

family liaison ask if Donald listened to the podcast, she said absolutely not, he didn't like true crime. We also asked the granddaughter, and she wasn't a listener either.'

'Does that mean the podcast is just inspiration to the killer rather than a place he finds victims?' Cal asked.

'We know that Cheryl took photographs of all our victims, this is our best link between our killer and Burns Night.' Nancy said.

'Could Cheryl be the murderer?' Isla asked.

'It's possible, but I think it's more likely that she's been another pawn in this man's sick plan.' Nancy replied.

'I've got access to Cheryl Wilson's social media,' Cal said scrunching up his nose. 'She is not a nice person, she doesn't like immigrants, spicy food, people with ginger hair, parents, dog owners or the majority of young women, although not exclusively *young* women. She spends a lot of time commenting on pictures telling people they look like whores and deserve to get raped, that if you dress a certain way, you're asking for it. Like I say she's unpleasant. She hides her real identity pretty well for the most part. I did discover that she has repeatedly turned down wedding photography jobs for same sex couples and mixed race couples. She appears on a wedding forum of businesses to avoid. I don't think she can know about that though seeing as she hasn't been on there giving her opinion on their reviews.'

'Let's have uniform pick her up and bring her in for questioning, I think it's time we see how much she really knows.' Nancy said. 'Did we get any further with the CCTV or doorbell camera footage for the carpet cleaning firm that went to Donald Stark's house?'

'Yes, it was genuine,' one of the CCTV officers said.

'What about the footage of the man with the suitcase

around the time of Owen's body being disposed of?' Nancy asked.

'Only one door picked it up, the man is wearing a cap and a scarf, it's not been possible to do much to improve the picture, If we had someone to compare it to then we can use things like height, facial structure etc to see whether there's a match.' Isla replied.

'Okay, we'll bear that in mind for when we make an arrest,' Nancy glanced around the room. 'Where's Grace, how did she get on with our hotline tip?'

There was silence from within the room, officers shuffling around looking at the desks and at one another.

Nancy felt ice creep through her veins, 'tell me someone has heard from Grace this morning?' She shouted at them.

'Sorry boss, I thought she must've been out on a call when I didn't see her first thing,' Isla said.

Rob lifted his mobile to his ear, 'her phone is switched off.'

'Somebody get me the details of that hotline tip right now.' Nancy said.

Chapter 37

Nancy had driven too quickly and taken a few too many half gaps whilst over taking. A quick call to her flatmate had confirmed that Grace hadn't come home the night before. The flatmate had put it down to her forgetting what shift rotation Grace was on. And now Grace had been missing for almost fifteen hours. The car shuddered slightly as Nancy bumped the wheels over the kerb at speed outside the caller's house.

She bounded up the concrete steps two at a time to get to the front door, knocking on the door louder and harder than was strictly necessary. The door was opened by a man in his eighties, dressed in black trousers and a pinstriped shirt as if he was about to go out to work for the day.

'Can I help you?' He asked frowning.

Nancy introduced herself. 'Can I speak to the lady that called our tip line yesterday please, presumably your wife?'

'My wife died three years ago, I can't see her calling anyone.' The man responded.

'Who else lives here with you?' She asked, trying not to lose her patience.

'I live alone, I have a woman come in every morning and evening to help me with a few bits, sometimes she walks the dog for me, but that's all.'

'Did you get a visit from Detective Constable Abbotts yesterday afternoon?' Nancy asked.

'I didn't get a visit from anyone, other than Lesley, the lady that comes in and helps me out.' The old man said.

'Can you give us Lesley's details please?' Rob asked.

No, no, I don't think I can, I don't think she would want me handing out her personal information to anyone.'

'I'm sorry that we've barged in here like this, but it is imperative that we speak to Lesley as soon as possible, she's not in any trouble, we think she can help us with our enquiries and I'm sure she would want to help us.' Rob said softly.

'When you put it like that,' the man replied before shuffling away from the door taking short steps without ever lifting either of his feet. 'This is her card.' He said handing it to Rob directly.

'Thank you, we'll get out of your hair now.'

The old man watched them as they walked down the steps and got back in the car, before closing his front door.

'If Grace was never here, where the bloody hell is she?' Nancy said.

'We don't know for sure that Grace didn't come here last night…'

'You heard him, he said no one visited yesterday.' Nancy interrupted.

'He said Lesley walks his dog for him, Grace probably came past here last night, saw Lesley leaving the house with the dog and spoke to her then. I bet when we get back to the station, she's going to be sat at her desk wondering what all the fuss is about.' Rob said as they got into the car.

'Or she could be being held hostage by someone we know has already killed three times,' Nancy said voicing the fear that had been growing in her chest every second since she realised Grace was missing.

'If, and I'm only saying if, that's the case then we have time, we know that he doesn't kill his victims right away.' Rob replied.

'I doubt that's much comfort to Grace right now.' Nancy said. 'Call the carer, let's see if you're right.'

Rob dialled the number on the card the old man had given him.

'Good morning this is Caring Together how can I help you.' The cheery female voice said.

'Hello this is Detective Sergeant MacDonald, I'm looking to speak to one of your carers, a woman named Lesley.'

'I'm sorry, Lesley is with a client at the moment, is it something I can help you with?' The voice significantly less cheery now.

'I'm afraid not, it's extremely important I speak to Lesley, can you tell me where she is right now.' Rob said.

'I'm sorry, I'm not able to give out client information, it's against GDPR.' The woman replied officiously.

'I understand that, however this is a life or death situation that I'm investigating and it is imperative that I speak to Lesley, can I take her mobile phone number.' Rob said, his patience wearing thinner with every response.

'Are you suggesting that Lesley is in danger?'

'I cannot discuss the details of an ongoing investigation with you madam,' Rob replied.

'I mean I suppose I could give you her phone number,

but I don't want to take responsibility for what happens if she's angry about it.'

'I will tell her I insisted,' Rob said.

'Fine.' She gave out the phone number with Rob checking it twice to make sure he'd taken it down correctly.

'Jesus Christ,' he said after hanging up the call. 'I swear criminals and gangs should be recruiting from call centres, these people are the most difficult, tight-lipped people I've encountered.'

Nancy allowed herself a small smile, she'd actually thought something very similar the last time she'd tried to book a doctor's appointment.

'Give her a call and see if you can find out if she saw Grace.' Nancy said.

It took four attempts before a grumpy Lesley finally answered the phone and then a further two minutes of conversation to discover that she hadn't spoken to Grace at all yesterday, nor had she phoned the hotline.

'Where does that leave us?' Rob asked.

'I've got a message out across Scotland to be on the lookout for her car, but anyone with any sense at all will have ditched it by now,' Nancy said. She drove back to the station painfully aware that there was no point driving around Dunfermline and the surrounding areas in the hopes of seeing Grace. Her time would be better spent investigating, finding out who had taken her before it was too late.

'Cheryl Wilson is in interview room two, uniform brought her in about twenty minutes ago,' Isla said as they returned to the office. 'I've put together the paperwork for a warrant to search her house as well, do you want me to take it to DCI Cooper,' she paused for a moment. 'Does he know about Grace?'

Nancy nodded, knowing that the information could only

come from her, she'd phoned as they drove back to the station. There had been a lot of silences and a few grunts, but Cooper had assured that she had his full support in doing what was necessary to find Grace.

'Take it to him and then if I'm not finished with Cheryl when it comes through, get on to the duty Sergeant and get some uniformed officers to accompany you to the search.' Nancy said.

Isla nodded and turned to leave.

'One more thing, no one goes anywhere by themselves until we've caught this bastard, is that clear. Just because he has Grace doesn't mean to say that the rest of us are safe from him. And pass that on to the duty Sergeant as well and anyone else who's working on this case. You need to at least be in pairs.' Nancy said.

'I'll let everyone know.' Isla confirmed. 'By the way, my contact at the auction house came back to me, the towels were bought by Cheryl Wilson's photography business account.

'Excellent work, thanks. Rob, you're with me, let's go and find out if our photographer can shed any light on the situation.

Chapter 38

'Interview commenced at 10:12, present DI Ravenscroft and DS MacDonald.' Nancy said into the recorder.

'Now Cheryl you understand that you're under arrest for the murder of Maria Fischer, Owen Fairmile and Donald Stark, I note your rights have been read to you and you have chosen not to be represented by a solicitor, is that correct?' Nancy continued.

'I haven't done anything wrong, I don't need a solicitor.' Cheryl said sitting back on the seat and folding her arms.

'When did you first meet Graham Smyth?' Nancy asked.

Cheryl's arms flopped down by her sides, 'what's he got to do with anything?'

'If you can tell me when you met, please,' Nancy repeated.

'Um about, eight months ago.' Cheryl said, she pressed the palms of her hands into the seat and turned them towards her body tucking her fingers under her bottom.

'June 2022?'

'It was actually the end of May.' Cheryl said.

'And how did you meet?'

'On a photography forum.' Cheryl said.

'Was Graham also a photographer?'

'No, he was looking for a photographer.'

'What for?' Nancy said.

'He wanted someone to do photos for his website, for his business.'

'And what was his business?'

'Holiday Chalets. You know, the log cabin kind, he has three on the edge of a bit of woodland he owns.'

'Did he ever take you there?'

'No, in the end he said he was going to sell them and put the money into something he'd enjoy.' Cheryl said.

'Did he tell you what that was?'

Cheryl shook her head.

'You hated Maria Fischer didn't you, you hated all women like her in fact, but you had to see her all the time, rubbing your face in the fact that you were getting older and you weren't getting any more attractive, and the offers for male company were getting thin on the ground, and there she was being offended by the attention she got.' Nancy said, hoping that the accusation would catch the woman off guard and encourage her to say more than she might otherwise have intended.

Cheryl's face was a hot red now, 'I didn't like any of them, all the girls that work there, they're all the same.'

'But you especially didn't like Maria though, after all not only was she young and beautiful, she was Australian and you hate outsiders don't you.' Rob said.

'When they come here that's one more job that's taken away from one of our own, don't tell me it doesn't bother you when you see someone getting ahead – getting a promotion because their skin is the right colour.'

'I'm doing alright thanks.' Rob said smiling.

'Did you tell Graham how you felt about Maria?' Nancy asked.

'No.' Cheryl spat.

'I don't believe you, last time we spoke you told me that Graham was interested in you, he came to your house, he admired your work, made you feel special. He must have seen pictures from Burns Night. And I don't believe you didn't start telling him about the people who worked there.' Nancy said.

'I might've said something about not liking her, but it's not like we talked about killing her or anything crazy like that.' Cheryl said.

'Did you know that Maria wanted to leave the club and go into childcare?' Nancy asked.

'Why would she tell me that, we didn't speak.' Cheryl responded.

'You might've overheard it?'

'Who would employ someone like that to look after their kids?' Cheryl said.

'So, you did know, did you mention it to Graham?' Nancy said.

'I can't remember.'

'Which of your photographs did Graham like best?'

'He liked the ones I did of charity events, he was kind like that. A lot of men would have taken the opportunity to look at the half naked girls in the photos, but he wasn't particularly interested in looking.'

Nancy frowned for a moment, 'you mean like the event at Burns Night?'

'Yeah, I suppose, I don't remember him having a specific favourite.' Cheryl said.

'But he definitely saw the pictures you took at that event?'

Cheryl pulled a face indicating she didn't understand why Nancy appeared to be fixating on this single event. 'He would've done.' Cheryl paused and smiled a moment, her cheeks slightly flushed. 'It wasn't long after that we, you know, for the first time.'

'At your house?' Nancy asked.

'Yeah, we did it at my house all the time, until he found out about the houses and then we did it there sometimes as well.'

'Did you ever go to Graham's house?'

'No.'

'Didn't you think that was a little bit strange?'

A knock on the door paused the interview, the interruption gave Cheryl time to ponder her situation, Nancy left Rob in the room and joined Cal in the hallway.

'Sorry to interrupt boss, it's just I thought you'd want to know. You remember a few days ago I was looking for places with compost heaps?' Cal said.

Nancy nodded quickly hoping that he'd get to the point before Cheryl decided she was no longer in a chatty mood.

'Well, I thought if all the bodies are disposed in various types of rubbish then it would be worth contacting all the local tips to have them be on the lookout for anything suspicious. I was thinking that the killer was probably going to want to get rid of the suitcase they transferred Owen's remains in. Anyway, one of the refuse workers at the Dalgety Bay one called in, said that they'd been doing more checks since I got in contact and they pulled a large black suitcase out of their landfill section which matched my description, black with two striped straps round the body. I got a uniformed officer to go and pick it up and take it to the lab.' Cal paused for breath.

'And?' Nancy encouraged.

'And, it had blood in it, a lot of blood, but that's not all, it had a luggage label on it and the name on the label is Cheryl Wilson. I double checked the address on the tag and it's the same Cheryl Wilson.' Cal finished.

Nancy raised her eyebrows, impressed. 'Excellent work, good thinking to get in touch with the tips. Did Daniel say how long before we'll have a DNA match?'

'He said he'll put it through as an urgent request.'

'Let me know as soon as you hear.'

'Will do, also Isla said to let you know the warrant came through and she's at Cheryl's house just now with a small team.' Cal said.

Back in the interview room Nancy looked at Cheryl, she was biting the skin around her thumb nail. Nancy sat back down.

'For the tape, DI Ravenscroft has re-entered the room.' Rob said.

'Tell me about your large black suitcase?' Nancy said, earning her a look of intrigue from her colleague.

Cheryl on the other hand coughed, almost choking on the air she was breathing. The change of subject had clearly thrown her. 'What?' She managed to spit out.

'You had a large black suitcase, where is it now?' Nancy asked.

'How do you know what luggage I've got?' Cheryl replied.

'Let me tell you what I know,' Nancy replied. 'I know that you had a large black suitcase, I also know that earlier this morning that same suitcase was pulled out of landfill and sent to our labs, where upon opening, it was apparent that it was stained with a lot of blood.' Nancy paused, giving her opponent the opportunity to let the enormity of that statement sink in.

Cheryl was pale, she'd gripped the edge of her thumb nail between her teeth and pulled, ripping it off leaving a jagged slightly bloody edge behind. She winced from the pain she'd caused herself. 'I gave that away, it's got nothing to do with me.'

'Who did you give it to?' Nancy asked.

'Charity shop.'

'Which one?' Rob asked.

'Don't remember?' Cheryl replied.

'When did you give it away?' Rob persisted.

'Ages ago, last year sometime.'

'You know what I think, Cheryl?' Nancy said. 'I think you gave that suitcase to Graham.'

'I don't remember.' Cheryl replied.

'How do you know Rachel Howgate?' Nancy asked.

'I've never heard of her.' Cheryl didn't look at them.

'You told us when we were at your house that you'd tried to call Graham several times the other evening. What you didn't know was that we found Graham's phone with Owen's body and the number that had called it wasn't one of yours, it was Rachel Howgate's. So I'm going to ask you again, who is Rachel Howgate?'

Cheryl frowned, her eyes darting around the room. 'I used a pay as you go phone to call him because he wasn't answering when I called from my regular phone. I don't know this person you're talking about.'

'I think you do, I think you created social media accounts for a fake person to help you catfish Owen Fairmile, was that your idea? It was very clever to use your skills to doctor the photographs like that. Did Graham have you talk to him on the phone as well, arrange to go on a date with him. Did you know that you were luring him to his death?' Nancy said.

'What?' Cheryl sat bolt upright in her chair. 'I haven't done anything wrong. It was all meant to be a bit of fun. Graham said he was winding up a friend, he said he needed my help,' she whined.

'That's what you want us to believe isn't it, that you're a helpless bystander. I think you were more involved than that. You picked the targets, you took the photographs and maybe by yourself or with your lover you chose who would live and who would die. You provided the secluded locations for the murders to take place and you provided the suitcase to get rid of Owen Fairmile's body after cutting it into pieces.' Nancy said.

Cheryl's eyes were wide now, her jaw had slackened causing it to hang open as she finally began to take in the seriousness of her position. 'I didn't do those things, I swear.' Cheryl said in a whisper, tears now cascading down her cheeks.

'You're involved, even if you didn't mean to be. What happened to Owen after you arranged to meet him at the restaurant.'

'I don't know, I asked Graham and he said the joke worked perfectly, that he'd turned up and met his friend, they'd had a laugh and gone out for drinks afterwards.'

'What did you think when you heard in the news Owen's body had been found?' Rob asked.

'Nothing, because I'd never known his last name. I didn't put two and two together, I swear I'm not involved in any of this, I wouldn't have done anything to actually hurt anyone. I rant online, but not in real life,' she squealed.

'If you're not involved then you need to help me catch Graham.' Nancy replied.

Cheryl sat silently crying for a few moments looking down at her trousers, sniffing as the crying intensified.

'It's not looking good for you at the moment Cheryl, but you can help yourself if you're willing to tell us everything you know about Graham,' Rob said passing her a paper handkerchief to blow her nose and dry her eyes.

'I thought he loved me,' she started in a hoarse whisper. 'He was interested in me…' she trailed off.

'But you knew something wasn't right, didn't you? That's why you didn't agree to keep having sex in weirder and weirder places.' Nancy said gently.

Cheryl nodded, still crying, pushing the tattered paper handkerchief into her eyes trying to stem the flow.

'When?' Nancy asked. 'When was it you started to suspect there was something not right?'

Cheryl looked at her, head cocked to one side, thinking. 'At first, I thought it was exciting, the empty houses. I mean I knew we shouldn't, obviously Mr Andrews wouldn't have been happy. Have you told him?'

'We had to, he needed to know we were sending people round to look at them.' Rob said.

'Was he very angry?' Cheryl asked, almost childlike.

'Disappointed really.' Rob replied.

'Did something happen that made you feel uncomfortable in one of the houses?' Nancy asked.

'Yes.' Cheryl said quickly, her mouth opened as if she was going to add more information, but no words came out.

'What happened?' Nancy probed.

'Graham was behaving really strangely, it started when he saw one address on my list, he kept pestering me to take him there. Two or three times a day he would ask about it, eventually I took him.'

'What had made you feel differently about this house compared to the other places you'd taken him?' Nancy asked.

'It had belonged to an old man who died, all his furniture was in the place, it seemed…distasteful I suppose. Then when we did go there, it was like he was on a high at the thought of having sex on the old man's bed. And…' Cheryl was blushing, she had picked so violently at the skin around her thumb nail that a small trickle of blood had run down the well between finger and nail. '…the sex was different too, he was rough, tried to choke me, even after I kept telling him I wasn't into it. But it was like he couldn't hear me, almost as though I wasn't even human to him anymore and it scared me,' Cheryl said.

'You continued seeing him after that though, why?' Nancy asked.

'Afterwards I spoke to him about it and he said he was sorry, he'd been watching pornography and he was just trying out some of the things he'd seen.' Cheryl said.

It seemed like a half arsed response to Nancy, the sort she'd have expected to hear from a teenage boy, not a fully grown man who should be able to differentiate between the fiction of porn and the reality of a sexual relationship.

'Did you have sex there after that?' Nancy asked.

'A couple of times and it was nice, normal. I still didn't really like doing it on the old man's bed, we used the other rooms instead. I figured he'd just got carried away, but it stuck with me and then when he was talking about having sex on a grave, it made me think about how he'd been at that house and I was scared that if I said yes he'd be like that again.' Cheryl said.

'I need you to tell me which house that happened in,' Nancy said putting the list of empty houses in front of the woman.

'That one.' Cheryl pointed and Nancy took the paper back circling the address with her pen.

'Tell me about the towels you bought for Graham.' Nancy said.

'How did you know?'

Nancy said nothing.

'I didn't buy them for him, I bought a job lot of linens at auction, they can be good for backdrops and props, I was going to throw the towels out, they weren't any use to me and then Graham saw them and asked if he could have them, something about them being perfect for a project he was working on.'

'Thank you.' Nancy said. 'Now I need you to tell me about the suitcase.'

Cheryl sighed. 'I lent it to Graham a couple of weeks ago, he said he needed one to move some things about, it was just before we broke up and after that I used it as a reason to call him, asking for it back. But he wasn't interested in speaking to me.'

'Is there anything else you're not telling me?' Nancy asked.

'Nothing.' Cheryl responded.

'Good, as we speak, I have a team of people searching your house and I'd hate for them to uncover something you've kept from us.'

Cheryl began to cry again, the tears falling into the pattern of the make-up streaked lines on her face.

Chapter 39

The address that had got Graham Smyth so hot and bothered was on the Fife Coast between Burntisland and Aberdour. A beautiful glass fronted home, built it the seventies, that looked like it almost jutted out over the water. Nancy and Rob had left the rest of the team back at the station going through past owners of the property to see if they could shed any light on why Graham had been so excited by it.

Daniel had arrived a moment or two after them. 'Have you spoken to the occupants?' he asked.

'Yes,' Nancy replied. 'They're none too happy but they got the gist that it wasn't an optional situation. They've gone out for a drive, and have asked that we're careful of their belongings, they've not long moved in. The wife is pregnant so let's see if we can do this as respectfully as possible.'

Daniel nodded, simply glad that the conversation hadn't been left to him, any time he'd been asked to speak at conferences or events he'd been reminded that one of the benefits of working in forensics was not needing to interact with the general public. 'We'll start with the bathrooms and the kitchen, those were the key areas at the last two properties and then we'll spread out.'

'We'll wait out here, give us a shout if you find anything.' Nancy said. She sat perched on the bonnet of her car silently staring out over the water.

'We'll find her,' Rob said.

'We'd better, I don't think I could forgive myself otherwise.' Nancy replied.

Two hours later when Nancy and Rob had moved to sitting inside the car trying to stay warm and avoid the random short bursts of rain, Daniel re-emerged from the house and gave them a wave. Nancy shot out of the car so quickly she caught her foot on the lip of the door shut and almost fell on her face, grabbing at the door to steady herself she felt the twinge of a pull in her shoulder.

On any other day Rob would have used this as a moment to gently mock his boss, but not today. Instead, he hurried round to her side to make sure she was okay.

She brushed herself down annoyed by her own actions and marched off in the direction of the Forensics Site Manager, leaving Rob to catch her up.

'We have blood spatter,' Daniel said as soon as they were in earshot.

'Where?'

'One of the bedrooms, would you like to see?'

After stopping to cover themselves in a white suit so as not to leave any traces of themselves in the evidence, Nancy and Rob followed him through the house to the open bedroom door, the outside of which was adorned with wooden letters spelling out "Lilly". The walls were a pretty pastel pink, a white cot was now placed in the middle of the room next to a changing table.

'The baby's nursery!' Rob said. 'Fucking hell, that's not great.'

Nancy didn't respond, he'd only voiced the same thought they must all have had. The skirting board had been carefully removed from the wall, brown blood stains now exposed on the unpainted segment of the wall.

'You'll recognise the blood spatter there, I'd suggest that this room perhaps didn't have any skirting boards when the murder took place, these look like direct spatter as opposed to blood running behind the skirting.' Daniel said.

'Is it enough to get a sample?' Rob asked.

'Yes, we're going to continue searching, next stage is to take all the furniture out of the room, remove all the skirting to see if there's any other staining, that will allow me to approximate where in the room the victim was when they were killed.' Daniel continued. 'I would suggest contacting the family and letting them know they'll need to find some-where else to stay whilst we fully process the scene.'

'I'm expecting this to be Maria Fischer's blood,' Nancy said. 'Our killer took a heck of a risk though, if he killed her here and then transported her body to Edinburgh for disposal, his car must've been picked up on some CCTV.'

Their conversation was interrupted by a uniformed officer informing them that the couple had returned.

'Aren't you finished yet,' the pregnant woman asked.

She looked tired, no, something deeper than that, more visceral, exhausted. 'It's Mrs Roberts, is that right?' Nancy asked.

'Yes, I really want to get in and get the weight off, you understand, we've been gone for hours.' Mrs Roberts replied.

'I understand. I am really sorry to tell you that I can now confirm your home is a crime scene which means we won't be able to let you back inside for some time.' Nancy said as gently as she could muster.

'What the hell do you mean, a crime scene?' Mr Roberts said.

'I'm afraid I can't give you many details as this is part of an ongoing investigation, the only thing I can share is that during the time it lay empty prior to you moving in, access to this building was unlawfully obtained and a violent crime was committed here.' Nancy replied.

Mr Roberts went to open his mouth, but his wife got in before he could speak. 'Where?' She asked.

'What do you mean?' Nancy replied, she knew exactly what the woman was asking but if she could avoid telling this woman that someone had been murdered in her baby's nursery then she certainly intended to.

'In what room?' Mrs Roberts asked.

Nancy closed her eyes for a fleeting second preparing herself for the barrage of emotions this woman was likely to experience in the coming minutes. 'In the nursery.'

Mrs Roberts turned white and seemed to sway uncontrollably before vomiting in the garden, narrowly missing one of the uniformed officer's shoes. Her husband held on to her, pulling her upright and into him as her body vibrated with sobbing. Nancy waited for them to compose themselves.

'What are we supposed to do now, all our stuff is in there.' Mr Roberts spluttered.

'I will have one of my officers escort one of you into the house to collect anything you think you might need for the next couple of weeks. We will also need to take fingerprint and DNA samples from you both so that we have them to rule out of our investigations.' Nancy said.

Mr Roberts glared at her. 'This is my home, I'm not

being escorted around it.' He gave a slight stamp of his foot as he finished the statement.

'If you're not prepared to co-operate then I will not allow you back in the house at this time, I cannot have you compromising an active crime scene. I'm sorry I know this sounds harsh, but I'd like you to take a moment to consider how you'd feel if your actions were the reason that another family didn't get justice for their relative.'

He humphed but conceded. 'Alright, but it's late, the DNA stuff will need to wait.'

'That's okay you can come in to the station at some point tomorrow and we can get them done there, it won't take long and it is completely unobtrusive. Do you have any family you can stay with in the meantime?'

'My sister is just in Dunfermline, she'll take us in.' Mr Roberts confirmed.

'If you prefer I can have someone drive your wife over to your sisters now, and you can follow up once you've collected some things?' Nancy suggested.

'No, I'm staying here, I don't want to go by myself.' Mrs Roberts said.

After a little persuading they managed to get her to sit in the back of her car and wait whilst her husband collected their belongings.

'Can't say I blame them being upset,' Rob said watching the car drive away from the house. 'Not sure I'd want to have my baby sleeping in a room I knew someone died in.'

'People die in houses all the time, I bet there's loads of people living in homes where one of the previous occupants died somewhere in the building.' Nancy said.

'There's a big difference between dying peacefully in your sleep and being stabbed to death though isn't there.' Rob replied.

'I suppose,' Nancy said as she lifted her mobile phone to her ear.

Rob frowned at her in confusion.

'Hi Mr Andrews, it's Detective Inspector Ravenscroft here, I need to know what happened to the furniture that was in the Burntisland property when it was sold?'

'A house clearance company took it away,' Mr Andrews said. 'You know I've already had Mr Roberts on the phone threatening to sue me for not disclosing their new home was a crime scene.'

'You can't be held responsible for that, we only just found out today so it's not like you had the information to disclose. What was the name of the company please.' Nancy said.

There was a moment of quiet whilst she listened to the clacking of a keyboard as the man checked his records. 'It was Williams and Son, do you want their contact details?'

'Yes please,' Nancy scrawled the address and telephone number into her notebook 'And can you send me over the sales brochure for the property as well please.' Nancy asked not waiting for the man to confirm that he would before finishing the call.

'What was that about?' Rob asked.

'We know that this house was furnished when Graham and Cheryl came here, and with there being blood splatter on the walls behind the skirting boards that makes me think he killed her on the floor, so surely the furniture would have got spattered as well so I want to check what it looked like in the sales brochure so we know what furniture might have been affected.' Nancy explained.

Nancy checked her emails, opening the one from the estate agent immediately. She clicked on the link to the sales particulars and began scrolling through the photographs. 'Bloody typical' she muttered.

'What is it?' Rob asked.

'It was the one room in the house with no furniture, it must've been some sort of storage room, there's a stack of boxes at one side. No carpet in there either.'

'We should check when Cheryl took these photos, if it was after she'd taken Graham there then he might've taken the flooring away with him, used it to wrap Maria up in, perhaps.' Rob said.

Chapter 40

It had been almost twenty-four hours since anyone had last seen Grace. If this were a TV show someone would have already said 'the first twenty-four hours are the most important.' At least she knew that wasn't true, not normally anyway. But in this case who knew. This morning she'd promised herself she wouldn't go to sleep tonight until she had Grace home safe and sound and now, she was facing the reality that she would have to.

Her phone buzzed, it was Professor Laing. Nancy had already ignored five calls from him, whilst she'd been driving around following up leads, trying desperately to find her officer.

'Hi Ewan, sorry it's been a bit of a day,' Nancy said answering the phone and finding that it had been on the tip of her tongue to tell him everything.

'Not a problem, sorry to keep calling you, it's just that I've had a look through all of the documents that you sent over and I can confirm that in my professional opinion, the Graham that messages with Diane, the Graham who talks to Cheryl, the User ID Omnipotent and the person that called themselves SusieV are one and the same. There's very specific sentence structuring that's used as well as interesting grammar formations.' He said.

'You're sure?'

'I'd be happy to stand up in court and confirm it. You should know it looks like the person has tried to change the way they speak or type, which gives me the impression that they are linguistically aware, but they're not as skilled as I think they think they are.' Ewan continued.

'Thank you so much, that helps tie everything together, just a shame linguistics can't tell me where to find him.' Nancy said trying to add some lightness to the conversation to mask her true feelings.

'Actually, maybe not where he is right now, but where he's been, that I can tell you something about.' Ewan said.

Nancy had only been jesting when she'd said it, now the professor had her full attention, 'what do you mean?'

'Linguistics allows us to compare how people use language against all of the data that's ever been collected, so regional accents, slang, that kind of thing, it can help age a person as well as give cultural or geographical pointers.' he explained.

'And what does the way this person communicates tell you?'

'I would say someone in their late thirties, early forties, there are words that adults that went to school in the nineties use more prevalently than other groups. He went to school locally, but he's spent some time out of the country, likely the USA, there's a couple of Americanised spellings in the things he says, I'd say as an adult though, not someone who went through his formative education in the states.' Ewan finished.

'And you can get all of that from those chats?' Nancy asked, impressed.

'Yep, linguistics is like magic, only better. Anyway, I know you're busy so I'll send over a detailed report so you can read through it yourself, but call if you need any further explanation, or pop up for a coffee if you'd prefer to do it in person.' he said.

'Thanks,' Nancy said before hanging up. If only she had a suspect to match to information that the professor had provided but she hadn't even got that. And soon the Chief Super would be breathing down all their necks.

Nancy might've sat at her desk torturing her brain trying to summon the identity of the killer for another few minutes if she hadn't been interrupted by Rob flinging the door open.

'We've found Grace, get your coat, she's on the way to the hospital, but she's still alive,' he gasped.

Nancy grabbed her jacket as she followed her sergeant through the office almost colliding with Cal as she went. Taking the steps two at a time, Rob was already nearing the bottom of the flight. She was catching her breath as she finally caught up to him in the carpark.

'Where…where was she found?' Nancy panted.

'In the back seat of her own car in the carpark down the road from Burns Night.' Rob said getting into his car and turning the key before he was properly seated.

'Who found her?' Nancy asked.

'You remember Natalie, the Australian Angle Grinder?' Rob asked.

Nancy nodded.

'She was parking for her evening shift, and by luck she parked next to Grace's car. She only noticed because she dropped her change for the meter and put her phone torch on, accidentally shining it into the back of the car and saw Grace collapsed on the backseat.' Rob said.

'Did she call 999?'

'Yeah, she called for an ambulance. After they left she called me, she had my card from when we met with her. Said she thought I might want to know, because it was so close to the club, she thought it might be connected. I managed to get hold of the uniformed officers who attended, and they confirmed it was Grace's car, they were just about to put a call in to let you know.' Rob said.

'Is it definitely her?'

'Warrant card, wallet, everything on her, and intact apparently.' Rob confirmed. He pulled into the carpark of the Victoria Hospital Kirkcaldy having made the twenty-five minute journey in a slightly terrifying fifteen minutes.

This time it was Nancy's turn to leave her colleague behind as she slammed the passenger door closed and ran across the road to the automatic doors. The hospital, bright white and illuminated by high efficiency strip lighting, felt almost uncomfortable to her eyes as she approached the nurse's desk in the A&E department. She had her warrant card out of her pocket before either of the nurses had a chance to speak.

'Grace Abbotts, Detective Constable Grace Abbotts, she was just brought in by ambulance, where is she and who is treating her? I need to know her condition immediately.' Nancy said.

Rob was now standing behind her, happy to let his boss take charge.

'She's in a private ward being examined, I'll take you to her,' one of the nurses said, making the good call that giving Nancy a series of left, right and through double doors style directions would not do in this circumstance.

The door to the room was closed with two plastic seats strategically placed against the wall for them to sit and wait.

'Can we go in?' Nancy asked, even though she had half a mind to barge in regardless.

'Let me speak to the doctor.' The nurse replied.

After a painfully long two minutes she reappeared from the room, 'the doctor says she's making sure Grace is stable and then she'll come out and speak to you, after that you'll be able to look in on your friend, but she won't be able to answer any questions this evening.' The nurse said.

Nancy sat down, she wanted to pace the length of the corridor. There were other patients in A&E, ones who didn't have their own room, instead had a curtain that barely gave them privacy. Many of them alone, probably frightened and definitely didn't need an agitated Nancy disturbing what little rest they were getting by pacing anxiously around.

Rob stood for a little longer before giving in and sitting down next to her, despite the chairs being designed for adults they still made Rob feel like he was back in high school, where he'd learnt just how far you could pivot on the back legs before you would topple and fall, not a skill that any of his teachers fully appreciated.

Neither of them spoke. Nancy leant her head back against the smooth concrete wall and closed her eyes letting the quiet hum of efficiency drift through her ears, interrupted randomly by a barking cough and a crying child.

Eventually the door to the room opened and the doctor emerged. 'You must be Grace's colleagues,' she said.

Nancy stood up offering out her hand, 'Detective Inspector Nancy Ravenscroft,' she said, her outstretched hand ignored.

'Sorry we don't do that anymore, not since Covid,' the

doctor said, clearly feeling a little awkward with the situation.

Nancy retracted her arm quickly, 'Of course, no problem. How is Grace?'

'Let me take you somewhere private to talk,' she said leading them to the room adjacent to Grace's. 'Thank you, in the circumstances I thought this would be more appropriate. I'm Doctor Wallis. Firstly, let me assure you that Grace is going to be alright, it looks like she's been through quite an ordeal, but given time and rest she'll recover, physically at least.'

Nancy wasn't ready to relax yet, Grace might be safe now, but she was dreading finding out what had been done to her. 'What can you tell me about her condition?' Nancy asked.

'She's been drugged, repeatedly by the looks of things.' Dr Wallis said.

'Drugged how?' Rob asked.

'Injected, looks like it's street grade heroin. I'm running some tests to see if there's anything else in her system.' Dr Wallis replied. 'And to test for any diseases that she might have contracted from the needle.

Nancy had done a stint in the drugs team, she knew how nasty heroin could be, then there was the risk of the needle that had been used, that sick bastard might have got off on using a dirty needle. The thought caused Nancy's stomach to contract, forcing bile into her throat causing her to cough from the burning sensation.

'What about any other injuries?' Nancy asked swallowing back the acrid yellow liquid.

'She's been restrained, I don't think she's been conscious long enough to struggle, but the restraints were tight enough they left a mark anyway. Some sort of nylon rope, there were some red and yellow fibres in her skin, I've extracted them. I assumed you'd want them sent over to your people?' Dr Wallis asked.

'Please,' Nancy said. 'Any sign of sexual assault?'

'No, we've taken swabs of course, but there's no vaginal or anal tears or bruising, no bruising on the inner thigh area. I'm confident she wasn't raped. She has however been physically assaulted, she has a nasty burn mark on her stomach. It's not very big, probably inflicted in the last six hours, looks like it was caused by a hot metal…'

'Does it look like a two tailed fish?' Nancy interrupted.

'A bit, it's not easy to make out. I was about to explain that it's become infected. We've started a course of antibiotics via IV,' the doctor paused. 'It is nasty, and I've seen this type of thing before, if the antibiotics don't kick in we'll be looking at doing a skin graft.'

'Christ.' Rob said.

'It sounds worse than it is, for now our focus is on beating the infection and helping Grace detox off the heroin.' Dr Wallis said.

'Do you think she'll have any trouble detoxing?' Nancy asked tentatively.

'By the time we discharge her she will be fully detoxed, whilst being drugged this way over longer periods of time can lead to dependency in the victim I would expect that Grace will not experience that kind of withdrawal. Although she's been given more than one injection, because it's been administered over such a short time frame her experience should be more akin to someone who's had to have morphine after an operation.' Dr Wallis replied.

'That's great news, thank you.' Nancy said. 'Can I check that you've kept her clothes?'

'Of course, they're bagged for you.' Dr Wallis confirmed.

'When can we see her?' Rob asked.

'I'll take you over so you can see for yourself she's okay.' Dr Wallis said.

'I'm going to have a couple of officers stay outside the room whilst she's here.' Nancy said.

'Of course, I understand.' Dr Wallis led them back into the corridor and through the door to where Grace lay in bed hooked up to a drip and a machine that let everyone know she was still breathing.

She looked peaceful, Nancy watched the young woman's chest rise and fall rhythmically. Tears pricking in the corner of her eyes, she blinked them away. Grace was alive and she was the best hope they had of finally catching the bastard that did this to her.

So caught up in her own thoughts Nancy hadn't noticed Rob walk round the side of the bed and gently stroke Grace's hair away from her eyes. His hand lingered against hers for a moment as he willed her back to full health. In the last twenty-four hours he'd been haunted by the need to tell her he was sorry how things ended between them. That he was, as she described, a bit of a bellend for letting her go and that if he could, he would change that. For now, he would be content that she was alive and safe.

Chapter 41

Nancy had been so fixated on finding Grace that she hadn't thought to check that the car she'd been found in was with Daniel and being thoroughly examined. Luckily the rest of her team had taken the reins and begun getting CCTV for in and around the carpark, forensics organised and had downloaded all the data from Grace's phone, to scroll through everything.

Now, sitting in DCI Cooper's office, the Chief Superintendent stood next to him, she felt small in comparison to the two men. Despite Cooper being considerably the larger man, the imposing nature of the Chief Superintendent made him feel like he took up the most space in the room.

'How long until you'll be able to interview DC Abbott?' The Chief Super asked.

'The doctor says it'll potentially be a couple of days before she's in a condition that she'll be able to talk to us.' Nancy responded.

'And you have someone positioned outside her room?'

'Yes 24/7. Dr Wallis has my mobile number and will call as soon as I can talk to Grace.' Nancy replied.

'We're confident that she was taken by our killer?' The question now directed to Cooper.

'Yes, the branding mark on her body is the same as the others. We're very relieved that she's going to be okay.' Cooper said.

'Of course, that's very important, but finding her hasn't brought you any closer to discovering the identity of a serial killer that is not only putting the public at risk but is making a mockery out of our ability to catch him. This needs to end, do you understand me.' The Chief Super looked at them both and then left the office.

'Are you alright?' Cooper asked.

'I'm fine,' Nancy said batting the question away.

'I've been in your shoes, thinking you're going to lose one of your team, it's never a good feeling. You'll catch this guy, I have confidence in you.'

'Thanks.' Nancy left her boss' office and returned to her team to give them the official update on Grace, although she was sure that news of her recovery was already around the building, let alone her team.

'Do we have any update from Daniel on Grace's car, anything that might give us any idea where he might keep his victims for the week before he murders them?' Nancy asked Rob.

'Nothing yet.' He replied, 'why do you think he let Grace go?'

'Because to him it's a game, he's messing with us, showing us how superior he is to us that he can take a detective from right under our noses.' Nancy replied.

'But he could have kept her and killed her like all the

rest.' Rob said. 'After all, to complete the crime he needs a policewoman.'

'But none of his victims have actually matched the original crime, and that's what's always bothered me about calling this a copycat killing. I've worked on copycat cases before, the perps are usually meticulous in selecting their victims in the same way as the original, they try to replicate all the known details. Our guy just barely stays within the parameters of the original crime.' Nancy said.

'Except when it comes to how he disposes of the bodies, that's been a lot more accurate, especially when you factor in that we're in a different country, and the original was almost 50 years ago.' Rob replied.

'I guess we can ask him when we find him,' Nancy said.

A uniformed officer appeared in the peripheral of her vision, standing on the edge of the investigation looking like he wasn't sure how far into the group of people he was permitted. Nancy waited to see what he was going to do.

He cleared his throat. 'I'm looking for DI Ravenscroft.'

'That's me,' Nancy walked towards him. 'What can I help you with?'

'I'm working on the hotline, and I got a call in. Sergeant West said I needed to come up and let you know.'

'Follow me,' Nancy said walking towards her office where she could shut the door and give him her full attention. As they passed Rob, she tilted her head indicating that he should come with them.

'Okay the floor is yours' Nancy said.

'I just took a call from the council, from their Civil Enforcement Office, one of their Traffic Wardens hasn't turned up for her shift, they called her mobile and got no answer and her emergency contact, her husband, he said she left for work at the normal time.'

Nancy and Rob exchanged looks.

'What's this woman's name?' Nancy asked.

'Destiny Popoola, she lives in Duloch, with her husband and their two children. She's been working as a Traffic Warden for the last four years, her boss said she's one of the most reliable people on his team that's why he worried when she didn't arrive for her shift cos it was so out of character,' the PC continued.

'Where would she have usually started her shift?' Nancy asked.

'Viewfield Terrace Carpark,' the PC answered.

The same carpark that Grace had been discovered in. 'Thank you, can you email me across your call and anything else you have found out.' Nancy asked.

The PC nodded and then took his cue to leave.

'I'm guessing Destiny isn't going to be so lucky as to be discovered unconscious in her car tomorrow.' Rob said.

Chapter 42

'Boss have you got a minute?' Cal asked as he stood tentatively in Nancy's doorway.

Nancy looked at her watch, she'd arranged to drive over to meet Lucas and Kayleigh, there had been some more commentary come through on the podcast forum they thought she might be interested in.

'Yeah, shoot.'

'I've been going through everything we have trying to see if anything gives us any indication as to where he might be keeping his victims before he kills them.'

'Uh-huh,'

'When I was reading through Cheryl's statement, she said she first met Graham when he approached her and asked about her doing some photos for his website. He told her that he had log cabins that he rented out. And I was thinking in the original case in the states there was a log cabin in the woods, what if our killer did the same thing.' Cal said.

'Which might be helpful if we had any idea where they were.' Nancy said.

'I thought about that too, and I started putting together a list of all the log cabins in a 50-mile radius, it's loads, but if you wanted, I can start going through them.' Cal replied.

Nancy pursed her lips thinking, it would be a lot of manpower hours to go through the hundreds of log cabins.

Cal continued 'My thinking was that a lot of them will be owned by limited companies like the ones in large parks, which would be unlikely to be suitable for holding someone or for moving them when the time comes. But if I focus on anywhere there are cabins by themselves or small clusters, Cheryl said he had three, then I might be able to use CCTV from around the areas to see if anyone comes and goes at the times that we know correspond with Owen's body being dumped.'

'Okay, but that's not a job for just one person, create a team of four, organise it however you want and let me know if you find anything you think might be suspicious,' Nancy said.

'I'm away to meet up with the podcast people again,' Nancy said to Rob as she passed him.

'Want me to come?' He asked.

'No, I'll not be long.'

'What happened to no-one is to go anywhere alone?' Rob asked.

'Given the developments in this case and the disappearance of Destiny Popoola I don't think we're at any risk anymore, and besides I'm going to pick up some print outs, I think I'll manage.' Nancy smiled.

'Alright, by the way the e-fit person has turned up, we're getting her set up with Cheryl just now, hopefully by the time you get back we'll have a face for this scumbag.'

Kayleigh and Lucas recorded their podcast from a custom-made summerhouse in Lucas' back garden. The exterior of the cabin was clad in oak horizontal boards, Lucas opened the door and invited Nancy in. The interior was brighter than she'd expected given that there were no windows for natural light. Looking up at the ceiling she realised that there were several small Velux windows in each of the eight slanted panels.

'It's good for the acoustics,' Lucas said watching her.

'I see.' Nancy looked around the room. One wall had a black deck of recording equipment, next to that were two chairs and a microphone. 'I take it this is where you do the chat for your podcast.'

'Yeah, we record and edit in here, it's really convenient to have a custom made space, we've got it insulated so that outside noise doesn't impact our recordings, Kayleigh often jokes that we could literally murder someone in here and no one would hear us.'

Nancy gave him a flat look.

'Sorry, inappropriate in the current circumstances, I wasn't thinking.' Lucas said.

'This looks like it would have been expensive.' Nancy said.

'I suppose it depends on what you call expensive.' Lucas replied smiling.

'You were able to pay for this with money you made from the podcast, explain how that works again?' Nancy asked.

'We have sponsors, different companies, their sponsorship money we use for the production of the podcast...'

'I thought you did that yourself?' Nancy interrupted.

'I do, but it pays for my time to do that and our research time, then in addition to the free podcast we have a member's only area, which includes access to the forum, our social media groups and we put out member only content once a month, it cost £9.99 a month and we have a decent amount of paid subscribers now, so it all adds up.' Lucas said.

'Very nice, you said you had additional transcripts from the forum that you thought might be useful.' Nancy said.

'Yes, I do, did the last ones prove useful?' Lucas asked.

'They have certainly helped to paint a picture of the type of person we're dealing with.' Nancy replied.

'You think your killer might be amongst our listeners?' Lucas questioned.

'It's hard to say, you told me that the conversations happened on your open forum so they could be anyone who stumbled across it and wanted to get involved in the conversations.' Nancy replied.

'I've been re-reading the conversations we gave to you, as I said before both Kayleigh and I have a real interest in linguistics.'

'Where is Kayleigh, I thought you were both going to be here.' Nancy asked.

'She called and said she'd got tied up with something, she can be a bit like that when she's researching a case, you know, goes off the grid.' Lucas said.

'Can't say I'd be overly amused if my partner randomly went incommunicado.' Nancy said.

'Oh, I'm used to it now, we all have our processes, every now and then she disappears for a few days and then when she reappears she's all full of energy and ideas. I guess some people really need their own company to recharge.' Lucas said.

'Has she always been like that?' Nancy asked.

'I think so, maybe a bit more now the show has got

more popular, anyway let me get you the transcripts, they're in the house, would you like a coffee?'

Nancy agreed that she would, the exhaustion of the last couple of days had been creeping up on her and in the warmth of the insulated studio she'd begun to feel like she could fall asleep on her feet. It was a relief to get out into the open air of the back garden, even with the wind blowing spots of rain into her face.

'You never thought about having the studio in your house, save you a rainy commute?' Nancy asked as Lucas slid open the bi-folding doors that led directly into the kitchen.

'We did think about it, I have enough room here, but Kayleigh likes to come and do work sometimes and this way she can let herself in and work away without having to disturb me or think about what I might be doing, I still do some lecturing and I have my study where I do that, it's all online. I teach courses in a couple of colleges in America so I can be working at strange times of the day. Kayleigh and I did a circuit of lectures around a few colleges last year, we were very popular and from that I managed to get a couple of lecturing gigs. It's quite an honour to have been asked, for a time it created a bit of a rift between Kayleigh and me. She became quite jealous of the attention I was receiving.' Lucas smiled as he watched the coffee drip through the filter of the percolator.

Not quite up to the professor's standards, but still head and shoulders above the machine in the station, Nancy thought.

'I can imagine that was tough, but you're through it now?' Nancy asked keen to stop Lucas going off on some random tangent. She had hoped to be in and out in no time, leaving her the option of dropping past the professor's house on the way back to the station. Instead, she was standing in Lucas' spotlessly clean kitchen listening to him harp on about his own importance all for the promise of a coffee and some transcripts.

'Of course,' Lucas poured the black coffee into two mugs. 'I only have oat milk, is that okay?'

'I'll take mine black,' Nancy responded, taking the mug from him.

'Okay, lets head through to the living room and I'll get those transcripts for you.' Lucas led the way out of the kitchen, through a short hallway and into the next room.

Another spotlessly clean space. Nancy wondered how anyone could use this space and keep it so tidy, she was about to take a seat on the cream leather sofa when she noticed it was covered by clear plastic.

Lucas put his mug down on a round cork coaster and walked across to a teak unit on the other side of the room. He pulled down a hatch that revealed a drinks cabinet, much larger than it looked from the outside. Nancy's eyes wandered across the row of alcohol, some of which were brands she'd never heard of. Off to the side next to a crystal decanter and matching glasses there was an ice bucket. Wooden on the outside and metal on the inside.

Cold darted through Nancy's veins when she saw the metal length of an ice pick peeking out from beside the bucket, then for a moment she locked eyes with Lucas.

Chapter 43

'Are you admiring my collection,' Lucas asked, not seeming to be at all perturbed. 'I'd offer you a drink, but you're on duty,' he smiled. 'I always find it odd when you watch police dramas on television, the amount of lead detectives that say, one won't hurt, or just half a pint,' he continued.

'Well, that's fiction, and I definitely don't drink on duty,' Nancy replied.

'That's good to know,' he smiled. 'But honestly most of the contents aren't even mine,' he paused to look at her. 'I mean the alcohol sure, it's a bit of a niche thing I'm into, I look for interesting brands of liquor and then invest in it, most of it hasn't ever been opened, but it looks good.'

'I thought I didn't recognise some of them.' Nancy replied.

'But the glasses and the bucket and this,' Lucas picked up the ice pick by its antler handle, 'they're not really me. I'm looking after this for Kayleigh, she inherited it when one of her grandparents died, her place is tiny, so she asked me to take care of it for her, as I've got all this room.' Lucas continued.

Nancy struggled to control the shiver that ran up her spine, she took a final drink of coffee, 'That was good of you, I'll put this back in the kitchen,' she said raising the mug slightly, she moved away taking care never to have her back to Lucas.

Lucas joined her in the kitchen, 'I've got the papers you came for,' he said handing her an A4 sized envelope.

'Thank you.' Nancy took them from him, her heart rate quickening. 'Well, thanks for the coffee, I'd better be going.'

'Swing by anytime, I'd love to have the opportunity to really get into the guts of some criminal investigations with you.'

Nancy smiled a polite non comital smile.

'And of course, I hope you get your guy…or gal, and the streets are safe for us all again.'

'Oh, I will, have no doubt.' Nancy said before exiting out of the kitchen door into the garden and round the side of the house.

Back in her car she took a couple of deep breaths, was he taunting her, letting her know that he was the killer, and she was alone and unsafe with him or had he just been his usual obnoxious self and inadvertently revealed his co-host as a murderer. Nancy wasn't going to wait here to find out.

Nancy clicked on Rob's name in her phone directory as she drove away. 'Hey do me a favour,' she said before he had the chance to speak. 'I need you to find Kayleigh McGuire, she was supposed to be meeting with me today as well, but when I arrived it was only Lucas, he said that Kayleigh has been AWOL for a couple of days.'

'You alright boss?' Rob asked seemingly ignoring the previous request. 'You sound stressed.'

'I think the murder weapon is in Lucas Martin's house, he had an ice pick in his drinks cabinet, he was showing it to me.' Nancy said.

'I'm sure plenty of people have one…'

'No they don't, no one else connected to this case has one. In fact, I didn't even know people had ice picks for crushing up ice for drinks, that's why they invented ice cube trays.' Nancy said.

'I told you I should've come with you, if this bloke is involved you put yourself in real danger.' Rob said.

'I'm fine, so no harm done, and I don't know if it is him – other than hosting a True Crime podcast there's not another single strand of evidence that connects him to any of our victims.' Nancy said.

'Maybe we need to look into him harder then.' Rob said.

'Get Cal on it, pull him off the log cabin thing and make this his priority. In fact get him to look into both of them and get uniform up at Kayleigh's place in Dundee, if Lucas is telling the truth and he hasn't heard from her in a couple of days then something might be up. But tell them to be cautious because she could just as easily be the killer, don't go ruling her out because she's a she.' Nancy said.

'You're coming straight back to the station, right?' Rob asked.

'Yes.' Nancy sighed. She could drop the additional transcripts off at the professor's house another time and if she was being honest with herself, she wanted to be back inside the confines of the station again.

Rob was at the main desk when Nancy returned to the station, she frowned, 'are you waiting for me?'

'Don't flatter yourself boss,' Rob smiled. 'I'm just down talking to the officers that went to Kayleigh's house. There's no sign of her there, looks like her place has been trashed, could be a break-in, there were signs of a struggle though, some pictures knocked off the walls and a couple of bloody handprint smears. I've got a forensic team going out there now.'

'Good, hopefully we'll know more soon' Nancy said. 'I'll see you upstairs,' she headed up the stairs whilst opening her phone contacts and calling the professor.

It rang for so long she was expecting it to click onto voicemail, so it took her a moment to realise that it had actually been answered.

'Nancy, are you okay?' Ewan asked.

'Yes, I need your help, I want to email over a document for you to check against the conversations you've looked at for me, I need to know if they could be written by the same person.' Nancy replied.

'You have a suspect,' he said. 'Don't worry I know you can't tell me, if you email it across, I'll clear my schedule for the day and make it my top priority.'

'Thank you, I'll send it as soon as I can,' Nancy said hanging up and hoping he would understand that she was busy not rude.

As she burst into the open plan office, for a second everyone seemed to pause what they were doing to look at her. 'Cal, my office please, she called over the noise of people working.'

Cal sprung up and weaved his way through his colleagues and their desk chairs.

'You want the information I've been able to dig up on Lucas Martin,' Cal said as Nancy took off her jacket, flinging it into the corner of the room.

'I do but give me a minute to send this email,' Nancy said as she went onto the internet and downloaded a paper written by Lucas on criminology throughout the ages to send to the professor. 'Right go for it what have you got?'

'Okay, born in Dunfermline as Lucas Millar, 39, lived in Scotland all his childhood, his parents separated when he was in his early teens, his dad, Graham was American, Lucas later went to live with him to go to college, he continued to live in the states until five years ago when he came back to Fife.' Cal said.

'Why did he come back?' Nancy asked.

'His mother was dying, he inherited her house, that's the address he lives in today.' Cal said.

'A bit different from the story he told us, he conveniently left out the part about growing up here,' Nancy said.

'After I discovered that he'd changed his surname it was easy to start digging into his past, I think the thing you'll find most interesting is the address where Maria Fisher was murdered...' Cal paused for dramatic affect. '...that house was where Lucas lived with his mum after his parents divorced, and assuming he went to the catchment area school, I'm still checking those records, he would likely have been taught by Donald Stark.'

Chapter 44

'Listen up people,' Nancy said to the team as they gathered for the morning meeting. 'We got some key pieces of evidence yesterday. This is the e-fit that was created by working with Cheryl Wilson, who for the time being has been released pending the Procurator Fiscal's decision whether to charge. She knows him as Graham Smyth. This is a photograph of Lucas Martin and I'm sure you can all see the likeness.' She went on to recap the information Cal had shared with her the previous evening.

'Are we bringing him in for questioning?' One of the uniformed officers asked.

'As we speak, a team have gone out to his home address to arrest him and bring him back to the station. Following that we'll have a search and a forensics team will comb through every single inch of his home and studio.' Nancy replied.

'Do you think that's where he keeps his victims?' Isla asked.

'Honestly I think it's unlikely, I was at his house

yesterday and I couldn't see anywhere that would be suitable for keeping someone locked up for days. It would be great if it was as we might then have the chance of saving Destiny Popoola.' Nancy replied, she turned to face Rob.

'Points of action for today,' Rob said standing and joining Nancy in the front of the room. 'Kayleigh McGuire, the co-host of the true crime podcast is missing and possibly hurt, we are canvasing her neighbours to see if we can get a timeline for her disappearance. We are scouring CCTV to see if we can get any further details on the disappearance of Destiny Popoola, we are on the lookout for any vehicles that pop up near all of our deposition sites. Please check the board for the assignments you will be working on and continue to check in throughout the day as these are obviously subject to change.' Rob paused to look around the room for his colleagues collective understanding. 'Isla and I will be visiting Grace in hospital today to take her statement, which we will feed into the case database. It is imperative that you update the database with any and all information and evidence that you uncover.' Rob said as he finished up.

Nancy dispersed the group to their various tasks and made her way to her office and sat down at her desk. Rob followed her sitting in the chair opposite.

'You sure you don't want me to stay and help with the interview?' He asked.

'No, the Chief Super was pretty insistent that DCI Cooper was in on the interview, understandable really, did you see the headlines this morning?' Nancy asked.

'Can't really miss them, not exactly complimentary towards our efforts in this case to date.' Rob replied.

'As far the papers and the public are concerned, we let 3

people die and one further person get kidnapped.' Nancy said.

'Yeah, with no consideration that all three people were dead before we knew they were in danger,' Rob replied with his arms folded.

'They were all reported missing, and we're being punished for the fact that the investigation into Maria's death was an absolute shambles of victim blaming.' Nancy said.

'Make that an international shambles,' Rob said before preparing to leave. 'I'll give Grace your love.'

'Thanks, tell her I'll pop in and see her soon, and don't forget to take a copy of the e-fit and the photograph. As Graham Smyth, he presented in a different way and after all she's been through, she might recognise that version of him better.'

'Will do boss.' Rob said.

'Thanks and let me know if you discover anything pertinent to my interview of Lucas,' Nancy said as Rob headed off to find Isla and go to the hospital.

Nancy swallowed down the remains of her mug of coffee, grimacing slightly at the realisation that it was now unpleasantly cold.

Sergeant West knocked on her door, 'Lucas Martin is in interview room three.'

'Thanks, any issues bringing him in?' Nancy asked.

'He was indignant at our audacity. Struggled during the arrest, was quite verbally abusive to my officers as they handcuffed him, but other than that all good. He's been read his rights and he's not asked for a lawyer yet.'

'Great thanks, does Cooper know?'

'He was passing through booking when he was brought in, so yes.' Sergeant West confirmed.

'Grand, I'll be down in a moment.' Nancy said.

She made her way down the corridor to meet her boss before starting the first of what Nancy suspected would be many interviews with Lucas Martin.

'Are you ready for this?' Cooper asked as they made their way to interview room three.

'Can't wait.' Nancy replied

As soon as she entered the room Lucas stood up angrily, 'What the hell is this all about, I welcomed you into my home just yesterday and then this morning you have your thugs come and handcuff me and drag me here like some dirty criminal.'

'Sit down Mr Martin' Nancy said ignoring his tirade. She clicked the recording on and noted that she and the DCI were in the room. 'You've been made aware you can ask for a solicitor?' She asked.

'I don't need a solicitor, I haven't done anything wrong.'

'If you change your mind, you can let me know.' Nancy continued. 'Tell me about your relationship with Cheryl Wilson.'

'I don't know anyone by that name,' he said leaning back in the chair, calm now, almost smug.

'When we first met you told me you were American, in fact everything I can find out about you online suggests you're American.'

'Because I am.'

'Except you're not, you were born in the UK, just down the road in Dunfermline Maternity hospital, to a Scottish mother and an American father.' Nancy said.

'I have dual nationality.' Lucas replied.

'Why hide the fact you were born here?' Nancy asked.

'I went to the US to be with my dad when I went to college, and it always felt more like home.'

'Then why come back?' Nancy asked.

'I had the opportunity to take part in a criminology programme of events that Dundee University were running and whilst I was over, I met Kayleigh, we became friends and when she suggested the podcast it was too good an opportunity to turn down.' Lucas replied.

'I see, I thought it was because your mother died and you came to sort out her affairs, that's who you inherited the house from isn't it?'

'Why are you even bothering to ask me these questions if you've already got the answers by snooping into my life.'

'It's not snooping, it's investigating. Why bother lying when the truth is so easy to uncover.' Nancy said.

'You've no business talking about my mother, leave her out of it.' Lucas said.

'I wasn't asking you about her, but seeing as you've brought her up let's talk about her, did you two get along?'

'No comment.'

'Did you have a difficult childhood after your father left?'

'Is this the part where you psychoanalyse me,' he laughed. 'Suggest that coming from a broken home messed me up in the head, you need to try harder than that.' He crossed his right leg over his left propping the heel of his right foot on his left knee.

'Do you get off on pretending to be someone you're not, seeing if you can trick people into believing you're whatever made up persona you've created,' Nancy asked.

He frowned, 'I've no idea what you're talking about.'

Nancy laid out the transcripts in front of him, 'when you gave me these, I bet you got a little thrill knowing that you were the author of all of them.'

'Why would I need to pretend to be someone else to comment on my own show's forum?' Lucas scoffed.

'I think you enjoyed the deception of it, and I think you used it as leverage. You got Diane Bridlington to tell you all about how disappointed she was in her brother whilst pretending to be another woman, then when she started to suspect something was off, you changed tack and created a new persona.' Nancy said.

Lucas looked at her shaking his head.

'Then when Diane realised she'd been manipulated into offering her brother up as one of your victims you threatened her and her children, made her believe that she would be considered culpable for her brother's murder.'

'This is all an interesting theory, but all you've said here is these random bits of correspondence were written by the same person,' Lucas pushed the papers across the table away from him.

'This morning I had a linguistics expert look at all of these and compare them next to this paper that you wrote and had published, he has confirmed that they were all penned by the same author.' Nancy said.

'What expert?' Lucas asked, the veneer of his confidence slipping ever so slightly.

'Professor Laing, recognised internationally as a leading academic in his field, he has assisted with a number of criminal prosecutions and has lectured across the world.' Nancy smiled.

'He's made a mistake then.' Lucas insisted.

'I doubt that,' Nancy continue, 'and what's really interesting is that it links these fake user IDs on your forum with these text and email conversations between Graham Smyth and Cheryl Wilson. So I'll take you back to my original question, tell me about your relationship with Cheryl.'

Lucas said nothing for a few moments. Nancy waited in silence and just as he had opened his mouth there was a faint knock on the door and Cal's face appeared in the small crack.

Nancy grimaced, it couldn't have been worse timing. She narrowed her eyes and glared at Cal, he didn't flinch. She scraped her chair back whilst Cooper announced to the recording that she was leaving the room.

Outside in the corridor Nancy spoke in an angry half whisper, 'this had better be important.'

'It is, I've been digging into Lucas' past like you asked, trying to see if there are any links to any of the victims, especially Donald Stark. Anyway I found a guidance teacher that was at the school at the same time he was there, she's retired now, and I think she was enjoying someone being interested in what she had to say.'

Nancy raised her eyebrows willing him to get to the point.

'I asked her if she remembered anything unusual about the time that Lucas was at school, what he was like as a pupil and that's when she told me about the scandal.' Cal said.

'What scandal?'

'Donald Stark and Morag Ellis, Lucas' mother, were caught having relations in the supply cupboard, the head-teacher walked in on them. Apparently Morag had been called in to see Donald about some disruptive behaviour Lucas was displaying in class and somehow that had ended with them, you know,' Cal said. 'Kicker of it all was that Lucas was sitting in the classroom just waiting for them to come back.'

'How old would Lucas have been then?' Nancy asked.

'Thirteen. Donald Stark almost lost his job over the incident.' Cal said.

'Did your source have any idea if this was a one off or is there a chance that the affair had been going on before or continued after?'

'She said it was the talk of the staff room, and that she suspected that it was a reasonably lengthy affair. She also said that the previous year Lucas had been happy, had a decent circle of friends and was doing well in school, then all of a sudden, he was hanging out by himself, grades dropped, and his attitude was terrible.' Cal said.

'I guess if you knew your mum was hooking up with one of your teachers that would be a good reason for the change.' Nancy said.

'Might also have been the reason he was so keen to leave the country and change his identity.' Cal added.

Chapter 45

Back in the interview room Nancy contemplated how long she would keep this newly discovered information to herself. 'Sorry about the disruption, you were about to tell me about you and Cheryl.' She hoped that in her absence he hadn't reconsidered sharing.

'What do you want to know?' Lucas uncrossed his legs and stretched them out under the table so that the soles of his shoes brushed against her feet.

'Why the fake name?'

'A bit of fun,' Lucas replied.

'What was fun about it?' Nancy asked.

'You could tell she was thirsty for attention, not that she did herself any favours,' he paused. 'Well, you've seen her, so you know what I'm talking about.' He cocked his head to one side. 'But on the other hand, she was gagging for it, and I knew she'd be an easy shag.' He grinned. 'Does that shock you detective?'

Nancy let out a short laugh, 'you think with everything I see that a man using a woman for sex would shock me?'

'Your job makes you cynical, which is a shame because you'd be not bad looking if you smiled a bit more, maybe let your hair grow out,' Lucas said.

Nancy ignored the comment, it was a pathetic attempt to bait her, and it wasn't going to work.

'Okay so you use a fake name and sleep with her once, there must have been something that made you keep going back for more.'

'She spoke her mind, even though what she thought wasn't PC at all, she didn't care, she was loud and obnoxious and there was something about that I admired, plus she was dirty, there wasn't much she wouldn't let me do to her in the bedroom.' He rubbed the palms of his hands back and forth enjoying the memory of his conquest. 'And if I didn't think about her soft flabby body, it was a good time.'

'You got excited when you found out she had access to all these empty properties didn't you?' Nancy said.

'It added a certain something to the experience and I liked pushing her to see how far she was willing to go, what she was willing to risk just to have me.'

'Did that make you feel powerful?' Nancy asked.

'I am powerful, that woman would do anything for me, I bet I could call her up now and she would take me back no questions asked.'

'But she wouldn't do anything though would she.' Nancy countered.

Lucas didn't reply.

'Wasn't that the reason you broke up with her, because she wasn't prepared to have sex in the graveyard. Whose grave did you want to do it on, was it your mother's,' Nancy said hoping that she had just pressed enough buttons to elicit a genuine raw emotion. She was rewarded with an outburst.

'How dare you!' Lucas slammed his fists onto the tabletop.

'You got really excited when you found out Cheryl had the keys for Seaview in Burntisland, was that because you recognised that address?' Nancy asked.

'You know I did, I lived there.'

'That's where you lived after your dad abandoned you and went back to America. It's a pretty fancy house, what did your mum do that she could afford that?'

'You're wrong about my dad, he didn't want to be with my mum anymore, but he still loved me. That's why he bought us that house, that's why I went to stay with him when I went to college,' Lucas said, spital flying out of his mouth and landing on his chin.

'Did she make you watch, or did you watch because you liked it?' Nancy asked.

'Fuck off.' Lucas replied.

'Maybe she just didn't care enough about you to bother whether you saw or not. Did you enjoy watching your mum with all those different men?' Nancy continued. 'Did the other kids in your class find out, is that why you didn't want to have friends around to your house anymore, you didn't want them to know that your mother was nothing but a cheap hooker.' Nancy hadn't been sure that her accusation towards Morag Ellis was correct, all she'd wanted was to make Lucas loose that cool persona, get angry and let something truthful slip. She smiled internally at hitting the nail so accurately on the head on the first go.

'She wasn't cheap!' Lucas shouted.

Nancy raised her eyebrows, 'Interesting, that's the word you object to? She was a high class hooker then, does that make it better?'

'She did what she had to.'

'She couldn't have got a job in an office like your friends mums?' Nancy asked. 'How did it feel watching one of your teachers with his hands all over your mum's body, listening to them over and over again. The creaking of the bedframe, the squeaking of the springs followed by the thump, thump, thump of the headboard…'

'Stop, stop talking.' Lucas covered his ears as he shouted the words.

Lucas' guidance councillor had thought it was an affair, but it was just business.

'When did the plan come to you?' Nancy asked. 'Was it when you started to research your latest case for the podcast, no I think you deliberately put this case up for consideration to Kayleigh, you were already planning on killing Donald Stark, weren't you, you just hadn't quite figured out all the details. Then you realised if you hid his death amongst others then we wouldn't be looking for a personal connection, we'd be looking for a serial killer.'

Lucas said nothing.

'You saw his photograph when you were dating Cheryl, did all that pent up hatred come flowing back?' Nancy continued.

'He made me sick, he paid more to make me watch. He liked to put his hands around her neck and call her names whilst he…' Lucas left the sentence unfinished. 'When I got into trouble at the school, he wanted me to know he could make her do whatever he wanted, wherever he wanted. I saw Cheryl's photographs and read the article about the fundraising, praising him for his charitable works, it made me physically sick.'

'Did you give any thought to the two families you utterly destroyed so that you could get revenge?' Nancy asked.

'They weren't without sin,' Lucas said. He was slumped

forward now resting his forehead on the table in front of him, his arms folded in loosely underneath his upper body.

'What sin had Maria Fischer committed?'

'She was a slut.'

'No. She wasn't. She was a young woman far away from home, that you lured with the promise of her desired career.'

'I didn't take any pleasure in killing her. She cried, begged for her life. Every day when I went to check on her she tried to be kind to me, promised if I let her go then she wouldn't say anything, that she'd get on a plane back to Australia and never come back. But it was too late, she had to die.' Lucas said.

'Why did you wait so long after Maria to kill Donald?' Nancy asked.

'I didn't expect there to be so much media involvement in her death, but with it being an international case I needed to wait until that all died down and I needed to make sure everything was perfect for killing that evil bastard.' Lucas said.

'You killed Maria in your old house, was that your old bedroom?' Nancy asked.

Lucas nodded.

'Did it turn you on killing her in there, all the memories come flooding back of you watching your mum with all those different men.' Nancy taunted him.

'It made too much mess.' Lucas replied.

'Is that why you killed Donald in the bathroom, you thought it would be easier to clean up, but then you didn't bargain for the old enamel bathtub, those things stain pretty bad.' Nancy paused. 'You've been clever though, making sure that the house was taken off the market, that Owen was the last person there, you wanted that, by then you'd already selected him as your next victim.'

'I am clever,' Lucas was sitting back upright again. 'I'm sure as hell smarter than you.'

'You can't be that smart, you got caught.' DCI Cooper said, speaking for the first time.

'Oh look, it speaks,' Lucas replied.

'If you were really smart, you'd tell us where you're keeping Destiny Popoola and Kayleigh McGuire,' Cooper continued. 'there's no reason to let them die, not now you've been apprehended.'

'Why should I care if they die? Three murders or five, it's not going to matter is it.' Lucas said.

'I think it would, I think a judge would look at you differently if you told us where those women are, and you let them go home to their families.' Cooper said.

'I don't care.' Lucas said.

'Kayleigh is your friend,' Nancy said. 'What happened there, she wasn't part of the plan, was she. Did she see something she shouldn't?'

'She came to the studio a couple of days ago, I wasn't home but she wasn't meant to be coming, I'd left my branding iron in there, I arrived as she was leaving, I could tell something was wrong. Then I realised and I couldn't let her come to you. I just wanted to give myself some time to think.' Lucas said.

'When I came to your house to get more forum transcripts you started to worry that I might be getting warm, and you realised you had an opportunity to point the finger of blame towards Kayleigh.'

'Like you said, I'm clever.' Lucas folded his arms and closed his eyes. 'I'm tired, I want a break.'

Chapter 46

'What did the search of his house turn up?' Nancy asked Isla.

'We found the branding iron and the ice pick is with forensics getting tested, I've asked them to put a rush on it. The house was rammed with things in the upstairs bedroom, it's going to take a bit of time to get through it all, we've had some extra officers drafted in to make it as quick a job as possible.' Isla replied.

'Nothing that would give us any indication where he might be holding Kayleigh and Destiny?' Nancy asked.

Isla shook her head.

'Okay well keep up the good work searching through his belongings, there's got to be something that we haven't come across yet,' Nancy said as her phoned buzzed, she glanced at the screen, it was Dylan. 'I've got to take this,' she said leaving Isla and striding to her office, closing the door behind her.

'Are you okay?' She asked aware that she must sound irrationally panicked.

'I'm all good, I was just checking on you, they said on the news that an arrest has been made on some murder case, which I'm guessing is the one you're working on.' Dylan said.

Nancy smiled. 'You know I can't tell you, but I think it will be a late one, will you be okay getting yourself some dinner and doing your homework.'

'I think I can cope, can I use your account to get a takeaway?'

'Of course, but don't stay up too late playing on your games console, alright.'

'Oh no,' he replied mockingly. 'You ruin all my fun, I suppose that means I should send all these party guests away now as well.'

'Ha ha.' Nancy replied. 'I'll see you when I get in.'

'Okay, make sure you remember to eat.' Dylan said before hanging up.

Nancy sat at her desk carefully flicking through the photographs taken from Kayleigh's house earlier in the day on her computer screen, zooming in on the images every now and then when she thought she might've caught sight of something. The blood smears on the walls looked more dramatic than they likely were, Lucy had assured her that even small amounts of blood can make that sort of mess. There was no reason to believe that Kayleigh was dead.

Rain rattled the building's old windows as the wind thrust the droplets against the glass at a ridiculous speed. Nancy hoped that wherever Kayleigh and Destiny were, they had each other for company and weren't being exposed to this awful weather.

Isla knocked gently on her door, 'Front desk just rang, apparently there's a man asking for you, says his name is Professor Laing.'

Nancy frowned, why the hell would the professor be here. 'Thanks, can you tell them I'm on my way down.'

Isla nodded.

Nancy jogged down the stairs persuading herself that her slightly elevated heart rate was from the exertion, not the anticipation of seeing her guest. She buzzed her way out of the secured area to the public seating section where Ewan sat, relaxed and smiling.

'Detective Ravenscroft, I hope I'm not disturbing you,' he stood beaming a smile in her direction.

'It's lovely to see you but I'm pretty busy,' she said, a pang of guilt detectable in her tone.

He held his hands up in mock surrender, 'don't worry I don't want to keep you back, after we spoke earlier I thought it might be useful to keep digging into any published writings of the person of interest you discussed with me.' Ewan said.

'Oh,' Nancy couldn't think of anything else to say.

'I hope that's okay, and I've not overstepped a boundary?' He asked.

'No of course not, just unexpected that's all, people rarely do more than the minimum.' Nancy replied.

'You need to start working with some new experts then,' he stifled a laugh. 'It's amazing the things that you can find online, anyway I discovered two things I thought might be helpful, the first is a piece of creative writing...' Ewan paused. 'Creatively it's not very good and the subject matter is a little disturbing, you can decide whether you think it's useful, especially given that it's pitched as fiction, and the other I suspect you might find relevant to your enquiries.'

'Okay,' interest now fully piqued, the professor had all of her attention.

'There's a linguistics professor I know, he's retired now,

but he truly is outstanding, he's been instrumental in building linguistic data bases, has travelled the world looking at regional data to feed in to help us really understand the cultural nuances in the way we talk and write.' he said.

Nancy smiled at him, as much as she was pleased to see him, she was hoping he'd get to the point soon.

'I know it sounds like I'm rambling, but the background is important. During lockdown he was asked to give a series of online lectures by a couple of universities across the world, something to help keep subjects fresh, they were for the main part attended purely by students attending college or university as full-time students, but there was one evening class that had some students sign up to them. Whilst I was looking through the texts you gave me, I was put in mind of one of his lectures which was on linguistic deception. It wasn't hard to give him a call and get a list of attendees.' He paused, whether it was for breath or dramatic effect Nancy wasn't sure. 'Your man Lucas Martin was on that list.'

'Oh wow, when did these lectures take place?' Nancy asked.

'During the first lockdown in 2020.'

'Almost three years ago.' Nancy said.

'Look I'll leave you to get back on with your investigation, I know you don't have time to socialise, and you probably want to get back to your desk and start looking at this stuff.' Ewan said.

'Yeah thanks, I really appreciate you going the extra mile like this, maybe we could do coffee some time after I'm done with this investigation?' Nancy found herself blushing.

'Talking of coffee, I made you up a flask, now granted it loses something not being straight from the stove, but it's got to be better than whatever you've got here, there's a bottle of cream and I brought some biscuits for your team.' It was his turn to blush. 'I hope that's not too weird, it felt like a nice gesture when I was at home, but now that I'm saying it out loud, I feel like it's weird.'

Nancy smiled. 'I could kiss you right now, you've no idea how much I need this coffee, and biscuits are always a good idea.'

The professor's cheeks flushed pink as he handed her a hessian bag containing the items, 'there you go then, you can return the flask the next time I see you.'

Nancy took the bag and watched as he left the building wrapping his coat around him tightly, lifting the collar to keep out the rain. She ignored the amused look on the desk sergeant's face as she passed him by.

The coffee tasted amazing from the metal cup of the thermos flask, she'd been tempted to close the door before opening the vessel in case the aroma drew in her colleagues when undoubtedly, she would have been expected to share. The brown hessian bag, far from containing a packet of shop bought biscuits held a Tupperware container of hand crafted Furniss Shortbread. She took a small stash for herself before setting the box aside telling herself she'd share them just as soon as she'd had the chance to look at the information Ewan had brought in.

It took Nancy a couple of attempts to get through the work of fiction, where Lucas had described the murder of his protagonist's mother, and the later dismemberment of her body. This was followed by the tale of revenge as the protagonist hunted down the lover that had wronged his mother, upon finding him he detailed the days of torture. He took pleasure in making the other man confess all his sins before he too was killed and fed to pigs.

The writing itself was amateurish, with no real plot development, but when it came to the description of the murders and the torture, it was detailed and littered with medical knowledge. The professor had taken the time to annotate sections noting how some of the podcast episodes had followed similar cases.

Nancy poured a second cup of coffee and took a moment to wonder at the organisational skill of bringing a small milk bottle style container of cream. She re-read the story this time taking notes, each of these two fictional murders were carried out in what was described as a wooden summer house.

Chapter 47

'Cal,' Nancy called from her doorway. She saw the sergeant look up startled out of what little world he was currently absorbed in.

He stood up from his chair so that he could see her better. 'Yes boss.'

She thought about conducting the enquiry by shouting over the office, but the tired looks on some of the faces around the room made her think twice.

'I'll come to you,' she called before darting back into her office and picking up the box of biscuits. A couple of moments later she was sitting beside Cal at his desk.

'Have a biscuit,' she said and he didn't put up any protest.

'Did you make these?' He asked innocently.

'Yes Cal, alongside conducting a multiple homicide investigation I had time to stand in Rob's kitchen and bake.' She gave him a stare.

'They're really nice,' he said.

'I'll let the professor know, now you remember you started to have a look at log cabins?' Nancy said.

'Yes.'

'How did you get on?'

'Um, I didn't get all the research done because Rob asked me to divert my attention into looking into Lucas and Kayleigh's background, but I'll run through what I discovered up till then. There are some privately owned cabins, nearly all of which are on managed parks, a few in people's back gardens and some that make up part of other holiday parks, sorry I think it's a bit of a dead end,' Cal said finishing a mouthful of biscuit.

'Can you see if there's any history of either Lucas or anyone in his family ever owning a summer house, you know one of those large fancy sheds, with a porch.'

'Why?' Asked Cal.

'Because in this god-awful manuscript that's where he does his killing and I started to wonder, what if this place actually exists.' Nancy said.

'Okay leave it and a couple of those biscuits with me and I'll see what I can find out.' Cal said.

She left him two biscuits with the promise of a third if he found anything useful. Lucas had been left to rest for hours now and their time was ticking away, the twenty-four hours she could hold him for would soon be gone. Time for another chat.

With DCI Cooper finished for the day she brought Rob in his place.

'I'm tired, can't we do this in the morning,' Lucas whined.

'No.' Rob said sitting opposite him and starting the recording.

'Anyone would think you're running out of time, you'll never have enough to charge me.' Lucas said.

'You mean apart from our conversation earlier today when you told me that you'd killed Maria and then Donald and Owen.' Nancy said.

'I don't think I said anything of the sort,' Lucas smiled.

'The ice pick found in your drinks cabinet had traces of all of your victims DNA on it.' Nancy said.

'I told you that belongs to Kayleigh, I'm just looking after it for her.'

'It has your DNA and fingerprints on it, but nothing of Kayleigh's, how do you explain that?' Rob asked.

'Your new friend is much more chatty than the last one.' Lucas said.

'Why did you kidnap Detective Constable Abbott?' Nancy asked.

Lucas shrugged, 'to see if I could,' he smiled, smug, 'I'd have loved to be a fly on the wall when you all realised she was gone.'

'You could have kept her as your fourth victim.' Nancy said.

'Too easy, and besides it was much more fun to mess with you, and whilst you were busy looking for your friend you weren't looking for me.' Lucas replied. 'You should thank me for letting her go.'

'Is it the being in control that gets you off?' Nancy asked.

He leaned back, 'I have enjoyed being one step ahead of you at all times.' He gave a breathy laugh.

'Did you know my officers have been through your house, they found the mess upstairs, I can understand why you wanted all of that shoved into one space, somewhere you didn't have to look at it. All your mother's knick-knacks, all the things that reminded you of your childhood. Doesn't seem like you're one step ahead anymore,' Nancy said.

'You had no right to go through all my things, you can't touch those things,' Lucas said.

'They're all evidence now.' Nancy continued. 'What do you reckon your mother would think about what you've done? Do you think she'd be glad that Donald Stark is dead?'

'She told me once that it was men like him that disgusted her the most, the ones that pretend to be good Christian family men but hide a darker side. They look down on people like her, call them names in public but in private they line up to pay to be with her. She said they were the most dangerous, because they all had something to lose and that meant they'd be prepared to do terrible things to keep their secrets hidden.' Lucas said.

'Was she afraid of Donald Stark?'

'I think so, he hurt her, she'd need to wear scarfs around her neck to cover the marks he left, he would spit on her, pull her hair, gave her a black eye once, because she didn't want me to see him doing those things to her.' Lucas paused for a moment. 'She'd be proud that I made him beg for his life, that he knew what it was to be afraid, to have someone else decide whether he got to breath or not.'

'Did he recognise you?' Rob asked.

'That was the worst of it, he tried to make out that I was mistaken,' Lucas stopped for a moment staring past them at the wall behind as if he was transported back to that moment. 'He was the only one I tortured, I had to, I had to make him confess. You understand that.' He looked directly at Nancy.

'Do you think you're better than him?' Nancy asked.

Lucas frowned, 'of course I'm better than him.'

'I think you're very similar, maybe you're worse.' Nancy replied.

'You can't think that, that man was evil, he took pleasure in what he did.'

'Do you need me to remind you of all the wicked things you've done?' Nancy looked at Lucas, he avoided the eye contact. 'You manipulated Cheryl, you deceived Diane, you lied and prayed on these women. You took the lives of two people who'd never done you or yours an ounce of harm so that you could kill one man.'

'You've got it all wrong, I'm the victim. I'm the victim.' Lucas' voice got louder until it was a shriek.

'No, Maria was a victim, Owen was a victim, Kayleigh and Destiny, they're victims, not you.' Nancy stared at him. 'And if you had even a shred of goodness in you then you'd tell me where you're keeping those two women, so they don't have to spend one more night away from their families. Destiny Popoola has two small children at home, scared not knowing if they'll ever see their mummy again. Would that make your mother proud. Would it?' Nancy could feel the anger burning in the pit of her stomach.

'Kayleigh was going to betray me.' Lucas spluttered.

'How could you be sure, she might have stood by you once you told her your story.' Rob said.

'I could see it in the way she looked at me, fear, and disgust. I had to go after her.'

'What did you do to her?' Nancy asked.

Lucas stared at her blankly.

'There were smears of blood on her walls.' Nancy explained.

'She tried to fight back, she threw a vase at my head, it hit the wall and smashed, she resisted when I tried to pick her up, I lost my balance and dropped her, she cut her hand on the broken glass, she did that to herself,' Lucas said.

'What was the plan – were you going to murder her too?' Rob asked.

'I hoped that if I gave her time she would calm down, it would give me a chance to get her to see my point of view.'

'And if she didn't?' Rob said.

'Then she'd have a tragic accident, I thought no-one would notice she was missing for a few days.' Lucas shrugged his shoulders. 'It doesn't matter anymore.'

'I'm going to give you one last chance to redeem yourself and tell me where she is?' Nancy said.

Lucas twisted his body away from the table and stared at the wall.

Chapter 48

DAY NINE, TUESDAY

'The Procurator Fiscal seems happy with the charges,' DCI Cooper said. 'You've done well.'

Nancy smiled flatly back at him, with two women missing for forty-eight hours she didn't feel like it was a job well done.

'He was never going to give their location up,' DCI Cooper continued. 'You got him to confess to the murder of three people, that's good going. And if we don't find Kayleigh and Destiny their murders will be added to his list of charges. The Chief Super is looking to get this case wrapped up.'

'I don't understand how he can stand down all the extra manpower when there's still an active missing persons case.' Nancy said.

'You've caught a murderer and that's our job, he's not going to authorise any more extra overtime on this case.' Cooper said.

'We could still find them alive, what's it going to look like

in the media if they die because we stop looking for them?'
Nancy said.

'I know, and I agree with you,' Cooper said putting his hand up to stop Nancy from talking. 'that's why I'm authorising you and your team to keep working on this case. I can give you one more week and that's it, after that they'll be presumed dead.'

'Thank you.'

'One week DI Ravenscroft, one week.' His use of her official title indicating that there was no room for negotiation.

Nancy hadn't made it back across the hallway to her own team before she was intercepted by a uniformed officer. 'DI Ravenscroft, there's a couple downstairs asking for you, something about their house being a crime scene.'

Nancy looked at the officer blankly.

'They've got a baby with them.' The officer added.

'Oh,' Nancy thought for a moment, 'the Roberts?'

'Yes, that's right.'

'Okay I'll come now.' Nancy followed the officer down the stairs and into the foyer. 'Congratulations on the new arrival,' she said looking at the pram.

Mrs Roberts said nothing, opting instead to glare in her direction. Nancy wished she could remind the couple that it wasn't her that had murdered someone in their house, but what good would that do.

'Thank you,' Mr Roberts said. 'We're staying with my mother-in-law for the time being.'

'That's good,' Nancy said, though judging by the look on the man's face the opposite was true. 'Good news though, you can get back in your house at the start of next week.'

Mrs Roberts made a scoffing sound.

Mr Roberts offered up a half-hearted smile, 'we'll not be going back to live there, my wife thinks it's bad luck, the estate agent has agreed to put it back on the market and cover the cost of the sale as a gesture of goodwill. We've found somewhere else we'd like to buy as soon as we have a buyer for our old house.'

'We'll take a loss on that property now though.' Mrs Roberts said.

Nancy didn't respond, Maria Fischer would have given anything not to have been murdered in that room, to be at home with her mother in Australia.

'We just wanted to know when we can go back and collect some of our belongings,' he looked nervously back at his wife, 'and we wondered if there was any compensation we could claim, for distress and rehousing, that sort of thing.'

'If you come into the station on Thursday morning, I'll make sure your keys are available to you for collection. You can complete forms with the duty sergeant here for consideration for compensation. It's not something I have any control over I'm afraid.' Nancy said.

'Great thank you.' Mr Roberts replied.

As Nancy turned and walked away she could hear his wife mocking him for thanking her. She took a deep breath and reminded herself that the woman had recently had a baby and could be excused being emotional, and selfish, and completely oblivious to the more acute suffering that had been caused by her home being a crime scene.

'Please tell me that we've found something?' Nancy said when she finally re-joined her team.

The room seemed eerily empty now with only the four of them in it, the hubbub of noise created by lots of people in one place all working towards a common goal now gone felt like failure.

'Nothing. Really!' Nancy said taking their silence as a no.

'Grace is getting to go home from the hospital tomorrow.' Rob said.

'And she has no recollection of where Lucas kept her?' Nancy asked.

Rob shook his head, 'none, according to the doctor it's not surprising given how heavily she'd been drugged.'

'Was Cheryl Wilson able to give us any idea of where to start looking for these log cabins Lucas mentioned to her when they first met?'

'No,' Isla said. 'She said that after he mentioned them to her the first time, he became pretty cagey if she ever asked about them. She thought that he didn't really have his own business and that he'd made it up to impress her.'

'What about you Cal, anything on summer houses?'

'Sorry boss, there's nothing connected to Lucas or any of his family.' Cal looked awkwardly at his colleagues.

'We've been given one week to keep looking into this and then this case is over whether we find Kayleigh and Destiny or not. And bear in mind that every day they're out there not being fed, possibly not having access to water and Kayleigh is injured, god knows what sort of state they'll be in. I want us to find living people, not corpses.' Nancy said.

'The boss is right, we need to get back over the evidence, we must've missed something, now let's find it.' Rob said.

Nancy made her way into her office, grateful to Rob for always having her back. He followed her in. 'We'll go back through everything, we'll find them.'

'I hope so,' Nancy said. 'Let me know if you find

anything at all that's worth following up and do me a favour and make sure the team are adequately fed and watered and I'll pay you back, don't put it through expenses.'

She opened her computer and began scanning her way through the pictures taken of Lucas' home, focusing in on the areas in the upstairs of the house where chaos seemed to rule, zooming in on anything that caught her eye. She was looking so intensely at an image that she almost didn't realise her phone was buzzing. When she zoned back into the room she look at the phone and realised she'd missed a call from Ewan.

She called him back, 'hi, sorry I missed your call.'

'No problem, I was phoning to say congratulations, I saw your boss on the tv saying you've charged Lucas Martin with murder, but I'm sensing from you tone that I'm a little premature.'

Was she that transparent? Or was his expertise in linguistics so advanced that he was able to pick up on her changes in mood already, she'd need to watch out for that in the future. Nancy blushed, what future was she imagining here. 'There's a few loose ends that I haven't been able to tie up yet,' she said.

'Are you talking about the missing women?' The professor asked.

'Yeah, Lucas refused to give up the location where he's holding them and as the days are passing it's looking more and more likely that I'm going to be looking for their bodies.

'Do you have anything to go on?'

'Not really, there was mention of log cabins in one of his early conversations with one of our key witnesses, but we haven't been able to locate anything.' Nancy shared.

The professor was quiet for a moment, Nancy could hear him scrolling on his computer, 'In episode four of the podcast he's talking to Kayleigh about his love of linguistics and when that started, he says that he noticed how people spoke to his American father differently to his Scottish mother when they were at their holiday home on the Fife Coast. I don't think it's a log cabin, sounds like a small cottage the way he describes it.'

'Any chance he said where exactly it was?' Nancy asked.

'He doesn't say, but he talks about swimming in the tidal pools in St Monans and Anstruther on the same holidays, says he and his cousins would cycle from the house together, his mum would give them money to get chips before coming home.'

Chapter 49

It had only taken Cal thirty-five minutes to locate Lucas' cousin, Glenn Williams, son of Lucas' mother's brother and only one year older than Lucas, and thankfully he still lived locally. Sergeant West and one of his PC's had interrupted the man's lunchbreak at work, reluctantly he'd agreed to come in to the station.

Now he sat in an interview room opposite Nancy and Rob. She looked at Glenn, he wasn't dissimilar in looks to his cousin, the same thick blonde hair, and blue eyes. But unlike his cousin Glenn's complexion was clear and his face looked kinder.

'Thank you for coming in to help us today,' Nancy said.

Glenn frowned, 'it wasn't like I was given much of a choice, is this about Lucas?' He asked.

'You're aware then that your cousin has been charged with murder?' Nancy asked.

'I'm aware, but honestly I've not seen him in years, not since we were teenagers.' Glenn said.

'How come?' Rob asked.

'Don't get me wrong, we were close growing up, both only children, close in age, similar hobbies, but he started getting weird as he got into his teens.'

'What do you mean by weird?' Rob asked.

'I don't know, he would make things up and then get angry when I didn't believe him.' Glenn said.

'What sort of things?' Rob asked.

'About girls, he'd say that he had a girlfriend and then brag about sex stuff, we went to the same school, I knew he was lying, but if you called him out about it then he went ballistic.'

'What sort of things did he say?' Nancy asked.

Glenn looked at his hands clasped in his lap, 'graphic stuff, I figured that he'd read it somewhere or seen a dirty movie. I knew he'd fallen out with his mates, and I figured he was trying to make himself sound cool. Thing is no-one believed him, it just isolated him more. I know he was my cousin, and I probably should've stuck up for him more, but high school is tough enough without hitching your wagon to the school weirdo, so I started keeping my distance. I don't think he ever forgave me for it.'

'Were you surprised to hear he'd been charged with murder?' Nancy asked.

'I didn't know he was back in the UK, but honestly not really. Not sure what help I can be though, like I said we've not talked in years.'

'The holiday property you stayed in when you were kids, do you remember that?' Nancy asked.

Glenn nodded his head and frowned, 'of course.'

'Who did that belong to?' Nancy asked.

'My mum, she'd been left it by her aunt.' Glenn said.

'And who owns it now?'

'Me, why?' Glenn replied.

'When was the last time you were there?' Nancy said.

'Um, about two years ago, I've been meaning to get up there, cos it needs a bit of work doing to it, but with the way things have been all my plans went a bit sideways and after a couple of years stuck at home, the wife was desperate for a bit of sun last year, so we went to Malaga. Why do you ask.'

'It might be nothing, but it would be helpful if you could let me have the keys and give us permission to search it.' Nancy said.

Glenn's face paled, 'do you think he used it when he was killing his victims?'

'We don't know, but I'm looking for two women that Lucas kidnapped shortly before his arrest and we're just exploring every possible location in the hopes of finding them and returning them to their families.' Nancy said.

'Yeah of course,' he took a bunch of keys out of his pocket. 'I keep everything on here otherwise I'd lose it and not have a clue where it was when I needed it.' He said as he fed a key off of the crowded keyring. 'Do you need directions?' He added a moment later.

Nancy took the directions and requested Glenn wait at the station until they'd completed the search of the property. He was initially concerned thinking that she was implying that he was somehow involved in his cousin's sordid mess, but in the end, he'd conceded and agreed to wait it out.

Reluctant to do anything that might jinx the successful discovery of the missing women Nancy opted for a low-key approach. She and Rob would enter the property with Isla and Cal on the outside, on the off chance that Lucas hadn't been working alone.

'This is certainly out of the way enough that no-one would hear you scream and enough off the beaten track that your comings and goings wouldn't be noticed by nosy neighbours,' Nancy said as they approach the small stone-built cottage.

'You really think no one would've noticed a strange car coming and going?' Rob asked.

'In a wee touristy village that arguably has several of the best chippies in the land as well as walking routes and a caravan park not that far away,' Nancy said frowning at her colleague.

'Fair point,' Rob mumbled.

They parked a little way down the rough drive, Isla and Cal in the car behind them, Nancy made her way around the perimeter of the building trying to peer in the windows. Lucas had been cautious, and each window was covered by a thick curtain. All the exterior doors looked to be intact.

Nancy put the key into the front door and turned it, relieved to hear a gentle clunk as the lock opened. She pushed it open and immediately gagged. A strong smell of ammonia and faeces wafted straight into her nostrils. Taking a moment to compose herself she covered her mouth and nose with her top and entered the building.

'You cover the right-hand side and I'll do the left, shout out if you find them.' Nancy whispered to Rob.

Nancy entered the first room, a traditional sitting room with a stone fireplace. The small sofa and armchair looked like they'd been sitting in the exact same places for the last 50 years. If it wasn't for the empty crisp packets and water bottles, she could have believed that the house had been left undisturbed since Lucas' childhood or even earlier.

Nancy took hold of the final door handle on her side of the hallway, it turned easily.

'In here,' Nancy yelled out.

She rushed to the corner of the room where a very pale

Kayleigh lay slumped on the lap of Destiny Popoola, both women chained to the base of a cast iron table.

Nancy reached out to feel for a pulse in Kayleigh's neck, it was weak, but it was there. Destiny's head was lolled to one side, dried crusty white saliva coated her lips. Nancy shook the woman gently, 'Destiny, Destiny, come on wake up now.'

A low groan was emitted from deep within the woman, her eyes flickering open, catching sight of Nancy, and closing again.

Rob had joined her in the room now, 'I've called for an ambulance.'

'She needs water, can you see if you can find any,' Nancy said to Rob before turning back to Destiny, 'I need you to wake up Destiny, open your eyes and look at me.'

Destiny blinked, raising her eyebrows to force her eyes to stay open, a few moments later Rob appeared with a bottle of water.

Nancy removed the cap and held it at Destiny's lips, helping her to take small sips, she indicated to Rob to take over as she looked at Kayleigh.

The cut on her arm and hand were crusty with dried blood, yellowy green puss leaked from the heel of Kayleigh's hand. Nancy put the back of her hand against the woman's forehead, she was clammy and hot.

'This wound is infected,' Nancy said, 'did you get an estimated time of arrival on that ambulance?'

'Twenty minutes,' Rob replied.

Destiny was more compos mentis now, she jerked her arm forgetting for a moment that it was tethered to the chain.

'Get the bolt cutters from the boot of my car,' Nancy instructed.

Rob left the room and headed for the front door.

'You're doing great,' Nancy said to Destiny as the woman's eyes locked on hers.

Wind blew against the front door causing it to bang into the wall, Destiny flinched and instinctively she wrapped her arm around Kayleigh.

'You're safe, you're both safe.' Nancy said gently.

Chapter 50

Kayleigh's wound had become infected in part through it not being treated but also because of the filthy conditions they'd been forced to live in. Destiny had tried to clean it up using the water Lucas had left her with to drink when he locked her up, and then she'd used Kayleigh's water to try and keep the woman alive.

Sitting up in her hospital bed Destiny looked like she was going to be fine, she'd been dehydrated and hungry, but otherwise physically unharmed.

'He had a knife,' Destiny explained to Nancy as she sat in the uncomfortable armchair next to her bed, the faux leather hot under her backside.

'Is that how he got you to go with him?'

'First he told me someone had blocked him in, I told him my shift hadn't even started yet, but I was in my uniform, so he was very persuasive, I thought hang it I'll see what it is that the man is complaining about.'

'But it was a trick?' Nancy asked.

'He took a knife from his pocket, told me to get in his car or he'd stab me and leave me to bleed out in the carpark.' Destiny said.

'Did he take you straight to the cottage?'

Destiny shook her head, not in disagreement, more like she was trying to dislodge a memory from where it was stuck. 'I don't know, I remember getting in the car and then I woke up and I was chained in that room, I've no idea what had happened in between.'

Nancy thought of Grace's experience, Lucas had repetitively drugged her, and it would figure that he'd done the same with his other victims.

'Was Kayleigh already there when you woke up?' Nancy asked.

'She was already in a bad way, I could see that she was injured immediately. I shouted at him that she needed medical attention, but he told me to shut up. He put a couple of water bottles down and said that would keep us going till he came back, but he never did.' Destiny said.

'No, because I arrested him.' She'd never felt guilty for arresting someone before, but the momentary pang was gone soon enough, the alternative would be that both Destiny and Kayleigh would be dead if she hadn't. Nancy doubted that Lucas would have waited his customary week to murder them, knowing that she was hot on his heels he would have killed them both and cut his losses.

'The doctor said that if it hadn't been for you Kayleigh would almost certainly have died in that room.'

'I did what needed to be done, honestly, I'd made peace with my maker, I was expecting to never see my husband or my children again. You were like a miracle, when I opened my eyes, I couldn't fully believe you were real.'

Destiny's husband tapped gently on the door. 'Is it alright to come in?' He asked, his arms full of flowers and gifts.

Nancy smiled and stood up, 'of course, we're finished now anyway.' She paused on the way out of the room to look back at Destiny Popoola being embraced by her husband.

On the way out of the hospital she checked in on Kayleigh. She was in a much more serious condition than Destiny, she was still too weak to give a statement.

DCI Cooper was waiting in her office when Nancy arrived. 'How are they?' He asked as she sat behind her desk.

'Alive, time will tell if they ever get over it.' Nancy replied.

'Your team will be rostered off for four days as soon as you turn in the remainder of the case reports.' Cooper said.

'We'll be fine,' Nancy protested.

'This is not a debate, your team are exhausted,' he glanced out into the main room where all four of her team sat hunched over desks staring at their computer screens. 'DC Abbott has been transferred to you on a permanent basis, given what she went through I've decided she'd be much better served being around those who understand her situation on a more personal level.'

'Thank you, sir,' Nancy offered him a small smile.

'And perhaps in your time off you can make some enquiries about finding yourself and your son a home. I'm sure DS MacDonald would like his back, as much as I think he's unlikely to tell you.'

'Yes sir, I'll do my best.' She thought of her small nest egg of savings and wondered if it would be enough to put a deposit down on something.

Cooper leant forward and placed a business card on her desk. 'Trevor Cutter is an excellent lawyer, you should give him a call and see if you can't get your money back from that arsehole of an ex of yours.'

Nancy picked up the card, 'will do.'

Chapter 51

AFTER THE CASE

'What do you think?' Nancy asked as she showed Dylan around the house.

'You bought a murder house,' he turned to look at her over his shoulder.

'I bought a house with a spectacular view and a low price tag.' She replied.

'Where someone was murdered.' Dylan said again.

'Yes, but I don't think that has to be this house's legacy, I thought together, you and I could turn it into something special.' Nancy said hoping that the teenager would show some enthusiasm for the project.

'I get to pick how I decorate my bedroom.' Dylan said.

'Sounds fair.'

'I can't believe you did this,' he said. 'I go away for one school trip.' He smiled.

'We couldn't keep on living at Rob's. It'll be a few weeks before it's officially ours, but no harm in starting to plan things now.'

'How's dad dealing with everything?'

'Your father and your aunt seem to think I've been very unreasonable asking for my money back and putting them in a position where they may have to sell the house. Living with the consequences of their actions isn't looking as pleasurable now. Have you spoken to him at all?' Nancy asked, conscious that as much as she hated her ex he was still Dylan's father and she had no desire to force him to cut contact with him.

'He text whilst I was away in Belgium, I didn't reply.'

'How would you feel about some family therapy?' Nancy asked.

Dylan walked back across the room and stood beside her looking out the large window pane to the water beyond. 'I know you think you need to fix this thing with me and dad, but you can't. He did this and if he really cared about having a relationship with me then me not responding to one text wouldn't put him off.' Dylan said. 'When you left, if I didn't reply to a text I would have five more within the hour, you never gave up on me or walked away from me.'

She put her arm around his shoulder, 'I made you a promise when you were just a little boy, that I'd always be there for you, and I meant it.'

'We should do a house warming barbeque when we move in,' Dylan said.

Acknowledgments

I would like to thank my husband, Gavin, for his ongoing support, for listening to all my story ideas, for reading my first drafts and for always believing in me.

The Wee Chippy and their excellent Gluten Free Menu.

To F&J for being by my side throughout it all.

About the Author

Born in the Kingdom of Fife, Angela spent her teenage years in Penzance before returning to Scotland. She had a varied career from Nursery Nurse to Bank Manager before becoming a full-time writer.

Angela now lives with her husband in the Scottish countryside. When she's not writing she can be found walking through woodland or touring the countryside in her campervan.

Also by Angela C Nurse

Jack In A Box, A Rowan McFarlane Mystery
Sally In The Woods, A Rowan McFarlane Mystery
What She Didn't See, A Rowan McFarlane Mystery
Lies She Didn't Tell, A Rowan McFarlane Mystery